Mending Hearts and Pastures New

Morag Clarke

MC

Mending Hearts and Pastures New
Printed by KDP, an Amazon.com Company
Copyright Morag Clarke 2024
The rights of the above author to be identified as the author of this work has been asserted in accordance with the Copyright, Designs and Patents Act 1988.

ISBN 9798336252231
All rights reserved. No part of this publication may be reproduced, stored in a retrieval system or transmitted in any form or by any means without prior permission of the copyright owner.
All the characters in this book are fictitious and any resemblance to actual persons, living or dead, is entirely coincidental.

Chapter One

Grey Lodge Bed and Breakfast; an impressive country manor in rural surroundings, run by the widowed Ursula Lloyd-Duncan, offered guests a place to relax and unwind in a spectacular and peaceful setting.

Unfortunately, the same could not be said for the staff.

Caroline had lost count of the number of people her mother had employed, only to have them leave a few days or weeks later. Which was why she found herself in the ridiculous situation of being the unpaid and vastly under-appreciated, helper.

She stacked the dirty breakfast plates onto a tray and wiped crumbs from the starched linen tablecloth with her hand.

Yes, she had been made redundant from her office job, and yes, she was grateful her mother had put a temporary roof over her head, following her divorce from Marcus. That didn't mean she wanted to be waiting at tables and cleaning rooms for some, quite frankly, unpleasant guests.

Waitressing was a job for youngsters, or students looking for part-time jobs, not someone approaching their fortieth birthday, whose career up to date had been clerical or secretarial work.

The dining room was empty, apart from one middle-aged man, sitting on his own at a table by the bay window that overlooked the sweeping lawns. Caroline gave him a cursory glance, as she tucked a damp cloth into the waistband of the frilly white apron her mother insisted she wore when she waited on the breakfast tables. Mr Dalton had been a guest with them for three days now and gave the impression he'd rather not be there at all.

'This coffee,' he said, 'is cold.' He held the cafetiere away from him as if it contained something distasteful.

Caroline straightened up and wiped her hands on the cloth. Her fingers were sticky with marmalade. 'I'm sorry about that. I'll get you a fresh pot.'

'Good.' He glanced down at his phone, which had beeped a message. 'In your own time.' He didn't even look at her.

Caroline tried to suppress the urge to throw the entire contents over him and gave him one of her most gracious smiles. It was a waste of time and effort, because he was more engrossed in his phone than her. She turned and stalked back to the kitchen, with the offending cafetiere balanced precariously on the tray of dirty plates.

Ursula was frying a pan of bacon with one hand and extracting toast from the toaster with the other.

'That's it!' Caroline said. 'I've had enough. That man is so rude and there's no reason for it. You should have heard the way he spoke to me.'

'Yes, well, I wouldn't take it personally.' Her mother levered the bacon from the pan with a spatula and left it on a warming plate while she started on the eggs. The delicious smell made Caroline's mouth water. She hadn't had time for any breakfast.

'I expect he's got a lot to think about.'

'Like what?'

'Oh, you know.'

Caroline didn't. She dumped the tray of dirty dishes on the worktop with a clatter.

'You don't have to like the guests. But they pay good money and we need to remember that.' Ursula shot her a sideways glance. 'What's his problem this morning?'

'He says his coffee is cold.' Caroline tipped the contents of the cafetiere into the white enamel sink. It did seem rather tepid, she thought. Definitely not cold. The dark brown grounds pooled in the plughole.

In the short time Mr Dalton had been with them, he'd found fault with just about everything; the draught from his windows; the creaky floorboard in his ensuite bathroom; the stiffness of the door, which didn't shut properly and would benefit from a good sanding down, and he was the most obnoxious man Caroline had ever had to deal with. Aside from Marcus, of course. Her ex-husband was definitely top of that list.

She flipped the kettle on to boil.

'The toast's ready if you want to take it out,' Ursula said, popping the hot slices into a silver rack.

'I'm making the coffee.'

Her mother's pointed glare left no room for argument.

'We need more staff,' Caroline said. 'You promised me, mother. You said this would be temporary until you found a suitable person.'

'Yes, well, I haven't.'

'Obviously.'

'The toast, Caroline. Else he'll be complaining that's cold as well.' Ursula turned her back to her daughter and flipped over the eggs.

Caroline scowled as she snatched up the toast rack and spun on her heel.

Ever since Marcus divorced her, Caroline's life had been one long and miserable mess. Not that being divorced was the problem. She had grown to dislike her husband almost as much as he disliked her. The fact he had gone off with a younger woman (one of the clerical assistants at the tax office where he worked) was the thing that rankled. Even she had to admit they had grown apart, and divorce was the next logical step for their failing marriage. But she hadn't expected him to take up with someone so soon after their last counselling session. That had been hurtful, to say the least. Finding out his girlfriend was also pregnant, made her wonder just how long their relationship had been going on.

'Thank you.' Mr Dalton glanced at his watch as she placed the toast in front of him.

He plucked a slice of granary bread from the rack and began to butter it. 'And the coffee?'

'Just coming.'

His audible sigh caused Caroline to bristle, as she stomped back to the kitchen.

This was not the life she had envisaged for herself when Marcus opted to buy her out of their marital home as part of her divorce settlement.

Her mother's suggestion that she move in with her until she found a place of her own to stay had seemed an attractive proposition at the time. She had rather fancied living in the old mansion house.

Grey Lodge stood in several acres of landscaped grounds, with sweeping views of the surrounding countryside, and a long, private, gravelled drive. No noisy neighbours—well, not counting that unfortunate incident with the travellers a few years ago—no trundling traffic to disturb her at all hours, nothing but birdsong and the rustling of the breeze through the trees and the occasional whinny from the horses in the nearby paddocks. It was a haven of peace and solitude.

It should have been bliss and would have been, till all and sundry decided to stay.

Caroline pushed open the door to the kitchen. A waft of fried bacon greeted her.

'Mr Dalton wants his coffee. Is it ready yet?'

'Over there.' Ursula wagged a spatula towards the table, where the cafetiere was gently steaming. 'You can take it in with his breakfast. It's nearly ready. He's the last one for the day.'

'Thank goodness,' Caroline said, taking the chance to catch her breath and sit down for a moment. Her feet were killing her. All this rushing backwards and forwards from the kitchen to the dining room was exhausting.

She still remembered the day her mother announced her plan to turn Grey Lodge into a bed-and-breakfast business. It had come as such a shock. Ursula had told her over dinner one evening, in that matter-of-fact manner she reserved for things she didn't deem worth discussing.

'But why?' she had protested. 'Grey Lodge is your home. You can't need the money.'

'Can't I? Have you any idea how much it costs to maintain a building this size, to say nothing of the upkeep of the grounds?'

'Well, no.'

'Exactly.'

'But there must be something else you can do?'

Her mother had given her a withering glare that suggested she had considered all other possibilities and found them wanting.

'I'm a pensioner, darling, and although some may say I was left well provided for, I beg to differ. Short of selling the place, I don't see what else I can do.'

So, the decision had been made, which was all well and good while Caroline drove off to work every day and didn't have to get involved with things. But since she got made redundant from her office job in town, it was far from ideal. Her mother automatically assumed she would pitch in, now that she had time on her hands. It was the last thing she wanted to do.

Caroline hated the fact that strangers were wandering round the house. The moment she showed her face, somebody somewhere wanted something, be it fresh towels, or a map of the local area, or a list of nearby restaurants. (Her mother didn't do evening meals. She was stressed enough trying to prepare the breakfasts).

And now Caroline found herself obliged to act as a temporary waitress until Ursula could secure a replacement for Shirley; who had walked out after an unpleasant confrontation over 'perks of the job', or so her mother had said. Shirley being the last of many.

Caroline placed the steaming cafetiere on a tray with a small jug of cream. The plate of grilled sausage, bacon and fried eggs, with mushrooms, tomatoes and black pudding looked and smelled delicious. Mr Dalton couldn't object to that, she thought. If he did, she'd have something to say about it. Her patience;

which was never one of her strong points, was wearing thin. Not helped by the fact her blood sugar levels had to be at an all-time low.

He grunted what sounded like an approval as she slid the plate in front of him, even managing to tear his attention away from his phone. Wonders would never cease. She'd done something to please him, at last. 'Can I get you anything else?'

'No. Thank you.'

'You're welcome.'

'Oh, but there is one thing.'

She hovered next to his table, with the smile glued so hard on her face, her cheeks were aching.

'I'll be going through some important paperwork in my room this afternoon and I don't want to be disturbed.'

'No problem,' Caroline said. Since she was the only person, apart from her mother on the premises, he could rest assured that neither of them would knock on his door. The less she saw of the man, the better.

'Good.'

His reply was so abrupt that the smile threatened to slip from Caroline's face. She picked up the coffee-pot and was about to fill his cup when he waved her away with a dismissive flick of his hand.

'Just leave it, okay? I think I can pour my own coffee.'

Caroline replaced the cafetiere on the tray, and without another word, turned and marched back to the kitchen, her cheeks burning. Who did he think he was, and why did he have to be so rude?

She had noticed the glint of a gold wedding ring on his finger. He was obviously married, but who in their right mind would marry him? Then again, she reflected ruefully, she'd married Marcus and look how that had turned out.

***

Vanessa—Caroline's younger sister—was feeling queasy. The smell of polished leather from the rack of new saddles and bridles she had spent the morning unpacking was overpowering.

She slipped into the stockroom at the back of the shop and poured herself a glass of water, leaving Sadie Mackinley, one of her regulars, eyeing up the array of brightly coloured children's jodhpurs that had been delivered to her tack shop the previous day.

'Molly's going to love these pink ones.'

'Hmm,' Vanessa said.

'I don't suppose you've got them in purple, too.'

'No.' Vanessa tried to smother a discreet burp. It must have been the sausage casserole she'd made last night. She'd thought it tasted funny. Jed hadn't complained. In fact, her husband had wolfed down two helpings, but then he'd spent the whole day helping Thomas at the stables, finalising the arrangements before he took over from him as Hollyfield Stables' new stud manager. He can't have had anything other than a bit of toast all day.

'Okay, well I'll take the pink, then. Vanessa? Vanessa, are you all right in there?'

'Just a minute.'

She swallowed another mouthful of cold water. She thought it might help. It didn't. She rushed to the toilet and shut the door.

If there was one thing Vanessa hated, it was being sick. But being sick in front of one of her customers, when trying to make a sale, was even worse.

Fortunately, her teenage nephew Adam chose that moment to wander into the tack shop. Seeing it unmanned, and presuming his aunt had popped to the loo (which indeed, she had); he took over.

'You're definitely looking peaky,' he observed, when she finally emerged from the toilet, clutching a crumpled-up tissue, some minutes after Sadie Mackinley had left. 'Do you want me to stay and help?'

Vanessa couldn't think of anything she'd like better. 'Haven't you got school?'

'Free period.'

'Skiving, you mean.'

Adam grinned. A shock of blond hair flopped forwards over his brow, and he brushed it back with his fingers. 'Nah, not really. It's study leave.'

Vanessa hiccupped. 'Which means you've got exams coming up.'

'Yeah, but not for ages.' He patted his shoulder bag that he'd dumped on the counter. 'And I've got stuff in here I can do.'

'Well, if you're sure.' She pressed the tissue to her lips. She really would be glad of the company, at least until the nausea passed.

'No probs, Aunty Van.' He opened his bag and took out a blue spiral bound folder.

The tack shop and saddlery had been bought for Vanessa by her mother, Ursula, when it became apparent she would not be a big name in the show jumping circuit. Despite having nothing in the way of business qualifications, she had somehow made the shop a success, helped in part by the support of her stepsister, Ella, a champion showjumper, and top-class riding instructor. Ella owned and ran Hollyfield Stables and Stud, the equestrian centre outside the village.

Hollyfield stables had an impressive reputation, and she was proud of her husband being promoted to the role of stud manager, following Thomas' impending retirement. She only hoped she hadn't poisoned him before he got the chance to take on the job, or to celebrate their first wedding anniversary.

One year, they had been married. Well, two weeks short of a year. She still couldn't believe her luck. She twirled her ring round her finger. Vanessa Harrison. She was Mrs Vanessa Harrison, and proud of it. Apart from this unexpected bout of food poisoning, all was perfect in her world.

Sadly, the same could not be said for her sister, Caroline.

Chapter Two

The calming and restorative effect of a walk in the woods, communing with nature on a breezy but mild spring morning, was not working for Caroline. She'd read somewhere that walking in the fresh air and enjoying the great outdoors would automatically lift her mood. It wasn't working. Not even the company of her mother's bouncy, and consistently happy springer spaniel, Monty, raised her spirits.

She was heading for forty, divorced, jobless (technically, since she didn't consider her stints at the bed-and-breakfast a proper job) and living with her mother. Her old school friends (and she'd never had that many) had departed to pastures new, with husbands, children, and glittering careers. Even her dumpy sister, Vanessa, had snared the most handsome man ever to come to Hollyfield stables.

So, what next? she wondered, picking up a stick and throwing it for Monty. The brown and white dog went bounding into the undergrowth, tail spiralling madly, then burst out through the trees, the bit of branch clenched between his jaws. If a dog could smile, this one had perfected the art. He charged up to her and dropped the stick at her feet, dark brown eyes gleaming as he pranced from side to side, waiting for her to pick it up and throw it again…and again…and again.

Caroline shivered and zipped up her fleece. The air had turned cooler. It was probably time she headed back. She picked up the stick for a last throw and made sure it was a big one, hurling it deep into the woods; Monty scampered excitedly after it.

'Oi!'

The shout came from somewhere to the left, through a thicket of brambles. 'What do you think you're doing?'

'Excuse me?'

'Don't you know how dangerous that is?'

Mr Dalton strode purposefully towards her, holding the stick aloft, with Monty barking excitedly at his heels. He had changed out of his business suit, and wore an open-necked checked shirt, dark jeans and stout walking boots. A thick sweater was tied round his middle.

Caroline's heart sank. This was all she needed.

'I'm so sorry. I didn't know anyone was there. It didn't hit you, did it?' she added. The man looked furious, and she couldn't fathom why, unless she'd clonked him on the head with it when she'd hurled it into the woods.

'Not me, you idiot.'

'Monty?' she said, crouching down and immediately fussing over the spaniel, who seemed delighted at the extra attention. 'But how…' She vaguely wondered how it could have hit the dog when he'd been by her side before she threw it.

Mr Dalton gave an exasperated sigh. 'This,' he said, waving the stick at her. 'Is sharp. It splinters. It causes untold damage to a dog's mouth, and yet people still think it's a good idea to chuck one and think it's a game. It's not a game.' He raised his knee and promptly snapped the bit of wood over it.

Caroline felt a flush of colour rushing to her cheeks. 'Well, excuse me, but I don't think what I do with my dog is any of your concern.' She stooped to clip on Monty's lead. Her hands were shaking.

'Really.' He stepped to one side as she straightened up. 'Then look at it as a bit of prudent advice.'

'I don't need your advice.'

'Plenty of people do.'

'More fool them,' she said. 'Come on, Monty. Home.'

She was still smarting with fury as she marched back up

the gravelled drive. A thin misty drizzle started falling, which didn't help her mood. Her fleece soaked up the moisture like a sponge, and her hair had frizzed. Besides that, she was conscious of him watching her as she stalked back towards the house.

Who did he think he was, talking to her like that?

'A vet, apparently,' Ursula said, as she made her a consoling mug of hot chocolate and slipped Monty a dried rabbit's ear to chew on.

'A vet?' Caroline repeated, her eyes widening in disbelief. 'How did you find that out?'

'He told me.'

'You never said.' She helped herself to one of Ursula's newly baked scones. 'Well, I'm glad he's not our vet. Not with his blunt manner.' She lathered butter on the scone and reached for the strawberry jam. She was starving. Her walk through the woods had given her an appetite. 'I wouldn't pay good money to see him.'

'Oh, I don't know. I've always favoured direct speaking. At least you know where you stand.'

That much was true. Her mother spoke first and risked the consequences later. It wasn't always the right thing to do, she thought. Sometimes tact and consideration worked better. She took a mouthful of warm, buttery scone. It was fresh from the oven and smelled and tasted delicious.

'So, if he's a vet, what's he doing here?'

'Oh, ah... he's... checking a few things out.'

Caroline eyed her mother with suspicion. She'd heard that tone of voice before. Shortly before she announced she was turning Grey Lodge into a Bed-and-breakfast, if her memory served her correctly.

She placed the half-eaten scone back on her plate and wiped her lips with the back of her hand. 'Mother, is there something you're not telling me?'

'No. Well, not really.'

'Mother?'

'Oh, all right, but I didn't want to tell you until I was certain.'

'About what?' Caroline's appetite had deserted her. She had the uncomfortable feeling that whatever her mother was going to say, she would not like it. Her eyes followed her as she pulled out one of the pine kitchen chairs, lowered herself onto it, and then propped her elbows on the table in front of her.

'As you know, I'm not getting any younger, darling.'

'You're not ill, are you?' Caroline started to panic.

'No. Well, not as far as I know, but it's all getting a bit much for me.'

'What is?'

'The house, the grounds, trying to keep everything going, and I've seen a lovely little retirement apartment in town. By the river, actually.'

'Wait, wait, wait! You're thinking of selling up?' Caroline was aghast. This was her home. She'd moved back here to be with her mother. All right, not exactly to be with her, but to live in grandeur for a change, while she got over the distress of her marriage break-up. Now, her mother was talking of selling up and going to live in a tiny retirement apartment in town? And what was she supposed to do? Where was she supposed to live?

'Yes. I'm downsizing. Isn't that what they say?'

'But…but you can't!'

'Actually, I can.' A hint of irritation had crept into her mother's tone. 'Nothing's settled, but that's what I plan to do.'

'But what about me?'

'Oh, you'll be fine. You've still got half the money from your house, and once I sell Grey Lodge, I'm sure I'll be able to help you out a bit. You'll be able to buy your own place.'

'I can't get a mortgage,' she said, her voice raising an octave. 'I haven't got a job. You could at least wait until I'm in full-time employment again.'

Her mother raised an eyebrow at her, as if that really wasn't her problem.

'Anyway, I don't expect it will be for ages. These things

don't happen overnight. You'll have plenty of time to look around.'

'For what?' she sniffed. 'A pokey flat, or a bedsit?'

'A job,' her mother said, gathering up the mugs. 'Goodness knows, you're nearly forty. You can't expect me to provide for you at your age. Not on my pension.'

The remark cut Caroline to the core. She didn't consider it her fault for being made redundant. These things happened. And she thought she'd been doing her mother a favour by helping her run the bed-and-breakfast, even if it meant changing sheets for strangers and scrubbing dirty toilets. She could have left her in the lurch, like Shirley had done, but no, she had helped out, and it would have been nice to be appreciated for it. Fat chance of that.

She swallowed hard, trying to control the tears that were threatening to fall. 'What has Mr Dalton got to do with this plan of yours?'

'Grant.'

'Sorry?'

'His name is Grant. Grant Dalton.'

'Please tell me you're not thinking of selling Grey Lodge to him.'

'Why not? His money is as good as anyone else's.' Her mother's voice sounded sharp.

Caroline shook her head. 'He can't buy it.'

'I'm sincerely hoping he will.' Her mother stood up and gathered the mugs in one hand and the plate with the half-eaten scone in the other.

'But, but…' Caroline was, quite literally, lost for words. This couldn't be happening. Her entire world was ending. No marriage, no job and now no home, and her mother seemed to think it was all fine and dandy, because she'd get to live in a retirement flat overlooking the river.

The woman in question stood by the sink, rinsing the mugs under the tap, her back turned to her. Deliberately, Caroline thought. Her mother had made her point and the discussion, it seemed, had ended.

Caroline scraped back her chair. It made a screeching noise on the tiled floor. Her heart thudded in her chest. 'I can't believe you're doing this, and you didn't think to tell me.'

'I didn't see the need until there was something to tell.'

'You could at least have discussed it with me. If you'd told me you were having problems, I could have helped you.'

'How, exactly?'

'I don't know.' She paused, thinking hard. 'I could have managed the business for starters if you'd said you wanted to retire.'

She was sure she would have made a better job of it, too. She could see herself in a managerial role, and even though she hated having strangers in the house, it might be different if she was the one in charge of things.

'Possibly.' Ursula dried her hands on the dishcloth and turned back to face her. 'But, let's face it, darling, you haven't been the easiest person to talk to recently.'

Caroline pulled a face. Was it any wonder?

'I know you've been unhappy after your divorce, and I understand that. And then, of course, you lost your job.'

'I was made redundant.'

'Exactly. But, darling, you can't let minor setbacks get you down. I've experienced being widowed more times than I care to think about, so I know what I'm talking about. Life goes on. It has to.'

Ursula patted her kindly on the arm, and Caroline resisted the urge to push her hand away. Her mother had lost three husbands and survived, apparently unscathed, so she supposed she meant well. But it didn't feel like it.

'You can't spend your days moping and feeling sorry for yourself. If you want things to change, you make it happen. No one else will.'

Her words were not what Caroline wanted to hear right now. She felt she had every right to feel sorry for herself, and this latest bombshell only accentuated that. Her eyes filled with tears, and she blinked them away before her mother noticed.

'Fine,' she said. 'Well, if you'll excuse me, mother, I'm going to my room. I need to think about what I'm going to do next, should this deal of yours go through.'

She stomped up the staircase and flung open the door marked private, that led to their suite of rooms—a sitting room and two bedrooms, with a small bathroom they shared—then slammed it hard behind her.

It was the shock of it all that she found so upsetting. How could her mother be so insensitive? She'd come to look on Grey Lodge as her home. Losing her job had put her plans to buy her own place on hold. Now it looked as if she'd have to find somewhere to rent, and that would soon whittle away her savings. If she could find somewhere, that is. Rental properties were few and far between, and those that were available tended to be expensive.

She stood by the window, staring down the long and gravelled drive towards the single-track lane that led to the village. The billboard, advertising the mansion as a bed-and-breakfast establishment, stood in the Gatehouse's garden, a single storey building at the end of the drive that Ursula used as a shed. On last inspection, it had contained the large ride on lawn-mower one of the village lads used to keep the lawns looking presentable, various gardening implements, chairs and tables, tins of half-used paint, and a load of packing crates that contained goodness knows what. But it had once been habitable.

Caroline wiped her eyes with the back of her hand and peered closer. The germ of an idea was forming.

Chapter Three

Grant Dalton studied the plans William Bracknell, the elderly architect from the neighbouring town, had drawn up for him.

'It's just a rough draft,' Mr Bracknell said. 'It'll give you an idea of the sort of things you could do if you decide to go ahead. I was thinking of operating theatres here.' He pointed at the rear of the building. 'And you'd want the waiting rooms here. Consulting rooms there and there. Reception at the front. Car park is more than adequate, and you could have living quarters upstairs, completely self-contained. Plus, you've got the bonus of the outhouses, which would easily convert to an apartment for a locum or a night nurse. It's all there. I'd say it is pretty damn perfect for what you want.'

'I had perfect,' he said. He didn't share the architect's obvious enthusiasm. Not yet, anyway, although he had to concede that the plans provided him with everything he needed for a new veterinary practice. But could he bring himself to part with the past and move forward? Leaving the life he had known and everything he knew behind him for a fresh start? He wasn't sure if he could do that. It seemed too soon, and yet, he knew, in his heart, that it would always feel that way.

The silence hung heavy in the air. Mr Bracknell stood up and walked to the bureau. 'Whisky? I've got a half decent malt.'

Grant nodded. 'Thanks.'

Purchasing Grey Lodge had been his daughter, Sabrina's idea. As a newly qualified vet, her aim was to specialise in equine medicine.

'I don't want to stay in Yorkshire, Dad. I did a locum job in Suffolk, and I've seen a place that would be perfect for us.'

'For us?'

'Yes, for you and me.' She held out her phone to show him the advertisement.

'Grey Lodge, Bed and Breakfast,' he read. 'A secluded setting in the peaceful Suffolk countryside.' He glanced up at her. 'You want me to stay there?'

'I want you to buy it.'

'What?' He thought he had misheard her, but by the eager look on her face, he suspected he hadn't. His eyes narrowed as he handed her back the phone 'Why?'

'Something has to change, Dad. You're living like a recluse. You need a challenge and I'm giving you one. We could set up our own family-run vet practice. I've heard, from a very reliable source, that the elderly owner is finding the responsibility of running the business too much and might be keen to sell for the right price.'

'What reliable source?'

'Her step-daughter,' she said with a grin. 'But that's between you and me. Ella will kill me if Ursula finds out.'

'Ursula?'

'Mrs Lloyd-Duncan to you, Dad.' She offered him the phone again. 'At least check it out. You could book in for a few days and have a look around first, before you say anything to the woman. Please? For me?'

Sabrina had her mother's instinct for a good thing when she saw it, and the guile to get her own way. He'd never been to this part of Suffolk, but here he was now, checking it out, just as she asked.

Mr Bracknell, an older man with a full head of grey hair that left Grant envious, since his was receding at an alarming pace, handed him a glass with a generous measure of whisky in it. 'Twenty-five-year-old malt', he told him. 'Brought it back from the Highlands on my last holiday.'

'Thanks.' He swirled the amber liquid round the bottom of

his glass and waited until the elderly man sat down again, before raising it to his lips and taking a mouthful. He swallowed and immediately coughed, his eyes watering as the fiery liquid hit the back of his throat. 'God, that's good.'

Mr Bracknell smiled. 'Thought you'd like it.' He leaned back in his chair, his elbows resting on the curved wooden arms, fingers steepled together. 'Now then, have you got any questions?'

Loads, Grant thought, placing the glass back on the leather-topped desk between them. But not ones he could ask the architect. He glanced across at him. 'If I bought the place—and it's a big if—how long do you think it would take to get things up and running?'

'Ah, now that's difficult to say. I would think four or five months, and that's a pretty rough estimate. Of course, you could be up and running in weeks, with work ongoing, but you'd have the noise and dust to factor in.' He gave a shake of his head. 'The poorly pets wouldn't like it.'

'True.' Most animals were nervous when brought to a veterinary practice. Loud noises wouldn't help. The building work would have to be finished before he could open for business, but that would give him more time to come round to the idea. And it would take time. He stroked his chin. 'Do you think there's a demand for another practice here?'

Mr Bracknell laughed. 'For horse vets, certainly. I'm presuming you've acquainted yourself with the area. You'll have seen how many livery yards there are.'

'I can't say I'd noticed,' he said. 'I expect my daughter would know. That's her area of expertise, not mine.'

'The location is perfect, Mr Dalton. I think it would work.'

'What about planning permission?'

'Again, I can't see it being a problem, as long as you maintain the character of the building. I made a few enquiries on your behalf,' he added. 'It's always handy to know these things before you go to the trouble of drawing up any plans. Saves everybody time, in the long run.'

Grant nodded and then drained his glass. 'Okay. Great. I'll give it some thought.' He stood up, his arm extended to shake the architect's hand. 'Thanks for your time.'

'My pleasure.' Mr Bracknell rolled up the papers. 'Take these with you. They're not official, at this stage, just suggestions for you to mull over. I've kept copies on file. If you want to proceed, just let me know and I'll get more detailed plans drawn up.'

Grant took the papers and tucked them under his arm. 'What's your schedule like?'

'Busy, but I'd make this a priority.'

'Thank you.' He shook his hand. The older man's grip was firm and assured. 'I'd appreciate that.'

He left the office in two minds about Grey Lodge. The building was old, some windows were draughty, and the upper floorboards, especially in the attic rooms, were uneven. It wouldn't surprise him if the roof needed some remedial work, too. But it was a magnificent house and the surrounding fields and land all went in its favour.

The attraction of living on site appealed to him. No more long commutes to work, with the bonus of a reduction in travelling costs. But moving away from the Yorkshire dales, where his life and his memories lay, would be difficult.

He'd met Helen, the love of his life, when he was studying to be a vet. Marriage and children had followed, and a partnership in Phillips, Dalton and Davies Veterinary practice. Life had been perfect, idyllic. Until it wasn't.

Stage four. Terminal.

The three words that had ruined their life together and lost him the only woman he had ever loved. The pain was still raw, the grief unbearable. Weeks became months, and months became years, but his feelings hadn't changed. He missed her so much.

Grant hitched the collar of his jacket up against the sudden, drizzly squall that swept in from the coast. The weather mirrored his mood. One minute fine, and the next minute gloomy. He had to stop thinking like this. It had happened and he couldn't change it. Helen hadn't wanted to worry him because he'd been stressed at work, so she'd said nothing about her own health concerns until it was too late. He should have noticed, but he'd been wrapped up in his own thoughts. Self-centred, as usual.

Grant kicked out at a stone, sending it bouncing over the kerb and into the road. He felt a wave of longing so intense it was almost painful.

The whisky had been a mistake, he thought, much though he appreciated the gesture. Apart from the obvious emotional reaction, he couldn't risk driving. He'd have to leave the car in town and walk back to Grey Lodge. This dismal weather wasn't the best for walking, but he had no choice.

Hitching his collar up and reminding himself that Suffolk was supposed to be one of the driest parts of the country, and the rain would soon pass, he set off.

It took him the best part of an hour to walk to the house down twisting country lanes and past acres of paddocks. Mr Bracknell had been right about the number of horse owners in the area. No wonder Sabrina had been so insistent that this was the right place to be.

'We could go into partnership, Dad,' she said. 'I could do the farm animals and horses, and you could specialise in domestic pets. You might even persuade Paul King to join us. He's not happy at Claremont vets. He told me so when I was doing my last stint there. He said he's looking to join an independent practice again.'

'I'm not the best person to work with these days.'

Grant was the first to admit that his patience was not what it used to be, meaning he often came across as blunt and unsympathetic when dealing with clients. If he could just look after the animals, and ignore the people, he'd be fine. But half the veterinary cases he saw were caused by ignorant owners, who thought giving a dog chocolate was a treat for them, or leaving food down all day wouldn't make their pet fat.

'We'll get you a good vet nurse. She can do all the talking.'
'You've got an answer for everything.'
'I'm being serious, Dad. I think this might be the change you need.'
'We'll see.'

He ambled up the long driveway towards Grey Lodge, trying to imagine it through a client's eyes. 'The Dalton veterinary practice.' It had a certain ring to it, he supposed. And it looked good. First impressions were favourable. The generous parking area helped. The estate had a lot going for it, all things considered. But could he leave everything behind in Yorkshire, sell up, and start afresh here? More to the point, did he want to?

The door sprang open as he approached, and a harassed-looking Ursula Lloyd-Duncan hurried out, a blue mac draped over her head and shoulders, the brown and white springer spaniel dancing round her legs.

'Get out of the way, Monty... Oh, hello.' A pair of owlish eyes blinked up at him from beneath the hood. 'Sorry. I didn't see you there. Just taking the dog for a run round the grounds. I don't know where he gets his energy from.'

Grant stepped to one side. 'He's a Springer, Spaniel,' he said drily. 'What do you expect?'

'Right. Yes, of course,' agreed Ursula, who'd previously told him of the years she had spent with a lumbering and overweight labrador, who slept all day. Monty appeared to have the energy of an endurance athlete and was keen to prove it. 'Have you...er... have you thought anymore about the house?'

'I've thought about it.' Grant replied.

'And?'

'I am interested. For the right price,' he said. 'I'll let you know once I've discussed things with my family and solicitor.'

He didn't tell her he'd spoken to his son on the phone that morning, and Greg was fully on board with the idea of his father moving to Suffolk.

'You need to get away, Dad. It sounds harsh, I know, but you've spent too long remembering and not enough time living. You can't change what happened. None of us can. Mum wouldn't want you to be stuck in the past. You know she wouldn't. She'd be telling you to go for it. A new adventure. Isn't that what she loved? Besides, it sounds like Sabrina has got you under her thumb already,' he added. *'I'd seriously consider doing it, if I were you.'*

'But you're not me.'

'Obviously. But what have you got to lose?'

Good question, Grant thought. He'd need to think about that.

'No, seriously, I think it sounds good, Dad. But if you really can't do it and you just want a break from things, you can always join me in the States.'

'And do what, exactly?'

Greg was a musician, currently touring with his fledgling rock band. Grant couldn't think of anything worse than hitting the road like an ageing rocker. He craved peace and solitude, not crowds of people.

'There's always loads to do backstage.'

'Nice thought, Greg, but I'll give it a miss, if it's all the same to you.'

Grant glanced sideways at Ursula, who had only managed a couple of steps down the drive. She still watched him with an expectant look on her face.

'When will that be?' she said. 'I mean, are we talking hours, days, weeks?' Her voice rose slightly.

'Soon,' he said.

'Oh, right.' She sounded peeved. Her eyes narrowed, and her lips tightened, giving him the impression of someone sucking a sour sweet. 'Well, don't take too long. There are other people asking about it.'

Grant knew she was lying. The house wasn't for sale on the open market. It was only because his daughter had heard she was struggling to employ and keep decent staff and might be interested in selling that he had approached the woman.

He had to admit; the place was in the perfect location for a new Equine veterinary practice. But he wouldn't let her know that.

He kept his face impassive as he stood, legs apart and arms folded, in the open doorway. Ursula had not made a move. The dog, however, was tearing down the drive, in hot pursuit of something, though, for the life of him, he couldn't see what.

'You'd better catch him before he reaches the lane,' he advised.

'Oh, Monty won't go far.'

Famous last words, Grant thought.

'Oh, bother. Monty! Here boy! Monty!' Galvanised into action, Ursula set off down the drive, the blue mac flapping behind her like a crusader's cape.

Grant closed the door behind her, and stood in the impressive hallway, glancing upwards at the sweeping, oak panelled staircase. He'd hate to lose that. It was a beautiful feature of the house. He climbed up to the landing, and peered back down over the wooden bannisters, imagining waiting rooms to the right, a reception desk in front of the stairs, and consulting rooms to the left. Yes, it might work.

For the first time in months, he felt a vague glimmer of hope. He might have found something to motivate him at last. He needed space to reflect and recover in a place where no one knew him. Maybe Grey Lodge was the place to do it. A place where he could get on with things without enduring the pitying backward glances and sympathetic looks. They didn't help. Nothing helped, not even the passing of time, which was supposed to be the healer of all things. Perhaps there could be a future for him here, in this peaceful part of the countryside.

And maybe, though it pained him to admit it, maybe his daughter was right.

Chapter Four

The small, enclosed garden of the gatehouse was about the only thing that didn't need any work doing to it. Caroline pushed open the white gate and stood for a moment, admiring the trim hedges and borders full of yellow daffodils and narcissus. A brick path meandered through the middle of a neatly tended lawn and led to a stout wooden door with a large padlock on it. The two leaded windows on either side were shuttered from the inside.

Caroline undid the padlock, and pushed the door open, casting a pool of sunlight onto the dusty tiled floor of what had once been a small sitting room. Now it was a storage area, piled high with crates and boxes, and an old leather trunk. It smelt musty and damp.

She flicked on the light switch, relieved to find it still worked. The place had electricity, if nothing else. Above her head, stretching to the shuttered windows, hung cobwebs of varying sizes, with dubious bits of insects hanging from them. A rustling noise in the far corner of the room made her jump.

She edged her way across the cluttered floor and peered into the small kitchen.

Someone had left a lawnmower by the back door, taking up most of the floor space. Bits of dried grass cuttings and clumps of mud were all over the tiles. The white enamel sink contained a yellow plastic bucket and some gardening shears.

She couldn't bring herself to look inside the kitchen cupboards. The smell in the room indicated something had gone off, and she had no desire to find out what caused the foul odour.

With one hand over her nose and mouth, she retreated to the sitting room, but not before she made enough noise to frighten off the rodents, she felt sure had taken up residence.

Stamping her feet, she made her way to the room on the right, which had presumably been a bedroom at one time, judging by the grimy floral curtains over the windows and the rusted metal bed frame that had seen better days.

A narrow corridor separated the bedroom from the small bathroom.

'Practically ensuite as well,' she said. 'What a luxury.' She hoped the mice, or (perish the thought) rats, appreciated her running commentary.

Caroline peered down at the cracked and stained toilet, and then up at the large, overhead cistern complete with rusty chain, and shuddered. She wanted to see if it worked, but nerves got the better of her. Goodness knows what might gush out of the pipes if she tried to flush it.

The washbasin showed cracks and appeared to have been used for cleaning something oily, based on the dark streaks and tide mark surrounding it. The bath had a pile of empty paint pots, brushes, tarpaulin, and other decorating equipment inside it. A set of wooden stepladders stood propped against the wall.

Caroline brushed a cobweb away from her face and gave an involuntary shudder. This was a stupid idea. She couldn't possibly live here. What on earth had possessed her to consider it?

***

'Actually, I think it's a brilliant idea.' Vanessa heaped a spoonful of sugar into the mug of coffee she had made and passed it over to her.

'Well, you would,' Caroline said, glancing round the immaculate kitchen, with its black worktops and gleaming white cupboards. 'You've got this place.' She carried it into the lounge and lowered herself down onto the settee, taking care not to spill any of it on the plush cream rug.

Years ago, this cottage had once been her home, too. She had hated living here and having to share a bedroom with her sister. It was probably the reason she had been in such a hurry to marry Marcus.

'Yes, which we bought from mother,' Vanessa reminded her, as she followed her into the lounge and placed a packet of open ginger biscuits on the glass and chrome coffee table.

Caroline didn't need reminding. It was a sore point. Vanessa and Jed had bought it at a bargain price in the run up to their wedding, and Ursula had been more than happy to sell it to them.

If only she and Marcus had thought about it first. It could have been theirs, instead of the box-like house they had bought on a rundown estate.

When their mother had married Michael Lloyd-Duncan and moved herself and Vanessa into Grey Lodge, the cottage had stood empty for years. The opportunity to buy it from her had never occurred to Caroline and Marcus. They were too busy settling into married life in their own house.

Caroline cleared her throat with a small cough and reached for a biscuit. There was no point in reflecting on the past and what might have been. It was the present that concerned her now. 'You've got a spare room,' she said.

'You're surely not thinking… No, absolutely not.' Vanessa plonked herself down on the soft and squashy chair by the window, her face a picture of horror. 'You can't move in with us.'

'I don't see why not,' Caroline said. 'I used to live here.'

'That was years ago. And anyway, it's Jed and mine's house now. We're the ones paying the mortgage. You haven't stayed here since you married Marcus.'

'Yes, well, don't remind me of him,' she said. She took a sip of coffee and pulled a face. It could have done with less milk and more sugar.

She thought Vanessa might have been a bit more sympathetic to her predicament, but apparently not. She was still in that honeymoon phase of deep and besotted love, and obviously didn't want her sister disturbing her love-nest. Not that she fancied being a gooseberry either, but if their mother sold Grey Lodge, she didn't know where else to turn.

'Look,' Vanessa said, her tone kinder. 'It might not happen for ages. You'd have plenty of time to do up the gatehouse. I think it would make a lovely little home for you.'

'You haven't seen it,' she muttered, dunking a biscuit into her milky coffee.

'Well, no, not recently,' Vanessa conceded. 'But think of the peace and the privacy, and that beautiful garden.'

'It's only beautiful because it's the first thing the guests see when they drive up to Grey Lodge. Mother made sure it looked good from the outside.'

'Exactly. And you can do the same with the inside. I don't mind helping,' she added. 'Decorating is a passion of mine.'

'Since when?'

Vanessa waved her arm around in an exaggerated gesture. 'Since I did all this. Besides, you'd be able to buy it for next to nothing, if it's really that bad.'

Caroline sniffed as she let her gaze wander around the pale green walls and cream woodwork. It looked nice. Her sister was cleverer than she gave her credit for.

'If Mother agrees to sell it to me, and it's not part of the deal she wants to make with Grant Dalton,' she said.

'Stop being so negative. He wouldn't be interested in the gatehouse, surely?'

She had no idea. Her mother hadn't expanded on the plans, and she hadn't been in the mood to discuss them. They weren't on the best of terms at the moment. 'Maybe you could have a word with her?'

'And say what? She hasn't told me she's thinking of moving.'

'Well, I only found out today.'

'Exactly, so you've got loads of time to plan. Look, if it's any help, I'll get Jed to look the place over and see what he thinks. But right now, I've got to get back to work.' Vanessa stood and brushed some biscuit crumbs off her lap. 'I've left Adam at the shop, but I can't expect him to stay all day.'

'I could help.' Caroline suddenly saw an answer to her

employment problem, or lack of it. She picked up the mugs and followed her sister into the kitchen. 'I'd rather work in the tack shop than wait on tables and change beds for mother.'

'I don't need help. Well, apart from today when I felt poorly,' Vanessa said hurriedly. 'Dodgy sausages, I think.'

'Yuck.' Caroline pulled a face. She hoped it wasn't that ghastly Norovirus that was doing the rounds. Ella said Rosie had been sent home from school with it the other day.

'Anyway, you need to go back and have a serious talk with Mother, and I'll get Jed to check the place out. How does that sound?' She picked up her jacket and bag as she spoke. It was, evidently, time to leave.

'Okay, I suppose.'

Caroline rinsed the mugs and placed them on the draining board. Talking with her sister had lifted her mood, slightly. Vanessa had a talent for recognising the positive in difficult situations. She wished she could follow her example. Maybe she would. Nothing was insurmountable, given time. It was the mantra she would remember when she talked things over with her mother.

***

Ursula, however, was not in the mood for any sort of discussion. 'I've lost the dog,' were the first words she said on Caroline's return to Grey Lodge a short time later.

'What do you mean, you've lost the dog?' She hadn't even had the chance to take off her jacket before Ursula bundled her out of the front door again.

'He ran off when I took him through the woods, and he hasn't come back. Go and look for him, darling. He likes you,' she added.

Caroline turned her collar up. 'I can't believe you just left him,' she said, snatching the lead from Ursula's outstretched hand.

Her mother had the good grace to look sheepish. 'I called him for ages. Only I got caught a bit short. I'd had three cups of tea. I really thought he'd be back by now.'

The drizzle, which started when she left Vanessa's, had turned into more of a squally shower. Monty hated the rain, although he did like a muddy puddle or two, which never did make much sense to Caroline. She pulled her hood up and put on her gloves.

'I'll take my phone with me. Call me if he comes home.'

'I will, darling.'

She strode down the drive and headed across the field that led to the woods. She had a soft spot for the bouncy spaniel that Ursula had bought to replace Bruno, their old labrador. A puppy had not been a wise choice, given she was heading for seventy when she got him, and trying to run a business at the same time. Consequently, the dog hadn't received the attention and training he needed at such a young age, and thought he was perfectly within his rights to roam off after the scent of a rabbit or pheasant, whenever the fancy took him.

'Monty!' she called. 'Here, boy. Come on, Monty.'

A flock of pigeons circled overhead before settling on the roof of the old mansion house. Caroline pushed open the swing gate and headed into the woods.

It felt marginally drier beneath the cover of the trees, but the ground was damp and slippery under foot. She had on her best trainers and wished she'd changed into boots when she heard the dog barking.

'Monty!'

He gave a few short yelps.

When she saw him, he was shivering by the trunk of an old oak tree, one that a lightning strike had blackened, but was still growing valiantly in the middle of a leafy copse of beech and ash. His front paw was raised, and though he seemed excited to see her, his tail swishing furiously from side to side, he didn't make a move.

'Come on, Monty.'

With a sinking feeling, she saw he appeared hurt. Caroline ran towards him, ignoring the mud splattering over her new shoes, and crouched down in front of him, fondling his head and ears with one hand as she took the offered paw in the other.

'What's up with you?' she murmured softly.

He gave a whimper and jerked the paw away.

She felt a sharp prick as she ran her fingers over the dog's pad, and saw, to her horror, a thin sliver of glass sticking out through the fur on his foot. It looked like it had gone in between the pads.

'No wonder you couldn't walk,' she said, gently stroking his head. She sat on the ground and leaned back against the trunk of the tree. Monty seized the opportunity to lie across her thighs, as she knew he would. He loved nothing more than lying on somebody's warm lap. His chin rested on her knees.

'Daft dog.' She waited until he was completely calm and still, before she took off her glove and felt for the shard of glass. She got hold of it between her thumb and forefinger. With one quick tug, it came free.

Though she could feel the glass slicing into her finger, that was the least of her worries. Getting him back to the house would prove more challenging. She couldn't carry him, but she didn't want him walking through the mud with an open wound, either. His paw still dripped blood. To make matters worse, the rain was coming down heavier, splattering off the overhanging leaves and soaking the pair of them.

She clipped on his lead and hooked it over her wrist before reaching for her mobile. It was time she called for reinforcements. Her mother would need to come and help her.

Fortunately, she answered her phone after one ring. 'What do you mean, he's hurt?' she said. 'He can't be. He only ran after a rabbit. Oh, my poor Monty. What's happened to him?' She sounded frantic.

And so she should be, Caroline thought, waspishly. This was her fault. 'He's cut his paw on some broken glass. I don't think he can walk. Or at least, I don't want him to until we get it cleaned up and bandaged. We're in the woods by the oak tree that was hit by lightning a few years ago. You know where that is, don't you? And bring something to wrap…' Her words tailed off as she realised her mother wasn't listening. She was talking to someone else. She could hear mumbled words like 'oak tree,' and 'lightning.' The voice in the background sounded like Jed.

'Mother!' she said. 'Are you listening to me?'

'Yes, darling. Yes, he's just coming.'

'Oh, thank God.'

Vanessa must have told Jed about the gatehouse as soon as she left her, which was a stroke of luck. He couldn't have called round at a better time. Vanessa's husband would know what to do. He wasn't just brilliant with horses, but could work his magic on almost any animal, using skills he had picked up when he worked on a ranch in Montana. He had a calming and confident manner that settled even the most anxious animal. Monty wasn't an anxious dog, but he was in pain.

'He won't be long,' Ursula said, and Caroline relaxed slightly. Monty was still lying on her legs, and she carried on stroking him, in the hope it would stop him from leaping up when he saw Jed, which he invariably did. He loved male attention. In particular, he loved Jed. The former actor and stunt rider, who they'd once thought of as an American cowboy, had won his place in all their hearts. Especially Vanessa's.

Caroline felt a slight twinge of envy at her sister's good fortune. If only someone as handsome and caring as Jed Harrison would sweep her off her feet, but she couldn't see that happening anytime soon.

Footsteps came crunching over twigs and bracken.

'Over here,' she called, holding tightly to Monty's collar. 'We're over here, Jed.'

Except it wasn't Jed.

Grant Dalton came striding through the thicket of trees, a black bag slung over one shoulder and a steely glint on his face.

Her jaw dropped in surprise. 'You.'

He dropped to his knees. 'Where's he hurt?'

'Front paw.' She tilted her head, still restraining Monty, who did his utmost to leap up and welcome this surprising new visitor to the woods.

'Broken glass?'

'Yes, I think I managed to get it out, but I didn't want him walking back through all that mud. There's a broken bottle over there. He must have stood on it.'

'Okay. Let's have a look, young man.' He worked quickly and calmly, examining every part of the paw, and gently wiping away the dirt with a sterile pad from his bag.

'Lift his head a moment.'

Caroline obliged, resting the dog's shoulder against her chest and hooking an arm around his neck.

'I'll put a temporary bandage on it for now,' he said. 'I can clean it properly when I get him back to the house.'

'Shall I carry him?'

Grant shook his head and stood up, brushing the mud and leaves from his jeans as he did so. Without another word, he hoisted Monty into his arms and hugged him to his chest.

'You can take the bag,' he said.

Without another word, he turned and strode back the way he had come, with Monty's tail wagging feebly, under his left armpit.

Well, that was her told. Caroline struggled to her feet and snatched up the black shoulder bag. As a precaution, she collected up the bits of broken bottle that were scattered round the base of the tree. People who had nothing better to do than trample through the woods had presumably smashed it and left it behind. This land was private, but short of installing security fencing, there wasn't much that could be done to keep the locals from trespassing on their land. Still, if things went as her mother planned, it wouldn't be their concern for much longer.

It annoyed her that Grant acted as if this was her fault. Monty's accident had nothing to do with her. It was her mother who had gone off and left him unsupervised. She had a good mind to tell him that too, if she could catch up with him.

He marched across the field carrying the dog as if he were light as a feather, and Caroline knew that, at twenty-five kilos, he was hardly that. Yet here she was, struggling with a backpack that weighed next to nothing as she slipped and slithered on the rain sodden grass. If she wasn't careful, she could see herself falling and cutting herself on the bits of broken bottle she clutched in her hand, and she doubted he'd be as sympathetic to her.

By the time she got back to Grey Lodge, Monty's cut had been freshly cleaned, treated and bandaged, and he was lying mournfully in front of the Aga, sporting a large plastic cone to prevent him from licking it. Grant had obviously come prepared, she thought. His car must be like a travelling vet practice. She dumped his bag on the floor and glanced round the room. 'Where's he gone?'

'For a shower,' her mother said, reaching for the kettle. 'He did look a bit wet.'

Caroline was dripping puddles onto the floor. Her long hair had coiled round her neck and was oozing rainwater into the folds of her shirt. 'Think I'll join him.'

Her mother jerked her head round.

'Oh, for goodness' sake,' she snapped, peeling off her wet coat and dropping it in a heap on the tiles. 'I didn't mean join him as in, well, join him.' She shuddered at the thought. 'And yes, I would like a hot drink, thank you.' She crouched down and stroked Monty's damp head. She was rewarded with a swishing of his tail on the quarry tiles.

'I must say, it's quite handy having a vet on the premises,' her mother said, as she presented her with a cup of hot tea and placed a biscuit on the saucer, which was either a peace offering, or to ease her guilty conscience.

Nevertheless, Caroline munched on it gratefully. 'I expect he'll want payment.'

'Do you think so?'

'Yes, and even if he doesn't, you should at least offer.'

'Why?'

'Because it was your fault.'

'Darling. You know what Monty is like. These things happen.'

'Really.' Caroline swallowed the last few crumbs of her biscuit and wondered if there were any more in the tin. She had lost loads of weight following the upset over her divorce, so she was sure a couple more wouldn't do any harm.

Her mother had turned her back to her and bent down to murmur words of sympathy to Monty. Her babyish voice made Caroline cringe.

She gave an involuntary shiver. It was time she changed out of her wet clothes. They were starting to cling rather unpleasantly and damply against her skin.

'I need to get changed.' She stood up. 'But after I've had a shower, we need to have a chat.'

'What about?'

'The situation. My situation. The house!' she said, exasperated. Her mother was looking at her as if she didn't have a clue what she was on about.

'Oh, that. Well, there's nothing much to say. Not until I find out whether he wants to buy the place. There's no point getting ahead of ourselves, darling.'

'Well, I'd like to be kept up to date, if it's all the same to you.'

'And you will be, I promise. In the meantime.' She handed her the folded-up newspaper left on the wooden dining table. 'You might want to take a look at this.'

'Why? What's in it?'

Her mother gave her a thin smile. 'The jobs page.'

Chapter Five

Caroline followed Jed through the door of the Gatehouse and watched as he picked his way around some old, rusty implements and abandoned tools. The place was so cluttered, finding a safe place to walk was almost impossible.

'You sister said I had to come straight from work,' he said. 'So here I am. Where do you want me to start?'

'Wherever you like,' she said, brushing a cobweb away from her face with a shudder.

She'd had some stupid ideas in her time, but clearing out the mess and filth from this pokey little hovel so she could actually live here had to be one of her most ridiculous ones.

She stood to one side, watching, while Jed examined the front room. He said nothing as he inspected the place, but he was being thorough. Every so often he stopped to tap on a wall or looked up to examine the ceiling. She felt like a spare part. 'Is there anything I can do to help?' she asked.

'Nope.'

She pursed her lips together. 'Should I wait outside?'

'No, you're fine. I won't be long.'

Good, she thought, trying not to breathe in too hard. The smell was unbearable. She planted her foot against the door, to keep it from swinging shut. Any air, even cold air, was better than nothing.

'It's really not that bad.' He ran his hands down the door frame of what was once the bedroom. 'I mean, the building's sound. Nothing that a thorough scrub and a lick of paint won't solve.' He pulled the floral curtains to one side to allow in some natural light. The thin material shredded and fell apart in his hands.

'It's filthy,' she said, holding a tissue to her nose. The dust was getting to her. Either that, or she was coming down with something. She tried to stifle a sneeze.

'Yes, and you can clean it. This is just surface dirt.' He dragged a finger along the skirting board and held it up for her to examine. His finger was black, but he had revealed a streak of cream coloured paint along the top of the board.

She admired his optimism, but her doubts remained. It would take weeks to get through all that engrained grime. Facing up to clearing everything out and scrubbing the place down was putting her off before she even started. The sneeze she had been trying to smother erupted in triplicate.

'Yeah, it is pretty dusty.' Jed undid the latch on the window and pushed it open. A welcome breeze of fresh air wafted into the room. Unfortunately, more dust blew into the air at the same time. Caroline held the tissue over her nostrils. Her eyes began to water and sting.

'I know it's looking bad at the moment but try to imagine the place cleared of all this rubbish; a new carpet, blinds at the window, a lick of paint. You must have watched those home makeover programmes on the telly. They've transformed some real dumps.' He glanced round the room as he spoke. 'Places a lot worse than this.'

'Yes, with an army of helpers.' She blew her nose.

He patted her on the shoulder as he strolled past her to the door. 'You'll have help. Come on, use your imagination. This place could be lovely.'

Caroline remained unconvinced. She felt sure Jed was only saying it because he didn't want her moving in with them. Vanessa must have told him to lay it on thick.

She trailed after him into the small bathroom, her feet crunching on scattered debris, including gravel and stones and an unmentionable substance that she fervently hoped was mud.

'The toilet's disgusting as well.'

'It's certainly vintage.' He reached up and pulled the heavy metal chain. A torrent of rust-coloured water gushed into the stained pan. 'Probably worth something too.'

'It's unhygienic.' Caroline stepped back to avoid getting splashed by the sudden rush of water.

'Right now, it is, but I can sort that out for you.'

She looked at him dubiously. 'Are you sure?'

'Yes, of course. Look,' he said. 'You'll get nothing better than this, at short notice. In this state, you could get it for next to nothing.'

'If Mother agrees to sell.'

'Why shouldn't she?'

Caroline shrugged her shoulders. Her mother was an enigma. She never knew what she was going to do next.

'Have you asked her?'

'No. I wanted to see what you thought of it first.' She followed him out of the bathroom and back into the kitchen.

He flicked the lights on and off. 'The electric's on, but you'll need to get the wires checked.' He crouched down to open the cupboard under the sink.

Caroline held her breath, the tissue stuffed under her nose. What was that disgusting smell?

'Rotten potatoes,' Jed said, holding up a dripping carrier bag. 'They're pretty much mush. I reckon one of the gardeners must have left them here and forgotten about them.'

She felt her stomach heave and stepped back to let him carry it at arm's length to the front door.

He tossed the leaking bag onto the lawn. 'Don't worry. I'll clear it up later.'

Then he started opening other cupboard doors, peering inside, shifting crumpled packets and dusty boxes out of the way, tapping and knocking on the walls behind.

Finally, he turned and scratched at his chin for a moment, as if considering what he should say. His expression was hard to fathom.

Caroline swallowed hard. She didn't know what to think.

Jed stuffed his hands in the pockets of his jeans and grinned. 'You want to have a chat with your mother about buying this place, and quickly too, before that vet chap gets his hands on it.'

She let out the breath she had been holding. 'Really? You think I could do something with it?'

'Absolutely.' He nodded. 'This is a sound little building. Yes, it's small, but what more do you need? It's got all the facilities right here; water, electrics, plumbing. Plus, you've got peace and solitude. You can't put a price on that. Beautiful views, lovely garden. I think you'd be mad not to go for it.'

His words seemed to work their magic.

Caroline leaned her hands on the dirty enamel sink and stared out of the grubby window, contemplating what he had said and trying hard to imagine herself in residence.

A new kitchen would transform the place; maybe even a new bathroom, although Jed's admiration of the vintage toilet made her wonder whether she should keep it on as a feature. 'There's no heating,' she said, rubbing her hands together, the damp chill reminding her of just how cold it might get in the depths of winter.

Jed pointed to a dusty metal grated object in the lounge. 'You've got a log-burner there. Be good as new, after a proper clean and service. The old boiler needs ripping out, but it makes sense to replace it, if you can afford to.'

Caroline nodded. With her half share of the marital home, she might be able to stretch to a new boiler and kitchen, depending on the asking price her mother wanted for the cottage.

She picked her way around the heaped-up boxes of goodness knows what, and stood in the front room, trying to visualise what it might look like with furniture, instead of rubbish. A sofa by the window, with cushions and cosy throws, a television and maybe a bookcase or two, and a coffee table. Whatever she liked, really, because it would all be hers. All hers.

She let that thought sink in for a moment.

'Talk to your mother,' Jed said. 'Don't ask her. Tell her. This is what you want to do. If she sells you the gatehouse, she might not need to sell Grey Lodge.'

'Oh, she will,' Caroline said, turning back to him. 'She's already admitted it's too big for her to manage.'

'But with your money, she could pay for some help.'

She shook her head. 'She's tried. No one wants to work for her.'

'That's understandable,' Jed murmured, adding, 'Sorry, but your mother's not the easiest person to work with, and word soon gets out. I'm surprised you've stuck it so long.'

'I don't have much choice. I have to live there.' She ran her fingers along the edge of the windowsill. But maybe not for much longer, she thought.

Outside, she could see the hazy glimmer of sunlight. The clouds were clearing. 'Besides,' she said, glancing over her shoulder. 'She wants this retirement apartment she's seen overlooking the river.'

'That's good. It means she'll be eager to accept your offer.'

'Really?'

'Of course. It gives her the cash for a deposit on the apartment she fancies. Even if that vet wants to buy Grey Lodge, I can't see the sale going through quickly. I'm presuming he's got a property to sell.'

'I don't know.'

'Well, let's assume that he has.' Jed started picking up tins of old paint and removing them from the bathtub. 'He's going to have to sell his house before he can think of buying, and then he's going to have to do the alterations before he can set up a new veterinary practice. It could take months before it's all settled.'

Caroline stared up at him with dawning realisation. 'So, if I give her the money for a deposit, by buying this place…'

'She'll be more than happy,' Jed said.

'She will, won't she?'

He grinned. 'So, what are you waiting for? Now, pass me

those bin bags. We need to remove some of this rubbish.'

Chapter Six

'We need to talk,' Caroline said, marching into the kitchen and tossing her jacket over the back of a chair. Even as she spoke, she realised she was using the precise words Marcus had said to her when he'd asked for a divorce. Well, she didn't intend to think about him right now. Not when she felt so motivated and positive; two things she hadn't felt in a long time.

Ursula was standing at the Aga, stirring a pot of something that smelt burnt.

Caroline could see smoke puffing from the stained bottom of the pan. Congealed grease, she presumed. Her mother had failed to wipe it off before putting the pan on the stove. Her eyesight wasn't good at the best of times.

'What about, darling?'

'The old gatehouse at the end of the drive.' She paused and sucked in a breath. The acrid fumes from the scorched pan caught in the back of her throat.

Her mother seemed immune to it. 'Oh, yes?'

'I want to buy it.'

Ursula turned, her beady eyes narrowing. 'What did you say?'

'The gatehouse.' Caroline pulled a chair away from the table and sat down on it. 'I want to buy it.'

'Why?'

'To live in, of course.'

Her mother let out a long and exasperated sigh. 'Don't be so ridiculous. It's not a house. It's a hovel. You can't live there.'

'I can, and I intend to, once it's done up. Jed's going to help me,' she added.

'What?' Her mother peered down at her over the rim of her glasses. Behind her, the pot on the Aga still emitted a strong, smoky aroma.

Caroline suspected it really was burning, now that her mother had stopped stirring whatever she was cooking. It certainly didn't smell appetising. 'Jed has agreed to help me,' she repeated. She waved a hand at the cooker. 'I think you need to give that a stir, mother.'

'It's simmering.'

Scorching, more like. Caroline folded her arms firmly in front of her. 'I need somewhere to live, since you're selling this place, and the gatehouse seems like the perfect solution.'

'It's a dump.'

'Yes, but in the old days it was once a home for the gamekeeper. I intend to make it one again.'

'For the gamekeeper?' Ursula looked puzzled.

Caroline maintained her outward show of confidence, though inside, she could feel herself weakening. Her mother had that effect on her.

'For me.' She met her mother's gaze with a determined stare. 'I don't have any other alternative. Other than moving in with Vanessa and Jed…'

'A perfectly sensible option, in my opinion.'

'Sensible maybe, but hardly fair. They've only been married a year.'

'I'm sure they wouldn't mind.'

'They would,' she said firmly. 'So,' she sucked in a deep breath. 'I propose to buy the gatehouse with the money from my divorce settlement. I can do it up into a cosy country retreat and *you*,' (She laid emphasis on the word you) 'can place a deposit on the apartment you like by the river, thus securing it until the sale of Grey Lodge goes through. Now, how does that sound?'

Her mother looked as if she was thinking hard. Behind her, the pot emitted puffs of smoke. The smell of burnt meat was making Caroline's eyes water.

'Is that stew….?'

'Oh, blast.' Ursula seized the handle of the pan and slid it to one side of the hob. In her haste, she had forgotten to use oven gloves, and the metal handle was hot. She rushed to the sink and stuck her hand under the cold tap.

'Mother, are you all right?'

'Yes, yes.' The water splashed everywhere. She had turned the tap on full blast.

Monty, who slumbered in front of the Aga, didn't take too kindly to a sudden and unexpected cold shower. He leapt up and started barking, his plastic cone banging against Ursula's legs as he did so, threatening to unbalance her.

'Monty, here.' Caroline leaned forward and patted her thighs. The spaniel happily obliged, trotting towards her, his tail wagging. She stroked his head until he calmed down, circled the rug twice, and then settled down by her feet.

With order duly restored, and scalded fingers soothed, her mother sat down heavily on a chair. Her floral blouse gaped open where the middle button had popped off. Caroline hoped it hadn't ended up in the pot of stew.

A thoughtful expression cemented itself on her mother's face. 'Hmm,' she said. 'Maybe it's not as ridiculous as it sounds. Except, there's one slight problem.'

'What?'

'Mr Dalton.'

Caroline stared back at her, her mind working overtime. How could he be a problem? The gatehouse was at the end of the drive, far enough away from the main building, so that she didn't have to see or speak to him if she didn't want to, and at this point in time, she most certainly didn't.

'I specified the sale of the entire estate,' Ursula said. 'He seemed interested in the outbuildings, in particular. I'm sure that included the gatehouse.'

'Can't you tell him it's not included?'

'And risk losing the sale?'

'Mother. Do you want to see me homeless?'

'No Darling. Do you want to see me bankrupt?'

Caroline gaped at her. Her mother looked weary all of a sudden, and old. She had taken her glasses off and was rubbing her eyes with the back of her hand. Her once blonde hair was a dull grey and white. She refused to pay the extortionate prices to have it coloured at the village hair salon, or so she said. But was that all bluster on her part?

'Are things really that bad?'

Her mother gave a small nod of her head.

Caroline couldn't believe it. 'But how? Why?'

'Blasted taxes.' Ursula replaced her glasses and gave a resigned shake of her head.

'What? Don't tell me you haven't been paying tax on the business?'

'On anything,' Ursula said. 'It was an oversight. You know how busy I've been with things, and I'm not getting any younger.'

'I don't think senility will count in your favour, do you?' Caroline couldn't believe what she was hearing. Her mother was usually so competent, so capable.

'I'm not senile,' Ursula insisted. 'Just forgetful.'

'That'll go down well in court. Sorry, your honour, I forgot.' She leaned forward, her elbows propped up on the table, her chin resting on her hands. 'Look, Mother, if I buy the gatehouse, surely that will help?'

'Yes, of course it will, but what about Mr Dalton?'

She thought for a moment. 'Well, he can't buy what isn't for sale. Since you've admitted to being forgetful, all you have to do is convince him it wasn't included in the estate. You can do that, can't you?'

Her mother was nursing her sore fingers, but she nodded her head as if considering the matter. 'Possibly. Yes, I'm sure I can find a way round it.'

'And you'll let me have the gatehouse.'

Ursula glanced across at her. 'Yes, I suppose so.'

Caroline gave a whoop of delight. 'That's brilliant. How much are we talking about? No, wait, I'll get it valued. There's that estate agent in town, Madisons. I'll get them to do a valuation.'

'You don't want to bother with their fees. No, no, I'm sure we can come to some agreement.'

Caroline wasn't so sure.

'I'm not trying to rip you off,' Ursula added, as if the thought had never occurred to her.

'Good. Because as far as I can see, this is the perfect solution for both of us.'

***

Grant Dalton was far from impressed by Ursula's revelation that the gatehouse was not included in the sale of the estate.

'It's not what we agreed,' he said, eyeing her with a suspicious stare.

Ursula placed the laden tray on the table in front of him and poured him a cup of tea.

'I don't recall any such thing,' she said. 'One sugar or two?'

'None.' He paced to the window and stared out over the rose garden. The tiled roof of the old gatehouse was just visible at the end of the drive. Surely it had to be part of the place? It stood to reason. She'd said outbuildings. It was an outbuilding. His architect had included it in the rough outline of his plans.

'If there's been a misunderstanding, I do apologise, but the gatehouse is not part of the sale. It never was. Scone, Mr Dalton? They're newly baked this morning.'

'No. Thank you.' He turned back to her. Was she angling to raise the price? Was that her game? Trying to get him to up his offer?

Ursula stirred a spoonful of sugar into her own cup and seemed oblivious to his concerns. Maybe it had been an oversight on his part. Maybe he had assumed too much.

The trouble was, the more he explored the house and the grounds, the more he saw it as the perfect solution. Grey Lodge could be the answer he was looking for. Helen always told him he worked best when under pressure. Said he was like a man on a mission. She used to laugh when he got his teeth into a new challenge. He missed that laughter now.

He breathed in deeply and exhaled slowly. 'Okay,' he said at last.

Ursula's lips hovered over the rim of her teacup. Her eyes watched him as he paced the room. He knew she was holding her breath, and he got a wicked delight in wondering idly how long it would be before she was forced to give in and take a gasp of air.

'Mrs Lloyd-Duncan.'

'Yes.'

He offered her his hand. 'I would like to buy Grey Lodge from you. Do we have a deal?'

Ursula's cup clattered onto the china saucer. She thrust her hand forwards and clutched his with a grip that was remarkably strong for an older woman.

'Yes, Mr Dalton, we do.'

'Good. I'll get on to my solicitor first thing in the morning.'

'Likewise,' she said.

It was as simple as that. He'd taken the first step towards a new future. His new future. It's not one he ever wanted, but without Helen, it would have to do.

Chapter Seven

With the sale of Grey Lodge underway, Ursula wasted no time in having the green and gold Bed-and-Breakfast sign removed from the garden of the gatehouse.

'The guest house is now closed,' she said. 'I'm fed-up waiting hand and foot on people who don't appreciate my hosting skills.'

What hosting skills? Caroline wondered, as she stacked the pieces of wooden hoarding on the lawn. She had been the one to deal with the guests. Well, ever since Shirley had walked out. Her mother had always stayed in the kitchen, out of the way.

She watched Jed reverse the Land Rover and trailer onto the grass verge, pleased that she had already begun with the business of clearing the rubbish before he arrived. She gave him a wave.

'How's it going?' he said, jumping down from the front seat and sauntering over.

He had come prepared, she thought. He wore dark grey overalls on top of his jeans and t-shirt. She wondered if he had a spare pair. Her navy trousers and burgundy sweater would go straight into the washing machine when she got home. Not only were they covered in cobwebs, dirt, and grease, but they looked and smelled disgusting.

'I've made a start,' she said, showing him the pile of black sacks on the drive. She pointed to where Ursula pottered round in the garden, her feet in wellington boots, on account of the wet grass. She wore a green waterproof coat that hung open over her portly frame, and her grey hair, tied back in a tight bun, was covered in a vibrant coloured headscarf. 'Mother's here to look the place over.'

Jed pulled a face. 'I'll be keeping out of her way, then.'

'That's probably best.'

Her mother stooped to pick up a fallen daffodil, (which she would later stuff in an old jam jar on the windowsill, to make the place look more homely). She looked her age, Caroline thought, with a wistful smile.

For as long as she could remember, her mother had dominated and bossed around the family, marrying a series of wealthy, and usually much older husbands, to maintain her affluent lifestyle. But had she been in love with any of them, she wondered, or had she only married them for financial security?

Admittedly, her mother's later years with Michael Lloyd-Duncan had appeared to be happy ones, and when he'd died suddenly from a heart attack, she had been bereft. The realisation that she now had to part with the family home, a place that had once brought her so much happiness, must cause her some distress, despite her attempts to convince herself otherwise.

'Can't you ask Ella for help?' Caroline had suggested when the extent of her mother's financial problems became apparent.

'Darling, I have my pride. Anyway, it will all be sorted, once the house is sold.'

That was Ursula all over. She hated to lose face. For years she had tried to convince her stepdaughter that she was a shrewd businesswoman with a head for figures. It had never worked. This latest incident proved it. So Caroline realised, no, her mother wouldn't be asking Ella for any kind of handout.

Caroline joined her by the door of the gatehouse, which she had left open to air the place. Her mother was elbowing cobwebs out of the way with the sleeve of her coat.

'It's going to take more than a lick of paint to make this place habitable,' she muttered. She peered into the dark interior of the cottage, as if wondering if she should venture inside. 'Darling, are you sure this is what you want?'

Want or need, Caroline thought. She had little choice.

'I mean, I can't remember when it was last lived in. Certainly not since I've been at Grey Lodge.' She shuffled through the door and tapped her knuckle against the loose plaster on the wall. A sizeable chunk fell off, scattering particles of dust over her wellington boots. 'I thought you told me Jed said the walls were sound.'

'He did. I mean, they are. Well, structurally. He said the brickwork was fine.'

'Hmm.' Ursula didn't look convinced. Her gaze rose to the ceiling, where a single grimy lamp-bulb cast a weak light onto the wooden floorboards. 'And that looks like a damp patch to me.' She pointed to a yellow stain in the corner.

Caroline followed the line of her finger and tried to stifle a sneeze. The air was heavy with dust motes, wafting about in the breeze coming in through the door.

'Well, it's decided. I can't possibly sell you this place.' Ursula brushed her hands down the side of her coat as she spoke.

'What? But, mother!'

'It's a dump.'

'Yes, I know it is.' Caroline trotted after her as she marched out of the front door, a handkerchief pressed to her nose. 'Please, mother.'

She needed this place. She didn't want to move in with a loved-up Vanessa. Nor did she want to find a pokey bedsit in town, which was probably the only thing she could afford, since she was quite sure no one would give her a mortgage.

'You can have it.' Ursula had taken off her headscarf, and was shaking it up and down, before putting it back on her head and tying it under her chin. 'If it's what you want, then it's yours. I'm gifting it to you,' she added. 'I always felt guilty about buying Vanessa the tack shop and not giving you anything, but at the time, you were with Marcus and working, and she had nothing. Well now, I'm giving you this. I know it's not the same, but it's a start.'

Caroline could feel her eyes filling with tears.

'There's no need for that,' Ursula said, getting back to her usual forthright self. 'You might not be so grateful to me when you see how much hard work and money are involved in putting this property to rights.'

'But don't you require cash for the deposit on your apartment?'

'Probably, but my solicitor can deal with that side of things. I'll get him to draw up an agreement for this place while he's at it. As long as I don't drop dead in the next seven years, it won't cost you a penny. There's only one condition attached.'

Caroline blew her nose and sniffed. 'What is it?' She knew things wouldn't be that straightforward. Anything concerning her mother never was.

'You'll have to take Monty.'

She stared, bemused, and pleased in equal measures. 'Is that all?'

'Well, they won't have him in the retirement complex. Cats are allowed, but dogs are a definite no, and I can't ask Vanessa to re-home him. Not with all those horses around.'

Caroline felt tempted to give her mother a hug, but the glimmer in her eyes suggested she perhaps better not. They'd never been much for hugging in their family.

'That's fantastic, and yes. Yes, of course I'll have Monty.'

'Excellent.' Ursula nodded, looking pleased. 'He'll be good at keeping the rats away.'

***

Vanessa parked her small blue hatchback on the grass verge at the end of the driveway, opposite the white gate leading to the tiny cottage. Sunday was normally her day of rest, after a hectic week in the shop, but Jed was working and Caroline had asked—well, practically begged—her to come and help with the mammoth clean up. She brought with her some heavy-duty rubber gloves, old clothes and a box full of cleaning essentials, including two bottles of bleach. (Jed had warned her about the toilet.)

The front door was propped open with a plank of wood, and all the windows were open. Black sacks were heaped up on the grass.

'Hello?' she called, peeping tentatively through the front door. 'Oh, there you are.' She spotted her sister on her hands and knees, her shoulders hidden as she leaned into the cupboard under the kitchen sink.

Caroline gave a muffled yelp as she jumped and hit her head on the underside of the enamel basin.

'Sorry.' Vanessa took a step inside. 'Goodness, I didn't realise it was this bad.' She scanned the pokey little room from side to side and held a hand over her nose. 'It smells funny.'

Caroline emerged from the cupboard and rubbed the top of her head. 'The bathroom's worse.' She struggled to stand, one hand using the rim of the enamel sink to give her support. 'God, my knees hurt. I should have brought mother's garden kneeler with me.' She stood on one foot and wiggled the other at the ankle, turning it left and then right in a circular motion, in what Vanessa presumed was an attempt to restore circulation.

'Got pins and needles,' she explained. 'Ah, that's better.' She straightened up. 'So, this is it. My humble abode. Or at least, it will be. Honestly, you've no idea how much better the place looks, now Jed's helped me remove most of the rubbish.'

Vanessa was glad she hadn't seen it before. She dumped her box of cleaning things on the worktop. 'Well, I'm here now,' she said. 'Where do you want me to start?'

'Anywhere you like. It all needs doing. I've been getting the clutter out of the way.' She motioned to a sack of old bits of metal, pots, pans, and broken crockery. A few ancient tins that could have been soup or beans, or anything really, lay on the floor. The labels had rotted and peeled off and rust had formed on the base of the cans.

Vanessa crossed the hall to the opposite room, which was the one and only bedroom. It was a reasonable size, she thought. Big enough to accommodate a bed (though probably a three-quarter one, rather than a double) with a dressing table and a wardrobe. Her sister had opened the windows, but the fresh air blowing through didn't disguise the musty smell of dampness.

She crossed to the window and peered out. The view was beautiful, stretching out over the fields to the distant thicket of trees. Peaceful too, with only the faint hum of a tractor ploughing, the chirping of birds, and the occasional car driving past on the single-track lane. But that was in daylight. She presumed it would be less inviting at night. She gave a small shiver, thinking of childhood tales of spooky old houses in the dark, owls hooting, foxes screaming (and they did scream, with a shriek like a crying baby) and rats. Her gaze rested on a heap of suspect droppings in the corner of the room, next to some yellowed and torn up newspaper.

Rather her than me, she thought, and pulled on her rubber gloves.

The nausea that had been troubling her for some time came over her in a sudden wave. She knelt on the dusty floorboards, and took in a deep breath, which was a big mistake. It made her cough and sneeze. In fact, she coughed so much that at one point she thought she was going to choke.

'Are you alright in there?'

Caroline's voice sounded concerned.

'Yes. No. Oh, I don't know.' Vanessa dabbed her eyes with a bit of tissue from the roll of kitchen paper she'd brought with her. They were streaming, and she wasn't sure if it was because of the dust, or the sudden realisation of what was happening to her.

'Well, what is it? Yes, or no?' Her sister stuck a puzzled head around the door. 'Vanessa? What is it? What's wrong?'

She gazed, blurry-eyed, up at her. 'I think I'm pregnant.'

'You're what?'

'Pregnant.' She blew her nose. 'I've been trying to deny it, because I didn't think it would ever happen. My periods have been all over the place and I'm hardly in the prime of youth, but recently I've been feeling sick. I've had days, no weeks of it —feeling sick, and tired, and, well, just different—and now I'm wondering if that's what's happening. If I'm actually pregnant.'

Caroline's mouth had, quite literally, dropped open.

'Really? Oh, my God!'

'I haven't done a test yet, so I'm not certain.' She blew her nose. 'You won't say anything to anyone, will you?'

'No, of course not.' Caroline knelt on the floor beside her and gave her an impromptu hug. 'But no more cleaning for you.'

'What?' Vanessa blinked tearfully back at her. 'Why?'

'Because, I say so. At least until you know for sure,' she added. 'Come on. Take those rubber gloves off. You need to get to a pharmacy for a test.'

'It's Sunday.'

Caroline plucked her mobile out of her pocket. 'There's bound to be one open somewhere. Ah, there we go.' She scrolled down the page. 'The supermarket pharmacy is open till mid-day. We've got loads of time. Come on. Leave your stuff here. We can take my car.'

Vanessa rose to her feet and steadied herself against the door frame. She felt light-headed as well as nauseous. Scared, too, if she was honest. What if she really was pregnant? And now that she'd come round to the idea that she might be, how would she feel if she wasn't?

Caroline was acting true to form and being her usual bossy self. Vanessa was grateful, for once, that her sister took charge, even so much as insisting she stay in the car, while she went into the pharmacy and bought the test for her.

Now, back at the cottage, and perched on the distinctly unpleasant toilet, (despite the quick wipe down her sister had given it with disinfectant and bleach) she could feel her heart racing uncomfortably fast inside her ribcage.

'You just have to wee on it,' came Caroline's helpful advice through the closed door.

'I know.' Vanessa had laid the sheet of instructions out on her lap. 'Don't rush me.'

She could hear her sister's impatient sigh.

Right, she thought. This is it.

'Well?'

The minutes ticked by. Vanessa was almost too frightened

to look.

'Oh, do hurry up. It says the results are ready in seconds.'

She looked down, and there it was.

Pregnant.

She gulped and swallowed hard. It shouldn't have come as a surprise. She'd been half expecting it, but to see it there, in unmistakable black and white, or blue, to be correct, was still a shock. She was expecting a baby. They were going to have a baby—her and Jed—they were going to be parents.

All of a sudden, she burst into tears.

'It'll be fine,' Caroline said, offering her a consoling shoulder to cry on as she emerged, weeping from the bathroom. 'There'll be other times.'

'It's positive,' she sobbed.

'Positive?' Her sister drew away from her, startled. 'As in, you're pregnant?'

She nodded.

'But that's fantastic.'

'I know.' The tears streamed down her cheeks, and she gave a hiccupping sob. 'I'm h… h… happy.'

'Well, you could have fooled me. You idiot.'

Vanessa felt herself enveloped in a bear hug that took her breath away and made her gasp. Caroline was not a touchy-feely kind of person, and this reaction was unexpected. She would have commented on it had she not been so overwhelmed with everything herself.

'It's a blinking good job I didn't decide to move in with you and Jed.' Caroline said, releasing her abruptly from the hug, as if suddenly aware of her uncharacteristic display of emotion. 'You'll be needing that spare room for a nursery.'

'Oh goodness,' she said. 'I need to tell him.' She rushed past her sister to the kitchen, where she had left her bag and phone.

'Not like this.' Caroline gently took the bag from her and closed the flap. 'Tell him tonight when he gets home. You can't break it to him in a garbled message over the phone. Give yourself time to calm down and gather your thoughts together.'

She was right, of course. Jed would think there was something wrong if she rang him in floods of tears, and practically incoherent as well.

'Does the test say how far gone you are?'

Vanessa hadn't looked. Her eyes had welled up with tears the moment she had seen the word "pregnant".

Caroline took the test from her and screwed her eyes up at the small print. 'Over three weeks. Well, that could mean anything. Have you got any idea?'

She shook her head. She couldn't remember when she'd last had her period. Although, come to think of it, it had been a while ago. She'd never been regular, so hadn't given it much thought. Her suspicions had only been raised when she kept feeling queasy.

'I expect they'll be able to tell you once you've had a scan. My advice is to get yourself booked in with the doctor as soon as possible.'

'Yes, okay.' She wasn't sure how quickly she could arrange an appointment. There was the question of the tack shop, for starters. She couldn't just desert the place, but she'd have to find some sort of cover.

'I can help in the shop,' Caroline said, as if reading her thoughts. 'It's not as if I've got anything else to do, now that mother has stopped running the bed-and-breakfast business, and I have done it before.'

That much was true, and Adam was always willing to lend a hand at weekends and after school.

'It'll be fine,' her sister assured her. 'Right now, do something useful, and pour us both a cup of tea. I packed a flask and some biscuits when I left Grey Lodge this morning. I need to get on with the cleaning and you need to sit down and rest.' She waved her hand at the fold-up chairs she had conveniently brought with her. 'You've had way too much excitement for one day.'

Vanessa couldn't argue with that. Her thoughts were racing, to say nothing of her heart. She loved being an Aunty to Ella's children, Adam and Rosie, but never thought she'd be a mother herself. And now, it was actually going to happen.

She rested her hands on her stomach. A baby. An actual little baby. A smile stretched so wide across her face she felt her cheeks ache.

'Hurry up with that tea. I'm gasping here.'

'Sorry. Yes, just coming.' She poured out the tea and opened the packet of biscuits. For once, she felt hungry. Taking out a couple, she offered them to her sister.

'When do you think you'll move in here?' she said.

Caroline was on her hands and knees, scrubbing the floor tiles in the kitchen. They were coming up a treat, though Vanessa secretly thought it was a lost cause. They were so cracked and chipped where the lawnmower had been that she felt certain they would have to be replaced.

'As soon as mother moves out of Grey Lodge. There's no point in leaving the house before then.' Caroline sat back on her heels, wiped her hands on a damp cloth, and took the tea and biscuits from her. 'Thanks.'

'Are you sure you'll be all right here? I mean, it's somewhat isolated, and you'll be on your own.' Vanessa didn't think her sister had ever lived on her own. She'd moved in with Marcus following her marriage, and back in with mother after her divorce.

'Yes, of course,' came Caroline's cheerful reply. 'I know it's not much to look at, but it'll be lovely once it's done. I'll have Monty for company, and all the peace and quiet I could wish for. Honestly, Vanessa, it's going to be perfect. I can hardly wait.'

Chapter Eight

Three months later, after a lot of sweat, tears, money and blooming hard work, Caroline could finally move into the gatehouse cottage.

A vast chunk of her divorce settlement had gone to pay the electrician, plumber, carpenter and plasterer to do the work she couldn't. But once the tradesmen had finished their work, she took over, doing everything else herself with a mixture of determination and sheer bloody-mindedness.

Yes, her painting might not be up to professional standards, but the newly plastered walls were now a warm, cream colour throughout.

She sanded, stained and polished the wooden floorboards. Learnt how to lay new tiles in the bathroom, courtesy of a video on YouTube, and conceded that Vanessa had been right about the kitchen tiles. They needed to be replaced. She begrudged paying a tiler, but the finished result more than compensated for the expense.

'You've done an amazing job,' Jed said. 'You should be proud of yourself.' He followed her through to the bathroom so he could admire the handiwork she was most pleased about. The cleaned, polished and re-vamped old cistern, with its shiny new chain.

He nodded, grinning. 'I'm impressed. I was right when I said you could do it, wasn't I? Stand aside, Laurence Llewelyn-Bowen. You have competition.'

'Oh, stop it.' She blushed, but inside, she felt delighted. 'I got the stains out of the toilet bowl as well, using a couple of mother's denture cleaning tablets. They worked a treat.'

'So, I see.' He glanced back at her. 'Well done, Caroline. Seriously, well done. Come on.' He turned back to the door. 'Let's get your stuff unloaded.'

He'd brought her things from Grey Lodge on the back of his trailer. There had been more than enough furniture for her to choose from.

'Take what you like,' her mother had said. 'I don't want any of it. I'm having everything new in my retirement apartment.'

She'd chosen the smaller of the sofas, and an upright chair, for reading. Her own bed, because it was comfortable and she liked it, and some bedside cabinets and drawers. The television and a bookcase, plus a nest of tables, completed the load.

Her mother had tried to persuade her to take more, but the cottage wasn't big enough. The tall fridge freezer would dominate her tiny kitchen. She would have to buy something smaller and more compact to fit under the worktop.

'What will you do with the rest of the furniture?' she asked. She wasn't sure if Mr Dalton realised he was being left with a half- furnished mansion. He was bound to have stuff of his own.

'The auctioneer is going to take some of the more valuable pieces. Anything Mr Dalton wants, he can have, and the rest can go to charity, or the tip. Frankly, darling, I don't care who has it. Out with the old and in with the new, that's what I say.'

Yes, but only if you can afford it, Caroline thought. She didn't think her mother actually could. And she certainly couldn't. Not the way her savings were rapidly dwindling.

She made herself a mug of coffee and sat down at the bespoke breakfast bar the carpenter had constructed, ensuring she had a place to sit in the small kitchen. It provided the perfect place under which to stow Monty's basket. It also suited the spaniel, not least, because he was near at hand for any stray crumbs that might tumble his way.

Her mother's dealings with Grant Dalton had not been without incident. A structural survey of Grey Lodge had shown several faults that would need rectifying. Since time and money were against Ursula, she had to drop her initial asking price, or risk losing her new apartment. It wasn't something she was best pleased about. Now, with the contracts exchanged and the completion date settled, her mother's departure and Grant Dalton's arrival were only hours away.

Hopefully, he'd mellowed in the intervening months since she last saw him. His brusque attitude left a lot to be desired. Stress probably played a part in it, she supposed, and in fairness to him, it was a stressful time, moving house. She could vouch for that, and she'd only moved a couple of hundred yards down the road. He was moving from Yorkshire and setting up a new veterinary practice.

Having said that, there was no excuse for rudeness, and he had been unpleasantly rude. Still, they were going to be neighbours now, whether he liked it or not. Probably not, she thought, but what did she care?

She sipped her coffee and gazed absent-mindedly out of the now clean and gleaming kitchen window. It was hard to believe that this room, with its built-in cupboards and fitted appliances, had once been the storage room for the lawnmower and other garden implements; that oil had pooled on the floor, and mice had made a nest under the sink.

Good for me, she thought. She felt she deserved a well-earned pat on the back. Things were finally turning out right for her at last.

Unfortunately, the same could not be said for Grant Dalton.

***

It was a five-hour drive from Yorkshire. Seven, if you factored in the inevitable delays caused by numerous road-works and hold-ups caused by goodness knows what. Grant drummed his fingers on the steering wheel and cranked up the volume on the latest traffic bulletin. He had been stationary, or crawling at a snail's pace, for what seemed like forever.

Knowing his luck, the furniture van, which had set off the day before, with a planned overnight stop near Peterborough, was waiting at Grey Lodge for him to open up. It wasn't going to happen anytime soon. Since Mrs Lloyd-Duncan had already vacated the premises and dropped the keys off with her solicitor, he reckoned he had about an hour to pick them up before they closed for the day.

An hour would not be long enough.

He tried his daughter's number on his hands free mobile, but she was out on a farm visit and couldn't talk. Not that she'd be much use, anyway. She was working in Berkshire, which was miles away, on the other side of the country.

Then he tried his own solicitor, but received the answering machine. Apparently, he was in court all day, which was blinking useless, when he needed to get hold of him urgently.

The number he had for the removal firm was similarly unavailable, with a recorded message giving him the office hours, which had now passed.

'Damn it!' Grant slammed his palm on the steering wheel, inadvertently blasting his horn at the driver in front. The bearded man in the pickup truck swung round and glared at him. Grant gave him what he hoped was an apologetic wave.

He leaned over to the passenger seat and started shuffling through the pile of papers he had put there; keeping one eye kept on the slowly moving traffic ahead of him. If he could just find the mobile number, the removal van driver had given him. It had to be here somewhere. He'd written it on a yellow post-it note.

The bit of paper with the elusive mobile number on it had fallen into the passenger footwell. He glimpsed it as he slammed the brakes on to avoid hitting the truck in front. Blasting his horn had been bad enough. He didn't think the man would appreciate being shunted from behind, either. It would have to wait until he pulled off the road at some services, though by the looks of the traffic jam in front of him, that may not be for some time.

Could this day possibly get any worse? It was his own fault for staying in a hotel north of Ripon overnight. His original intention had been to leave the area the previous day, once the removal men had packed up everything into their lorry and driven off. He saw no point in hanging about in the empty shell of a much-loved, family home that reminded him of his loss.

Things hadn't quite worked out as planned. He hadn't expected the wall of emotions that hit him when he drove away, watching everything he had loved and strived for fade into the background in his rear-view mirror.

A few miles out of Whitby, he literally broke down. He couldn't do it. Parked up in a layby, his chest aching and tears pouring down his cheeks, he realised he was in no fit state to drive. He booked himself into the nearest hotel, shut out the rest of the world, and took time out to reflect and gather his thoughts.

Emptying the house had been a painful experience. Sabrina had helped him sort through years of accumulated stuff and decide what to take and what to get rid of. He didn't think he could have done it without her, but she had commitments to honour before she could join him in Suffolk. She had to leave him on his own for the last week to take up a temporary post in Berkshire.

'You'll be fine, Dad. You've got everything under control, and I promise I'll join you as soon as this stint as a locum has finished. It'll give you a chance to weigh things up before I arrive and start bossing you about.'

'Huh. You wouldn't dare.'

'I would. Especially if we're partners.'

'A junior partner,' he reminded her. 'Anyway, *there's a lot of work to be done before we get to that stage.'*

'I can be patient.' She laughed before giving him a parting hug. 'The question is, can you?'

No, was the answer to that. He tapped his fingers incessantly on the steering wheel, cursing under his breath as the queue rolled forwards a few yards and then ground to another halt. He, most definitely, wasn't patient.

He had contracted the builders to start work the following

week. Everything was in hand for the alterations to be done on Grey Lodge. Now he just wanted to get there and get his teeth into the project. It didn't look like that was going to happen anytime soon.

By the time he could stop at the next service area, he knew he had missed his chance to pick up the keys. Contacting the removal van driver on the mobile number he had been given was just as frustrating for him. His call went straight to voicemail. He tried twice, in between a fortifying strong coffee and a sandwich, with no response. On the third attempt, he left a message stating that he was delayed in traffic. It was all he could do. What they did with the information was beyond him.

He didn't think they'd relish spending a night in the lorry, but he didn't want them dumping his worldly goods on the drive and heading for home either. In the end, he left a last message, suggesting they head to the nearest hotel with a secure parking area, and he would see them suitably reimbursed for their trouble the following day.

By six thirty, he was back on the road. One and a half hours later, he headed into the sleepy rural village that was soon to become his new home.

He drove up the gravelled drive to Grey Lodge with a renewed sense of optimism. Maybe, just maybe, the furniture van would still be there, and he would find a way of gaining access to the property. But it was not to be. By the rutted tyre marks on the fine gravel, he suspected the removal van had been and gone. The doors to the Lodge were secured, and even in the dimming evening light, he knew nobody was home.

Unless…His gaze stretched down the drive to the flicker of lights from the gatehouse bordering the road. Unless someone had left a set of keys at the cottage.

He reached into the car and pulled out his jacket. Although the day had been a warm one for the time of year, now the sun was setting, the air had turned chilly. Apart from that, he needed the stroll. Hours spent sitting hunched over a steering wheel was not good for his posture, circulation, or mood.

He stretched and yawned before slipping his arms into the padded jacket and locking the car. Then he walked round the building, trying to peer through the windows, but most of the curtains on the ground floor had been closed. There was definitely nobody home.

The cottage it was, then.

The white gate creaked as he pushed it open, and he could hear the frantic barking of a dog. He hoped it was friendly. A smart rap on the front door, and then he stepped back a pace, just in case the dog came hurtling out to see him off the premises.

'Who is it?' came a voice from behind the freshly painted door.

'Grant Dalton,' he said. 'I'm the new owner of Grey Lodge. I wonder if I could have a word.'

The door swung open, and a brown and white spaniel came hurtling towards him, tail wagging with excitement.

'Sorry, sorry, I meant to catch him.'

The woman came rushing out of the door, a slip lead dangling from one hand, and Grant took a double take as he recognised her, and the dog, instantly.

'You!' he said.

She looped the lead over the dog's neck and pulled him back towards the cottage.

'Are you living here?' he asked. He couldn't quite believe it. Mrs Lloyd-Duncan's daughter, Caroline, and that scatty spaniel. He'd had no idea.

'I am.' She shoved the dog inside and quickly pulled the door shut after him. Monty barked and started jumping and scratching at the door.

'Is that a permanent thing?'

She frowned. 'I own it, if that's what you mean.'

He detected a hint of hostility in her tone.

'What can I do for you, Mr Dalton?'

He gave a resigned sigh. 'The thing is, as you've probably guessed, I was held up in traffic and I haven't been able to pick up the keys to the Lodge from the solicitor's office. I don't suppose you have a spare set?'

'You suppose right. I don't.'

Of course, she didn't. Grant sighed and stroked his chin. 'And your mother? She wouldn't have kept a spare key?'

'No. Why would she?'

'Right.'

He glanced back over his shoulder.

'Your removals van arrived this afternoon,' she said. 'The driver asked me the same thing. They've left,' she added. 'I think they got fed up waiting.'

'Did they say where they were going?'

'They didn't. No.'

'Or when they'd be back?'

'No.' She gave him a measuring look.

Probably wondering how he could be so unorganised, he thought.

'Haven't you got their number to call?'

'Yes.'

'I suggest you give them a ring, then.'

'Right.' He stuffed his hands deep into the pockets of his jackets.

Well, that was a load of help, he thought, stomping back up the gravelled drive. He marched briskly round to the rear of the property and stared upwards, wondering if, by any chance, a window might have been left ajar, to let fresh air into the building while it was empty. But no such luck.

Besides, he reckoned he was past shimmying up a drainpipe, like a teenager sneaking back home after a forbidden night out. The way his luck was going, he'd fall and break his blinking neck.

Letting himself back into his car, he slipped into the passenger seat and stretched out his legs. His knees, he knew, would give him trouble in the morning.

He tilted the seat back and closed his eyes at the precise moment that his mobile rang. It sounded unreasonably loud in the quiet stillness of the countryside.

'Dad, hi. How's it going?'

'Sabrina, hello.'

'Yes, sorry I couldn't get back to you earlier. Difficult birth. The calf was stuck. I was up to my arms in it. Quite literally,' she laughed. 'How's the house?'

'Um,' He peered through the steamed-up windscreen of the car. 'Yes, looks good.'

It seemed pointless worrying his daughter. She'd find out the truth, eventually.

'I can't wait to get there. Be a couple of weeks at best.'

'That'll give your old man time to get the ball rolling.'

'You're hardly old, Dad.'

Old enough, he thought. And feeling older by the hour.

'Anyway, I'll let you get settled in. You must have loads to sort out, but I just wanted to check all was okay.'

'Perfect,' he said. 'Bye, darling.'

Wide awake now, Grant called the van driver's mobile, and was rewarded by a gruff, and sleepy sounding 'Yeah?'

'Oh hello. Grant Dalton here. Did you get my message?'

'Yeah.'

'I take it you've found somewhere for tonight.'

'Yeah.'

'So, you'll be back here in the morning?'

'Yeah.'

The line went dead. Grant wondered if he was the one with the problem, or the driver of the lorry. "When, in the morning?" he wanted to ask, but decided it was probably unwise to ring the number again. The man hadn't sounded too happy about being disturbed.

A sudden shiver came over him, and he zipped up his jacket. He was cold, hungry, and parched with thirst. The last thing he'd eaten had been the sandwich at the services. He was also exhausted. It had been a long day, and it wasn't over yet.

Searching for a hotel where he could spend the night and get some much-needed sleep would have to be his next priority. That's if he could sleep, given all that was going on in his head at the moment.

The trouble with living in a remote and rural part of the country, however, was the complete absence of hotels and the unreliability of the mobile phone network.

After a fruitless tour of the surrounding sleepy villages, he'd gone full circle and ended up back on the drive, opposite the gatehouse cottage.

The lights were still on.

He parked on the verge and took a deep breath before climbing out of the car. He had run out of options. There was nothing else for it. He tapped on the door, and was rewarded with a volley of barks and a stern, 'Who is it?'

'Grant Dalton… again,' he replied.

He was sure he caught the sound of an exasperated sigh, before the door swung open and the dog came bounding out. This time, he managed to catch hold of its collar.

'Sorry about this,' he stooped to stroke the dog's silky fur. 'I still haven't been able to gain access to the house.'

'No,' Caroline said. 'I don't suppose you have. Not without the keys.'

'Exactly. And I haven't been able to find a hotel in the area.'

'Not in the immediate area, no,' she agreed.

'I was wondering… I mean, I don't like to intrude, but… is there any way…'

She tilted her head to one side, her eyes narrowing.

'I mean, just for one night. I'd pay, of course.'

Her eyes widened again in what looked like disbelief. 'You mean you want to stay here?'

'Well, yes. If possible. I mean, I could sleep in my car…' He looked over her shoulder, and could see a perfectly cosy little lounge, with a comfortable looking sofa, covered in many throws. He suspected those were for the benefit of the dog. 'But, I'd really rather not.'

She stared back at him, her gaze implacable.

'Or…maybe you can suggest somewhere else that's close by, bearing in mind it's quite late.'

'Ten thirty-seven.' She glanced at her watch. 'And no, I can't.'

He could have sworn it was later than that, judging by how weary he felt. 'I'm sorry. I realise it's a huge imposition, but the truth is, I'm desperate. It's not like we're strangers,' he added. 'I mean, we have stayed in the same house before, and we are going to be neighbours.'

Her stiffened shoulders relaxed slightly.

He hoped she was considering his words. 'And I'll be gone first thing,' he said, trying to look reassuring. Since he had no idea when his furniture was going to turn up, and he would need to collect the keys to the house before that, this much was true.

She sighed and pushed the door open wider. 'I suppose you'd better come in.'

Hallelujah! Grant felt like punching the air. But he didn't. He followed her into the small lounge and peeled off his jacket. A log burner flickered in the corner, and the room was warm and toasty.

'Thanks. I can't tell you how much I appreciate this.'

'I suggest you try.'

He gave her a sideways look, wondering if she was serious.

'There's only one bedroom,' she said. 'You can sleep on the sofa.'

'Believe me, I could sleep anywhere.'

'I don't doubt it, but I'd rather you slept there.' She swept the dog blankets onto the floor. 'I'll get you a throw and a pillow.'

'Thanks.' He sat down, testing his weight on the padded cushions. They felt soft and squashy. Perfect for one night, he thought, even if he had to share it with the dog.

'Bathrooms through there.' She pointed down a short hall after dumping a folded up travelling rug and a pillow on the sofa beside him. 'You can help yourself to tea and coffee.'

'I don't suppose you've got anything stronger?'

She gave him a stony stare.

Apparently not. Tea would have to do, then.

'Goodnight, Mr Dalton.' She paused by the door. 'Oh, and

I'm a light sleeper. Try not to snore.'

***

Grant was surprised how soundly he slept on the sofa, curled round the snoozing spaniel. Monty had provided a welcome bit of warmth once the fire died down.

He rubbed his eyes, yawned, and stretched. The dog shifted to one side but seemed content to doze. Grant pushed the rug away, swung his legs to the floor, and sat up.

Sunlight flickered through a gap in the curtains, but a glance at his watch reassured him it was still early. He strolled through to the tiny kitchen and switched on the kettle.

Coffee first, then a quick wash, and hopefully, he'd be out of Caroline's way before she got up.

He didn't want to face her. In the cold light of day, he felt embarrassed about showing up on her doorstep and pressuring her to let him stay the night. Yes, he'd been tired and more than desperate, but for goodness sake, she was a single woman on her own. He should never have put her in that situation.

He took out a handful of notes from his wallet and stuffed them into an empty mug, hoping it would be enough to pacify her and relieve his guilt. Then he slipped his feet into his shoes, picked up his jacket, and tiptoed to the door. Monty still rested, though he raised one eyelid when he heard the click of the latch. He obviously decided Grant wasn't worth bothering about and closed it again.

Grant pulled the front door quietly shut behind him and breathed in an invigorating lungful of fresh morning air. It was a little after seven. The birds were singing, the grass was wet with dew, but already the sky was a clear and cloudless blue. It was going to be a lovely day... he hoped.

Chapter Nine

'You've got to be mistaken,' Vanessa said as she buttered a piece of toast. Jed had been up since dawn, exercising some horses that had been boarding at the stables. He always came back starving, so she'd made him a fried breakfast. 'She wouldn't have a man staying there. She would have told me.'

Jed raised an eyebrow at her and stabbed his fork into a plump sausage. 'Well, I know what I saw, and I'm telling you; Caroline had a man staying at her cottage. I saw him leave with my own eyes. I was riding back from the bridleway, and he came out of the gatehouse and got into a black car parked on the grass verge.'

'At seven in the morning?'

'Yup.' Jed chewed slowly. 'He turned the car round and headed towards the village.'

Vanessa poured herself a mug of tea and joined him at the table. She had eaten a bowl of porridge earlier. Fried foods gave her heartburn, though the smell of the sausages was making her mouth water. She rested her hand on her swollen belly. She was six months into her pregnancy and couldn't be happier.

'Did you recognise him?'

'Nope.' Jed crunched down on a bit of toast.

'I'm going to have to ring her.' She grabbed her phone.

'You can't do that.'

'Why?'

'Because she'll think I've been spying on her.'

'Well, you were.'

'Not intentionally.' He grinned and pushed his plate to one side. 'Thanks, love. That was just what I needed.' He scraped back his chair, picking up the piece of toast as he stood. 'Got to go.' He leaned over and kissed the top of her head. 'Look after that little guy for me.'

'Don't you mean little girl.' She rested a hand on her stomach. They had decided not to find out what the baby was in advance. It was part of the fun, trying to guess if they were having a boy or a girl.

Jed grinned. 'You're lucky I stopped gambling; else I'd be placing a bet on it. See you later, love.'

She could tell he was as eager to be a parent as she was, much to her relief.

When she had found out she was pregnant, her main concern had been what Jed would think. They'd never discussed having children, because she didn't believe it was an option. Everyone said it was hard to conceive at her age, so she had convinced herself it would never happen. But, now that it had, he couldn't be more attentive or enthusiastic.

He'll be a brilliant dad, she decided, watching him stride past the kitchen window. He was calm, and gentle, patient and loving. What more could a baby need? Or a wife, for that matter.

She watched him pass the stables, stop to have a quick word with Ella, who was rinsing hay-nets under the outside tap, and then go into the black barn.

Satisfied that he wasn't coming back anytime soon, she picked up her phone. She would ring her sister to confirm what shifts she might cover at the tack shop. It would pave the way for Caroline to tell her what was going on.

Besides, the mid-wife had given her a string of extra appointments, on account of her age, so she needed to arrange something with her. Geriatric mother indeed. She had been quite affronted when she'd spotted that written on her notes. Apparently, it was becoming more of the norm these days, she was told. Well, that might be the case, but it didn't mean she had to like the terminology.

Caroline answered her phone on the first ring.

'Blimey,' Vanessa said. 'That was quick.'

'That's because I was about to call you.'

'Really?' Vanessa tried to contain her excitement, whilst waiting for her sister to tell her everything. Because she would, she was sure of it. But she didn't.

'Yes. I wondered if you needed any help in the tack shop. Grant Dalton is moving in to Grey Lodge today, and I don't want to be around when he arrives.'

'Oh. Why's that, then?'

'I just don't.'

Vanessa detected a trace of irritation in her tone. From what Caroline had told her previously, the man had stayed with them as a paying guest and she didn't like him. Her mother wasn't too keen on him either since he forced her to drop the asking price on Grey Lodge.

'Well, yes, if you want to come over,' she said. 'I'll be glad of some help. I'm opening at ten.'

'Fine. I'll see you shortly.'

'Great.'

That was odd, she thought. Why was her sister being so secretive? Especially with something like this. Maybe she didn't want to lose face?

After her divorce, she insisted she was finished with men for good. She was much happier on her own, thank you very much, and nobody was going to make a fool of her again.

Vanessa cleared up the breakfast dishes, loaded them into the dishwasher and considered how to broach the subject. Despite what Jed said, she was desperate to find out who the mystery man was. If her sister was seeing someone, then she felt she had a right to know. They never kept secrets from each other.

The saddlery and tack shop were in the next village, a couple of miles from Hollyfield Stables, and on the same road that led past Grey Lodge. The country lanes were narrow, with thick, overgrown hedges on either side. The council couldn't cut them back on account of the nesting season. It wasn't the best place to meet a huge furniture removal van; one that had no intention of giving way to her small hatchback.

The driver—an older man with the implacable scowl of someone who meant business—indicated, with an explicit wave of his hand, that Vanessa should move out of his way. The youth beside him in the cab grinned broadly.

Reversing had never been one of her favourite manoeuvres. At six months pregnant, and wedged under the steering wheel, it was nigh on impossible.

Vanessa glanced over her shoulder. There was nothing behind her, as far as she could see, but she couldn't twist round enough to be absolutely certain. She turned back and gave him a helpless shrug.

At this point, he blared the horn.

There was no need for that, she thought, trying to avoid his angry glare which made her feel flustered. It could have accounted for why she put the gearstick into first, instead of reverse and, for a terrifying moment, felt the car lurch forward.

The man had his head out of the lorry window in an instant. 'Back up, lady,' he shouted. He looked as furious as he sounded.

Vanessa felt her cheeks redden. She shoved the car into reverse gear and pressed her foot on the accelerator—too hard. Shooting backwards, her exhaust hit the grass verge and made a screeching clunk as it did so. Wrenching the steering wheel to one side, she veered back onto the road in time to see the shiny black bonnet of another car rapidly approaching her rear end.

She slammed on the brakes.

Fortunately, the driver had razor-sharp reactions. Either that, or he was used to emergency stops. He pulled up behind her with inches to spare.

The lorry driver banged his steering wheel with clenched fists.

Vanessa could hear a string of expletives through his open window.

The soft tap on her door made her jump, and she turned to see the driver of the other car, a middle-aged man in a blue shirt and dark jeans, crouching down beside her.

'Do you need some help here?'

'Get her to move that bloody thing out of our way,' shouted the lorry driver, gesticulating with a meaty arm. 'Hasn't she read the Highway Code?'

The man ignored him. 'There's a farm track a short distance behind us. I'll move my car and then come back to move yours. Okay?'

Vanessa nodded. She didn't think she had been more grateful to anyone in her entire life. 'Thank you,' she said.

He straightened up and gave the lorry driver a thumbs up signal, which appeared to appease him. Then he proceeded to move both cars until they were safely reversed onto the farm track, and the removal lorry could be on its way.

'You must think I'm pathetic,' Vanessa said, as he handed back her car keys.

'Not at all. My wife couldn't reverse either, but we all have our own strengths and weaknesses.' He held the car door open for her and waited while she levered herself into her seat. 'He was a bully,' he added. 'I'm not surprised you panicked. I'll be having words with him later; him and his gormless mate.'

'You will?'

'Yes,' he said. 'When they unload my furniture. I'm moving into Grey Lodge, the old mansion house on the outskirts of the village. Used to be a bed-and-breakfast place. Do you know it?'

'I do,' she said, reaching for her seat belt and clipping it into place. 'Very well.' She was about to tell him it had been owned by her mother, but she didn't get the chance.

'Actually, I'd better double back to catch up with them. I missed them yesterday. Long story,' he added. 'I don't want to do it again.' He closed the car door, and gave her a brief wave, before hurrying back to his car.

Vanessa switched on the ignition and glanced back at him in her rear-view mirror.

So, that was Grant Dalton, was it? Well, he certainly didn't seem rude and obnoxious to her. Caroline must have pushed him the wrong way. On reflection, she decided, that really wasn't difficult.

***

Caroline parked her car in the small yard behind the tack shop, and left Monty barking on the back seat. She busied herself moving bags of feed the merchant had delivered to the storeroom door. It wasn't like her sister to be late. She glanced at her watch. She had said ten o'clock and it was nearly twenty minutes past.

One disgruntled customer had already complained that they had made a special trip to pick up some stirrup leathers, not expecting the shop to be shut; and why on earth didn't she have a key?

It was something she would ask Vanessa about when she finally turned up. If she turned up. She was about to ring her mobile number when the small blue hatchback clanked its way into the yard, with what looked like the exhaust pipe, bouncing off the ground behind her. Puffs of smoke were emitting from under the chassis. A clod of grass and soil hung from the rear bumper.

'Where have you been?' she demanded, striding towards her. 'And what's happened to your car?' She brought herself up short. 'Are you alright?'

Vanessa didn't look her normal cheerful self. She looked exasperated.

'I'm fine.' Her sister heaved herself out of the driving seat. 'But the blasted car isn't. I've clattered through the village. I think it's the exhaust.'

'I'll say.' Caroline stooped to peer under the boot. 'You weren't driving cross country, by any chance? There's half a field on your rear axle.'

'Hilarious. No, I had to reverse out of the way of a removal lorry. Well, not me personally.' She fumbled in her bag for the shop keys. 'It was your Mr Dalton.'

Caroline froze.

'He moved it, but that was after I'd hit the verge.' She clicked open the lock and pushed open the door. The shrill ring of the alarm jolted Caroline out of her trance.

'Do you know the number?' Vanessa was asking.

'What? Oh, yes.' She was distracted, wondering what her sister meant when she said, "Your Mr Dalton". Had he said something to her about last night?

'Well, put it in, then. It's best you get used to doing it, for when I'm not here.'

'What did he say?' She jabbed the code in, hoping that it worked.

'Who, the lorry driver? Oh, he was foul. Honestly, you've never heard such language.'

'Not him, Mr Dalton.'

The shrill ringing of the alarm stopped and a green light flashed on the display. Caroline exhaled the breath she'd been holding.

'He was lovely. I don't know why you took such a dislike to him. I found him utterly charming.'

'Did he say anything about me?'

Vanessa gave her an odd look, as she flicked all the lights on and walked into the back room to unlock the door to the yard.

'No. I didn't have time to tell him who I was, so why should he mention you?' She propped open the door as she spoke. 'Can you drag those bags of feed in? It looks like it's going to rain.'

'In a minute. I'll just get Monty out of the car.'

'Did you have to bring him with you?'

'I can't leave him in the cottage,' she said. 'He's not used to being left. Besides, he needs time to settle in.'

'He'd better behave himself.'

'He will,' she said, and fervently hoped that he would.

She wasn't sure why she didn't just come out with it and tell Vanessa that Grant Dalton had stayed the night. It had all been perfectly innocent. But, knowing how tongues wagged in a small village community, it was probably best she kept quiet.

Someone somewhere was bound to get the wrong

impression. Apart from that, she didn't think her mother would take too kindly to hear she had allowed him to stay. Not that she'd had much choice in the matter. She might not like the man, but she couldn't have let him sleep in his car. That would have been petty of her.

She suspected her mother would disagree.

She had dragged all the bags into the storeroom and busied herself with a rush of customers while Vanessa phoned the garage and arranged for them to come and look at her exhaust pipe; by which time, she had forgotten all about it.

The money she put into her handbag that morning, however, was a blatant reminder. She felt peeved that Grant had gone without even the decency to thank her. He had folded the rug into a neat bundle with the pillow, washed up his cup and left without saying a word.

Then she had found the wad of notes stuffed into a coffee mug.

It was a kind gesture, but somehow, it rankled. She would have to return it to him. He hadn't taken money for treating Monty's paw, so she could hardly take money from him now. It wouldn't be right. She'd visit him when she got home, give him his cash back, and call it quits.

Chapter Ten

The rain, which had threatened to fall all morning, turned into a thundery downpour; a typical summer storm. Streaks of jagged lightning flashed across the sky. It wasn't a great start to Grant's first day at Grey Lodge. Fortunately, most of the furniture and boxes had been unloaded before the sudden deluge began.

Grant watched the men cart the last of his belongings into the house and up the oak panelled staircase. Everything had been taken to the second floor, apart from the stuff for the kitchen because of the building work he had planned and the resultant dust and mess that it would entail.

The removal men weren't pleased. He gathered that from the amount of muttering and cursing that went on, but they had been paid to do the job, and adequately compensated for the extra night, so they could jolly well get on with it. He was the one in charge. They couldn't bully him, like they'd tried to do with that pregnant woman earlier.

'If that's everything, we'll be off now,' the older man said, puffing his way up the stairs for the last time. Dark pools of sweat stained his grey and white t-shirt. His navy jogging bottoms hung low beneath his protruding belly.

'Right.' Grant gave him a cursory glance over his shoulder. 'Good.'

He was in what had once been the front bedroom overlooking the rose garden but was now going to be his lounge. The sofa, armchairs and television were already in place. A pile of boxes sat in the far corner, waiting to be unpacked.

He rested his hands on the windowsill and leaned forward to admire the view down the long drive towards the distant barns and paddocks of Hollyfield Stables. Green fields, lush from the storm, wooden post and rail fencing, horses grazing in the meadow. It was quite stunning, even under the shadow of thick, black clouds.

'I said, that's us finished now.' The rain battered against the window panes, and the man had raised his voice to be heard.

Grant knew he was hovering in the doorway, presumably, hoping for a tip. There was fat chance of that. 'It's not the best weather for driving.' He strode across the room and picked up one of the cardboard boxes. 'You have a safe journey now,' he added.

'Right,' the man said, his chest wheezing. One grubby hand rested on the door frame.

He might have been waiting to get his breath back, but Grant didn't think so. It was a well-known ploy, and he wasn't falling for it. They could hang about all day, as far as he was concerned. He ripped open the cardboard box and focussed his attention on unpacking the stack of books and files it contained.

The driver cleared his throat. After an awkward moment, when neither man spoke, he gave up.

Grant heard heavy footsteps clumping down the stairs. A short time later, the front door slammed and an engine roared as the empty lorry trundled down the gravel drive.

Silence descended, apart from the pattering of rain and the distant rumble of thunder. He sat back on his heels and ran his hands through his hair.

This was it, then. He was here. He'd finally done it.

But the exhilaration he'd expected at the start of this new chapter in his life was tempered by the realisation that he was achingly and crushingly alone.

***

'How are you doing, Dad?' Sabrina's cheerful phone call broke the silence. but came at a somewhat inopportune moment.

Grant switched his phone to loudspeaker, so he could talk

to his daughter hands free, while he toasted some bread and heated a bowl of beans in the microwave. He hadn't eaten all day, relying on strong coffee and adrenaline to keep him going. He was starting to flag. Mind you, it was after six, so it was hardly surprising.

'Hi darling. I'm fine. Bit swamped by all the unpacking, but I'll get things sorted, eventually.'

Sabrina laughed. 'You don't have to do it all in one day, Dad. I know what you're like. By the way, how was last night?'

'Last night?'

'Yes. You know, first night in your new home. Did you sleep okay?'

He sucked in a breath. 'Yes, surprisingly.'

He'd been more than comfortable on Caroline's sofa. The cosy room had been snug and toasty, and he had the benefit of Monty's warm body to keep him company. Whether he would sleep as well tonight was another matter entirely.

'Oh, that's good. I'm useless when I stay in strange houses, and you know how often I move around.'

'Well, I was pretty shattered after the long drive.'

'Didn't you set off the day before?'

'I did.' He stirred the bowl of beans. They were piping hot and he could feel his mouth watering. He licked the spoon. 'I split the journey,' he said, omitting to tell her by how much.

'That was sensible. Look, I've got to go. I'm on call, but I wanted to check everything was okay.'

'Yes, all good here.' He tipped the beans onto a slice of toast and carried the plate to the solid pine dining table with six matching chairs that Ursula had left behind in the stone-flagged kitchen.

'Bye Dad. Love you.'

'Love you too. Bye.'

Who would have thought such simple fare could taste so delicious? Grant hadn't realised how hungry he was. He wiped the crust round his plate, gathering every bit of delicious tomato sauce he could manage.

Tomorrow, he would head into town and stock up with essentials for the week ahead. He suspected he wouldn't have much time for cooking with the builders due to arrive on Monday. He was fully prepared for this to be a hands-on job. The sooner it was completed, the sooner he could return to his true vocation in life; working with animals.

Buttering up clients wasn't his best attribute, but it was a necessary part of business. He could turn on the charm when needed, but he preferred the rest of the team to handle that side of things. The trouble was, he didn't have a team.

Starting from scratch and finding colleagues he admired and trusted would take time and effort. He hoped his daughter could help him. With her knowledge of the area and the contacts she'd made while working as a locum vet, Sabrina was in an ideal position to assist with recruiting nurses and reception staff; all of whom would be vital for the smooth running of the practice. He couldn't wait for her to arrive.

In the meantime, it was just him, this huge empty house, and a million thoughts going round in his head. Some that he'd rather not think about.

He dumped the dishes into the sink and headed for the stairs.

Outside, the rain continued to batter against the windows. It was a thoroughly miserable day, though not a cold one.

He would sort his bed out first. That was the plan. Once it was made up and ready, he could crack on with some more of the unpacking, and hopefully fall exhausted into it later in the evening.

He'd forgotten about the bottle of brandy buried deep inside the box containing the bedding. An expensive bottle given to him by the practice manager as a parting gift. He had wrapped it in the duvet for safe-keeping during the move.

Perfect, he thought, removing it from the box and placing it reverently on the table by his bed. It was exactly what he needed. A small glass of this, and he'd sleep like a log. He'd only have one. He didn't enjoy drinking alone, but it had been a long and stressful day. It might help him relax.

The bedroom was the one he had slept in previously, although it looked completely different with his own furniture in place. The dark wood chests of drawers that Ursula favoured were not to his taste, but she'd left them behind, saying they'd never fit into her retirement flat, and he was welcome to have them. He reasoned they would come in useful in some of the other rooms. A cleaner, sleeker, more modern style was what he preferred for his own room.

Draping a fitted sheet over the bed, he topped it with a duvet and a couple of pillows. With his sleeping arrangements sorted and a comfortable mattress to lie on, he was all set for the night.

He picked up the brandy and headed downstairs to the kitchen, found and unpacked a box of glasses, and poured himself a generous measure. It was a shame about the lack of ice, which was his preference. The fridge and freezer were up and running, but it would take a few hours before they reached the right temperature to make some. He'd have to drink it neat, without the rocks, and without company, just him and an open bottle of brandy.

It was a bad combination.

Chapter Eleven

'Hello? Mr Dalton.' Caroline rapped firmly on Grey Lodge's heavy oak front door.

The lights were on, and she could see his black BMW parked on the drive. He had to be home. She knocked again, wishing he would hurry up. The rain was coming down heavier now and soaking her, despite her efforts to shelter under the lintel.

She tried the handle and was surprised when the door opened. He hadn't locked it. She stepped into the hallway and shook the water from her hair. It trickled down the back of her neck, and she wished she'd brought an umbrella. 'Hello?' she called again.

A light from the kitchen shone under a gap in the door. 'Mr Dalton, are you in there? It's Caroline.'

She edged nearer. She could hear something. It sounded like snoring. Puzzled, she pushed it open.

Grant Dalton lay slumped forward over the pine table, his head resting on his arms. A half bottle of brandy had fallen on its side. The crystal glass beside it was empty. Fumes of alcohol emanated from him. In between the grunts and snores, he was muttering and mumbling.

Tip-toeing forwards, she righted the bottle and moved it out of harm's way. Then filled the glass with water and placed it in front of him.

She didn't know what to do. He was drunk and semi-conscious. She couldn't leave him in that state. But she didn't fancy trying to wake him, either.

A glance round the kitchen showed he had done little in the way of unpacking. The kettle was plugged in, and dirty dishes were steeping in the sink. A pile of packing crates was stacked by the patio doors. The stone-flagged floor was covered in muddy footprints, presumably left by the removal men. If she could find a mop, she'd give it a wipe down, but she wouldn't know where to look.

It felt odd to be standing in her mother's kitchen, with none of her mother's things in it, apart from the sturdy wooden dining table and chairs. The shelves were empty, the cupboards bare and the huge American fridge freezer looked oddly out of place.

She would wash the dishes, she decided. She draped her damp jacket over the back of a chair and rolled up her sleeves. The water was piping hot, and she found a bottle of washing up liquid under the sink. It was open, so presumably her mother left it behind when she moved. She was up to her elbows in soapy suds when she heard him cough and splutter.

Oh God, she hoped he wasn't going to be sick.

He had managed to prop himself up from his slumped position, but his head was buried in his hands as he groaned.

Caroline promptly tipped out the washing-up bowl, grabbed it, and rushed towards him, plonking it in front of him. He lifted his eyes, and stared, transfixed, first at the soapy plastic basin and then at her.

'What…are you doing…here?' His words were slow and slurred and by the look on his face, he was having trouble focussing on her.

'I did knock,' she said. 'The front door was open.'

'Was it?' He shook his head, as if trying to clear his thoughts.

'I only came to return your money. I don't want it.' She plucked the notes out of her jacket pocket as she spoke. 'Here.' She placed them on the table. They felt soggy and looked wrinkled. 'I couldn't leave when I saw the state you were in. You could have choked to death.' She slid the basin closer. He had an unhealthy pallor about him, and she had the horrible feeling he was going to vomit.

He took a swig from the glass of water. 'I'm fine.' His voice was gruff and croaky.

'You don't look fine to me. What you need is a strong coffee.'

'I don't want one.'

'No, but you need one.' She filled the kettle as she spoke. 'I'm presuming you've got coffee.'

He waved vaguely towards one of the boxes on the granite worktop.

She found a jar of instant coffee, tea bags, and sugar. No milk, but that couldn't be helped. Black and strong was what he needed right now anyway. She topped it up with cold water from the tap and placed the mug in front of him. 'Go on. You'll feel better for it.'

He groaned. 'I doubt it.'

'How much did you have to drink, anyway?'

'Too much.' His hands shook as he raised the mug to his lips, sloshing coffee onto the table. 'I'll sleep it off. Be…fine…tomorrow.'

Caroline doubted that. Brandy tended to give killer hangovers. She'd been married to Marcus long enough to have experienced the after-effects of his many works social events. Lots of back-slapping and alcohol rarely mixed. Once, he'd been laid up for two days in a darkened room with an ice pack, and she'd had to tell his boss he had severe food-poisoning. So no, she didn't think Grant Dalton would be fine tomorrow, but she was more concerned over whether he would be fine overnight.

He drank half the coffee, but his eyelids were heavy, and he kept lowering his head into his hands, until one elbow slipped off the edge of the table, and he almost fell off his chair.

'Bed,' he mumbled and stood up. He swayed and rested one hand on the table for support.

'I think you should drink some more coffee.'

With a shake of his head, he lurched towards the door.

He was going to fall and crack his skull open at this rate. Caroline hurried to catch hold of his arm. 'Here. Let me help you.'

He swayed, one hand gripping the wooden bannisters. 'Why...' His eyes narrowed as if he was trying to focus on her face. 'Are you here?'

'God knows. Believe me, I wish I wasn't.' She hooked his arm over her shoulder. 'Come on. Lean on me and let's get you to bed.'

It took an age to negotiate the flight of stairs, and longer still, to find a bedroom that he could sleep in. Grey Lodge had eight guest bedrooms, including the converted attic rooms. She sincerely hoped he hadn't decided to pitch up in one of those.

'This one?' she said, as he slumped back against the wall. 'The room you stayed in before?'

He nodded.

She pushed open the door and was relieved to see the bed already made up. All she had to do was fold down the duvet. She guided him gently towards it and was about to suggest he take off his shoes, but she was too late. He thumped down on the mattress, keeled over sideways, and was asleep before his head hit the pillow.

Now what? Caroline thought, straightening up and standing over him. She couldn't leave him. He was a danger to himself in this state. What on earth had possessed him to down half a bottle of brandy? It was hardly a celebratory drink; more like he was trying to drown his sorrows, whatever they might be.

She undid the laces of his smart leather shoes, tugged them off and placed them on the other side of the room, in case he stumbled out of bed and tripped over them. Then she covered him in the duvet, checked he was on his side, and used a spare pillow as a bolster behind his back, should he attempt to roll over. (She'd seen that on a television drama once).

He didn't stir. He was out for the count, mouth half open, and one arm hanging limp over the side of the bed.

She didn't envy him the stonker of a headache he was

going to have in the morning.

What is your problem? She thought, realising she knew next to nothing about him; whether he was married, divorced, or even if he had a family she could contact, if anything bad happened. Oh God, she hoped not. She peered closer. He was still breathing, but very faintly. The smell of his aftershave mingled with the heady fumes of brandy was intoxicating.

Maybe she should try and wake him? On second thoughts, she'd better get the empty washing-up bowl first.

She hurried downstairs to retrieve the basin and a large glass of cold water.

By the time she got back to his room, he was snoring. He looked peaceful enough, but she wouldn't feel comfortable leaving him.

In the corner, over by the window, she spotted a plush chair in blue velvet, which was draped in a grey woollen throw. She would sit there for a while, she decided, watching the sunset. The rain had stopped and rays of weak sunlight were appearing as the sky dimmed into hues of purple and pink.

For a while, she gazed at the clouds drifting and fading away, like distant puffs of smoke. It felt strangely hypnotic and relaxing. Her eyelids grew heavy.

He coughed, and she sat bolt upright in her chair.

It was a false alarm. He grumbled, cleared his throat and settled back down again. The snoring resumed.

This wouldn't do. She wouldn't be much use to him in a crisis if she fell asleep. No, it was far better she did something useful, like clearing up some of the dirty footprints that trailed across the carpets, or washing the greasy fingerprints from the paintwork.

She found a brush and pan in the kitchen, and the under-sink cupboard held an assortment of cleaning things, including cloths and a pair of her mother's rubber gloves.

Months of doing up her cottage had given her a new found enthusiasm for housework, and making things clean and comfortable. She started in the kitchen first, then made her way up the stairs and on to the landing, removing all traces of the mud and dirt that the removal men had trailed into the house.

Every so often, she stuck her head round the bedroom door to assure herself that Grant was asleep and still breathing.

Then she tackled the bannisters, polishing the oak panelling on the walls and the curved handrails until they gleamed.

Next, she sponged down the paintwork, removing the dirty handprints and grimy fingerprints, with a mixture of soapy hot water and elbow grease. The fresh, lemony scent made a welcome change to the brandy fumes.

Finally, she ventured into his bedroom and drew the curtains. It was dark outside. She switched on the bedside lamp and looked down at him. He was breathing steadily and peacefully.

The furrowed lines on his brow had disappeared. He didn't look half as unpleasant when relaxed and asleep. He was actually quite handsome.

She waited a moment or two longer, watching him, but he didn't stir. He looked fine; settled and stable. Thank goodness for that. She needed to get home to feed Monty and take him for a quick walk. The dog would be going frantic by now. He wasn't used to being left alone.

Except he wasn't on his own.

Caroline had no recollection of leaving any lights on in the cottage, but as she picked her way down the drive towards the gatehouse, she could clearly see a light on in the sitting-room window. Aside from that, the curtains were closed, and she knew for a fact that she hadn't drawn them shut before she left. It had been broad daylight.

The front door opened as she approached the white gate, and she froze in surprise as she saw her sister trying to back out of it without letting the boisterous spaniel escape.

'Vanessa?'

Her sister jerked her head around. Monty chose that moment to burst through the gap. He ran towards her with a joyful volley of barks, leaping up at her as if she had been gone for weeks, let alone for a few hours.

'Get down, Monty. Oh, for goodness' sake.' She grabbed at his collar. 'What's going on?" She glanced sideways at her sister. 'What were you doing in my house? More to the point,' she added, straightening up. 'How did you get in?'

'You left a key under the plant pot by the back door.'

True. She had left one there in case she ever found herself locked out by mistake. It had happened to Marcus once, and he had never forgiven her for not leaving a spare one for emergency use. Now, living on her own, she had deemed it a sensible thing to do. But not for anyone to let themselves in. She deserved some privacy, surely.

'I thought something had happened to you,' Vanessa said. 'Monty was barking. Your car was there. What was I supposed to think?'

'That I was out.'

'Well, yes, maybe. But you said nothing about going out tonight when you were at the shop.' Vanessa followed her into the front room. 'I thought you might have had a fall. An accident. Anything.' Her eyes narrowed suspiciously. 'Where were you, anyway?'

'Out.'

She opened the kitchen cupboard and reached for a tin of dog food. She was conscious of her sister watching her, as she emptied it into Monty's bowl, and placed it on the floor for him. He wolfed it down in seconds, his tail wagging from side to side, so that it whacked against her legs.

'Well, excuse me for being nosey, but you're stuck in the middle of nowhere. You wouldn't go anywhere without your car, unless...' She took a step closer, her nose wrinkling. 'You've been drinking.'

'I have not.'

Vanessa looked triumphant. 'I can smell it. That's the thing about being pregnant. Your sense of smell is amazing, and I can smell...' She paused, sniffing, '...brandy. You've been on a date, haven't you? Oh, do tell.'

'I don't know what you're talking about.' Caroline washed her hands under the kitchen tap before turning to face her. 'I haven't been drinking, and I certainly haven't been on a date.'

'Well, I think you're lying.'

She reached for the kettle and switched it on, trying to act casual, if that was possible, with Vanessa watching her like an over-excited child.

'Oh, go on. I won't tell anyone. Who's your mystery man?'

She hesitated for a moment, shocked by her sister's words. 'Excuse me?'

'The man Jed saw, leaving here first thing this morning,' Vanessa said. She had a knowing smile on her face. 'I've been dying to ask you about him all day, but we were so busy in the shop, and what, with my car and everything, I completely forgot. That's why I popped over tonight. So, go on, who is he? Tell me all the juicy details.'

Caroline popped a couple of tea bags into two mugs and topped them up with boiling water. She felt mortified knowing that Jed had seen Grant leaving her house, and she wondered how to explain things, without looking as if she was hiding something. Which, she wasn't, but the fact that she hadn't told her sister about him, in the first place, patently looked like she was.

Vanessa handed her the carton of milk from the fridge. 'Well? Who is he?'

'It's not what you think.'

'You don't know what I'm thinking.'

No, but she could hazard a guess. 'It wasn't a date,' she said, picking up the two mugs and carrying them into the lounge, with Vanessa following on her heels like an eager puppy. 'He had nowhere else to stay.'

'You took in a homeless person?' Her sister's eyes widened in disbelief. 'Really?'

Caroline set the mugs down on the coffee table. 'No... although, yes, I suppose; in a way, he was homeless, but only for one night. It was Grant Dalton, the vet who bought Grey Lodge. He arrived too late to pick up the keys from the estate agents.'

'Grant Dalton? But you said you hated him.' Vanessa picked up her mug, and pushed one of Monty's throws to one side, so she could sit on the sofa. 'Why on earth would you let him stay?'

'Believe me, it wasn't my idea,' she said. 'And before you ask, no, I haven't changed my opinion of him. If anything, I felt sorry for the man. He was obviously exhausted and stressed, and it was late. Short of letting him sleep in his car, I didn't have a choice. So, I let him sleep on the sofa.'

Vanessa shifted in her seat and looked uncomfortable, as if she shouldn't be sitting on the spot he had recently vacated.

'He went before I got up, so I didn't see much of him, thank goodness.'

'And you didn't think he was worth a mention?'

She took a mouthful of her tea and swallowed it. 'No. And I didn't expect anyone to see him, either. Trust Jed to spot him leaving. I hope no one else did. You do realise that's how rumours start.'

'Hmmm.' Vanessa raised the mug to her lips. 'Interesting.'

'What?'

'Well, if it was all so innocent, I'm surprised you didn't tell me sooner.'

Caroline gave her an exasperated stare. 'Do I have to tell you everything that happens in my life?'

'You usually do.'

This much was true. She sighed, and plonked her mug down on the table, slopping tea onto the polished wood. 'We were busy in the shop, and I forgot about it. For your information, Grant Dalton is the last person I would go on a date with, let alone sleep with, and you can tell your husband that. Okay?'

She stood to fetch a cloth from the kitchen and caught a glimpse of Vanessa's contemplative expression. She seemed to be considering her words and finding them wanting.

'So, where were you this evening?'

'What?'

'This evening, when I called round. You weren't at home.'

'No.' She reached into the cupboard under the sink for some kitchen roll. 'If you must know, he left some money on the table for me, and I didn't want to accept it, so I walked up to the house and returned it to him.'

'Did he ask you in?'

'No.' She stooped to mop up the spilt tea before it stained the wood, while trying to act dismissive, as if it wasn't important. In any case, it wasn't a lie. Grant hadn't asked her in. He'd been unconscious at the time.

'Only, you were gone for ages.'

'Was I? Why? When did you get here?'

Vanessa glanced at her watch. 'Oh, about a couple of hours ago.' A satisfied smirk spread across her face.

'What is this? An interrogation.' She stomped back to the kitchen with the damp cloth. 'Honestly, you're worse than mother. I went for a stroll.'

'In the rain?'

'Yes, which was why I didn't take Monty with me. You know he doesn't like it, and I fancied some fresh air after being indoors all day. Now, is there anything else you'd like to ask me, or have I satisfied your curiosity?'

'I suppose so.' Vanessa stood and brushed dog hairs from her trousers. Monty was moulting, and they seemed to go everywhere. 'I'm disappointed, that's all. I thought there was a new man on the horizon and you were keeping him a secret from me.'

'Hardly.' She held the front door open for Vanessa, whilst attempting to restrain the dog. 'But, should I be lucky enough to find someone, I promise you, you'll be the first to know.'

Chapter Twelve

Sunlight slanted through a gap in the curtains and darted across his face. Grant groaned and stirred, stretching beneath the crumpled-up duvet. He felt rough. Worse than rough.

He was lying in bed but had no memory of how he had got there.

The room tilted around him as he struggled to prop himself up on one elbow and dragged a hand through his hair. His mouth felt parched, dry, and disgusting. He could taste something sour in the back of his throat.

Pushing the duvet to one side, he sat up and gingerly swung his feet to the floor, noting, as he did so, that he was fully clothed, which was strange.

Beside the bed stood a large glass of water. He frowned, puzzled, then picked it up and drank from it, swilling it round his teeth and tongue before swallowing.

He had vague recollections of opening the bottle of brandy. The way his head pounded indicated he had done more than just open it. He glanced at his watch and found it hard to focus on the time. He closed one eye and squinted at the clock face. It was after eleven, and he was bursting for the toilet.

The small, ensuite bathroom could not have been more conveniently placed. A short stagger across the carpeted floor, and he could get some relief from the pain in his kidneys, that had eventually stirred him from his semi-comatose slumber.

Resting one hand on the wall, he stared at his bleary-eyed reflection in the cabinet mirror, and saw an old man, with thinning, sandy brown hair and the beginnings of stubble on his chin. He shuddered. The face looking back at him could have been that of his long-dead father. Not a confident, capable and highly respected veterinary surgeon who had recently turned fifty.

Pull yourself together, Grant. He hung over the basin and splashed water on his face. What sort of idiot drinks neat brandy, by himself, in an empty house, for God's sake?

Well, he'd have plenty of time to regret that stupid mistake. The next twenty-four hours, if he wasn't mistaken.

He stripped off his clothes, leaving them in a heap on the floor, and stepped into the shower cubicle. The sudden blast of cold water almost took his breath away; but served its purpose. By the time he'd finished and draped a towel round his middle, he felt wide awake and marginally more human.

Naturally, he had done nothing useful, like unpack his suitcases. The wardrobes stood empty. Closing the doors, he glanced over to the corner where his cases were stacked among a heap of packing crates and cardboard boxes. He was not in the mood to sort through them right now.

Steadying himself against the wall, he made his way to where he'd left his overnight bag. Fortunately, it contained enough to tide him over. He found a clean pair of socks, boxers and a t-shirt. The sweatshirt and jeans he had slept in would have to do until he felt better.

Coffee and paracetamol were the next things on his to-do list.

He groped his way down the stairs to the kitchen. The fresh lemon scent puzzled him. The smooth, polished bannisters puzzled him more. At the foot of the stairs, the black and white floor tiles positively shone. The muddy footprints that had been there the previous day, on account of the pouring rain, and the removals men tramping backwards and forwards, had miraculously disappeared.

Grant thought he was hallucinating.

He pushed open the door into the large, old-fashioned kitchen, surprised to see that it too appeared neat, tidy, and gleaming, as if someone had freshly cleaned it. What was going on? Had he got up in the middle of the night and blitzed the place in his sleep?

His plate, cutlery, and mug lay clean and dry on the draining board. The half empty brandy bottle stood on the worktop. His glass had been washed and left to dry on the rack. And on the table—he squinted and stepped closer — lay a wad of money.

His brain hurt too much to think. A memory stirred of someone being there with him. Someone who had helped him upstairs. Sabrina? His gaze returned to the money. No, not Sabrina.

Caroline, he realised, with a sickening feeling in the pit of his stomach.

Oh God, he'd done it again. As if he didn't feel bad enough about what had happened the night before, and now this. What was wrong with him?

He switched the kettle on, and as he did so, remembered her doing the very same thing. Snatches of memory were coming back to him, and he disliked what he was recalling.

'You need to drink some more coffee.'

'I don't want it.'

'No, but you need it...'

Caroline must have helped him to bed, he realised. He had the vaguest recollection of stumbling up the stairs; of holding on to someone and resting against the wall, whilst the bedroom door was pushed open.

'This one?'

He steadied himself, planting his hands on the worktop. Oh God, what had he done?

Drawing in a deep breath, he shook his head, as if it might clear his thoughts, but the blankness remained. He exhaled slowly, feeling dizzy. He'd been drunk. That much was certain. Too drunk to do anything, surely?

Oh, God! Oh God! Oh God!

Why would she clean the place from top to bottom? Why would she do that? Unless…

His hands shook as he tipped a heaped spoonful of coffee into a mug. It didn't bear thinking about. He'd never forgive himself if he'd…. But, no, he couldn't have. It wasn't possible.

Helen used to tell him he was a lightweight when it came to drinking. The memory came back to him in a sudden rush of nostalgia.

"It's pointless wining and dining you," she'd said. "You fall asleep the moment your head hits the pillow."

He remembered a time they had been enjoying champagne to celebrate their twentieth anniversary. She had prepared a special meal, and he'd been exhausted after a period of night calls and long hours without rest. He'd picked at the food, and quaffed the wine, and when she suggested an early night, he couldn't have been happier. Because he craved sleep, and lots of it. It was a sore point, and a recurring joke.

His spoon bounced off the rim of the mug, scattering dark brown coffee granules over the immaculately polished work surface. He tried to scoop them up in the palm of his hand, but only succeeded in making more of a mess. With a muttered curse, he brushed them into the sink, then sloshed boiling water into his mug and breathed in the familiar, heady aroma.

It was a start.

Next, he had to find some painkillers for his blinding headache, though where on earth he was going to find them was another matter.

He slumped into a chair and tried not to think of Helen, and what she would have said to him, although something along the lines of "self-inflicted misery," came to mind.

At least his daughter hadn't been here to witness the sorry state he was in. God, he was such a fool! This gap in his memory was going to take a while to fill.

The only thing he was certain about was the fact that he had a lot of apologising to do. It wasn't something he excelled at, as his late wife would testify.

'You never back down,' Helen had told him, in a rare moment of irritation. 'You never admit to anything being your fault. But you did this, Grant. Nobody else.'

The shattered remains of her favourite crystal vase lay as evidence on the tiled kitchen floor. He had knocked it over while rummaging through the letter rack, and accidentally nudged it with his elbow.

'If you hadn't left it so close to the edge.'

'See! You're doing it again.' She knelt to sweep up the broken bits with a brush and pan. 'Trying to blame me for it.'

'No, I just said…'

'Don't!' She held up her hands and waved him into silence. 'Just don't.'

She had been right, of course. He wasn't good at losing face. Not then, and not now. But he'd have to apologise to Caroline at some point, and sooner, rather than later.

It would keep, he thought, taking a tentative sip of black coffee. At least until he recovered from his hangover.

The pounding in his temples eventually lessened as the painkillers he had fortunately found in his toilet bag worked their magic. The grogginess remained. Grant decided a bracing walk in the fresh air might help. It would also give him a chance to re-acquaint himself with the land he now owned.

The house stood on several acres of its own grounds. In addition to magnificent lawns and gardens, which included a vegetable plot and a small orchard, the Lloyd-Duncans had set aside part of the estate for woodland, meadows, and wildlife.

Dog walkers and locals frequently walked in the woods, despite the efforts of Mrs Lloyd-Duncan to dissuade them by erecting warning signs for trespassers.

Grant strolled through the trees, sticking to the well-worn path that had obviously been a favoured route for Monty, judging by the number of half-chewed bits of branch he came across.

By the blackened trunk of the oak tree, he found more broken bottles and the remains of a campfire. A disposable barbecue tray lay abandoned on the ground. A plastic carrier bag stuffed with empty beer cans hung from a branch. He could smell the distinct stench of urine. Someone had been having their own little party here in the woods.

Considering the quantity of drugs that would be stored on the premises once the business was operational, Grant decided that installing new fencing and security cameras would be a necessary precaution. He couldn't afford to be complacent.

In his previous practice, the police had warned him about the dangers of thieves who searched for ketamine, a powerful tranquilliser, and nitrous oxide, commonly known as laughing gas. Vigilance, they said, was the key. Grey Lodge was in an isolated position. Security would be one of his major concerns. That, and hiring staff. He'd need to talk to Sabrina about that. Plans had to be put in motion.

His foot squelched into something soft and smelly, and he dragged the sole of his shoe over a pile of soggy leaves. As he bent down to check it was clean, he staggered forward and thumped his head against the solid, gnarled trunk of a tree. It hurt like hell.

'Jesus!' he swore, rubbing his forehead with his fingers. They came away damp. He stared at them in disbelief. He was bleeding profusely, the blood coming from a cut above one eyebrow. So much for feeling better in the fresh air, he thought. It was time he headed home.

The remoteness of the property meant he could return to the house and patch up his forehead before anyone spotted him staggering out of the woods with a head injury.

It was another blatant reminder, should he need one, of the folly of drinking vast amounts of alcohol on his own.

Grant spent the rest of the day indoors, sorting out boxes, unpacking, and suffering in silence, since there was no one with whom he could commiserate.

His plans for the house included making the second-floor and attic rooms their own personal living area, complete with a modern fitted kitchen. The current one downstairs would be for the use of the practice, once it was up and running.

Sabrina would have her own living room, bedroom,

and adjoining bathroom. Because Grey Lodge had already been partially modernised to accommodate paying guests, it wouldn't require much in the way of conversion. If Sabrina wanted more privacy, she could use the rooms in the attic. He'd leave that for her to decide once she arrived.

In the meantime, he arranged the lounge to his own satisfaction, and even hung up a picture or two. He thought he could hammer in a few nails, although it was probably against health and safety guidelines.

Instead of going on his planned shopping trip, owing to the amount of alcohol he felt sure still flooded his veins, he purchased some groceries online with a promised delivery from the supermarket for the next morning.

As an afterthought, he also ordered a large, and extortionately expensive bouquet, plus a luxury box of chocolates, to be delivered to Caroline at the gatehouse. It was the least he could do, he thought, and might save him from the humiliation of having to face her in person.

By the time he crawled into bed that night, he was exhausted and looking forward to a sound night's sleep. The builders would be arriving first thing in the morning.

Chapter Thirteen

'What do you mean, you've come to seize my goods and assets?' Grant followed the burly, shaven-headed man in the padded waistcoat and black trousers, who had pushed past him and stood in the middle of the hall, gazing up at the magnificent oak staircase.

'Just what it says here.' The man thrust a piece of paper at him. 'This is a warrant from HMRC, giving us permission to seize goods in lieu of unpaid taxes.'

'I don't have any unpaid taxes.' Grant snatched the piece of paper from him, aware that the builders, who were currently spreading dust sheets over the floor, had stopped what they were doing and were listening with interest.

'That's not what it says here.'

Another black jacketed man stuck his head through the open front door. 'Car is registered to a Grant Dalton. We can't take that.'

'Pity. It looks like it's worth a bob or two.'

Grant slapped the paper against the man's bulky chest. 'I think you'll find you've made a mistake.'

'Yeah, yeah.' The man rubbed the side of his nose with a stubby finger. 'That's what they all say.'

'I,' he said coldly, 'am not Mrs Lloyd-Duncan.'

'Her husband, then?'

'Absolutely not. She was the previous owner of this estate.'

The man looked unsure for a moment or two. He frowned and scratched his head. 'Who are you?'

'Grant Dalton.'

'Owner of the BMW outside?'

'Yes. I also own this house, and I'd thank you to leave it. Now, if you don't mind.'

The man held up a hand to silence him and reached for his mobile phone.

Grant swore under his breath and paced the floor. That bloody woman! This was all he needed. The builders looked like they were considering downing their tools and packing up for the day. Probably thinking he wouldn't be able to pay them either. 'This has nothing to do with me,' he said.

'Right.' The foreperson looked unsure.

The bailiff glanced back at him, with the phone still clamped to his ear. 'I need to see some proof of identity.'

'What?' Grant was incensed.

'Driving licence, utility bill, phone contract…'

'Yes, yes, whatever.' He reached for his wallet and plucked out his driving licence.

The man spent an age studying it, before handing it back to him with a curt, 'Thanks.'

He said a few more words to whoever was on the other end of the phone, presumably his head-office, before ending the call, and pocketing his mobile. 'Dave, job's off,' he called to his colleague, who was in the kitchen with a clipboard and pen, noting down items of interest.

'Sorry about that, sir,' he said, though Grant didn't think he looked the least bit apologetic for having burst into his home uninvited and with a thoroughly unpleasant and threatening manner. 'I don't suppose you've got a forwarding address for this… er… Mrs Lloyd-Duncan, the previous owner.'

'I don't. No.' Grant held the front door open for them. 'But her daughter lives at the gatehouse, at the end of the drive. She might be able to help.'

The two men climbed into their white transit van and started up the engine.

He slammed the door shut and glanced round the empty hall, hoping Caroline wasn't at home. They weren't the sort of people he thought she should deal with. It was wrong of her mother to put her in that situation, and he regretted telling them where she lived. Still, it wasn't his problem.

He had enough of his own to contend with. Getting the builders to crack on with the work again, for one. The unwelcome intrusion had seemed to be the decider for an unofficial tea break, and the chance of a smoke or two in the garden.

'Everything all right, guv?' asked the foreperson, poking his head round the kitchen door.

'Never better.' Grant drew in a deep breath. It was time to get started.

Mr Bracknell, the architect, had arranged for the plans to be drawn up and approved in an incredibly short period of weeks, rather than months, and for that, he was grateful.
Converting the downstairs living space into three consulting rooms, a waiting area and a reception desk, would be straightforward enough. Planning had also included alterations to make two operating theatres at the back of the property.

The oak staircase would be left as a feature of the building. It would mean constructing a partition wall on the landing, but the builder assured him he could do it with the minimum of disturbance to the upper floors.

The carpenter was currently measuring up to build a framework, which would keep the living quarters completely separate from the workspace on the ground floor.

It was all systems go.

Grant decided he was more use out of the builders' way, and would spend his day clearing the adjoining outhouses, which had once been part of a stable block. They could be again, if Sabrina approved. He had earmarked the large, double garage for general storage, and the redundant brick coal shed for a locked and secure drug store.

Eight weeks was the estimated time frame for most of the building work to be completed. Grant was banking on less.

In the meantime, he would arrange for adverts to go in all the veterinary magazines and websites, hoping to attract suitable staff, for what he hoped would be state-of-the-art facilities for both small and large animals.

On that note, he had booked a visit to the nearby stables and stud, with whom his daughter had already been in touch.

Hollyfield Stables was owned and run by Ella Trevelyan, who, he discovered, was the step-daughter of Ursula Lloyd-Duncan. He viewed the visit with some trepidation, having had quite enough of that blasted woman to last him a lifetime.

Sabrina had assured him she was nothing like her stepmother and that they had become the closest of friends during her previous stay in the area.

'She used to be a champion showjumper,' she'd told him. 'But she concentrates on teaching these days. She's good. She might even persuade you to get on a horse.'

'That,' he said, 'will never happen.'

'Never say never.'

He smiled to himself on the short drive to the neighbouring stables. His daughter had a knack for repeating his oft-used phrases, and that was one of them.

The car park was busy, which had to be a positive sign. Grant pulled up between a green, battered Land Rover, and a dark red mini.

To the right, he could see a sand school, where a children's pony class was in progress. The youngsters were being led round by teenagers and reminded him of the times Sabrina had begged to be allowed to help out at their local riding school in exchange for a free lesson or two. At fourteen, she'd loved mucking out and poo picking, and had won an award one summer for best kept stable. If only she'd kept her own room as clean and tidy, he reflected.

He followed the path across the lawn and up to the house, where a sign pointed to the reception office.

The woman behind the desk could not have been more pleasant. She was the same sort of age as his daughter, he guessed, with short spikey hair, scarlet-rimmed glasses and a warm and welcoming smile.

'You must be Sabrina's father.' She stood up to greet him. 'I'm Sally. How lovely to meet you. We've heard so much about you.'

Grant didn't know if that was a good thing or a bad one.

'Ella's expecting you.' She ushered him towards an adjoining room and tapped on the door. 'Mr Dalton is here,' she said, popping her head round. 'Go in,' she added, turning back to face him. 'I'll put the kettle on. Tea, or coffee?'

Ella Trevelyan was not as he had imagined her to be. He'd expected her to be full of airs and graces, and a tad pretentious, which had been his experience with other "horsey" people, but this woman could not have been more down to earth if she tried.

'I'm so excited that Sabrina is going to be working in the area permanently,' she said, over a cup of freshly brewed coffee. 'I couldn't believe it when she told me you were a vet as well.'

'Not a horse vet,' he said. He had studied basic equine medicine as part of his course but had opted for small animal medicine after an unpleasant incident with a young mare, who had objected to being examined by a novice. A well-aimed kick had let him know what she thought. The resulting bruise and limp had lasted for weeks. 'I'll be concentrating on the dogs, cats and other small pets.'

'Sounds like the ideal combination.' Her cup clinked as she placed it back on the saucer. She leaned back in her chair, crossing one leg over the other. She wore black jodhpurs and a cream sweatshirt, with the Hollyfields logo stitched on the front. Her long blonde hair was tied at the nape of her neck and secured with a black velvet ribbon. She looked casual, but smart, he thought. She seemed totally at ease with herself. He liked that. Her manner helped him to relax after what had been another stressful morning. He suspected she had the equivalent effect on her horses.

'How are you settling in to Grey Lodge?'

'There's been a few problems.'

'Like what?' She leaned forwards, looking genuinely interested.

He shrugged, not wanting to tell her the complete saga of his first couple of days. The edited highlights would have to do.

It was strange, but she was having the same effect on him as a counsellor might; the patient and expectant silence as she waited for him to continue. He had to admit, it felt good to talk to her. To talk to anyone, in fact.

'Oh, just little things,' he said. 'The usual sort of problems, when you move house, I suppose. Well, apart from the bailiffs,' he added, with a reflective smile. 'They turned up this morning, wanting to "seize my assets", as they so politely put it. It appears your stepmother has got herself into a spot of bother with the tax people.'

'Not again,' Ella groaned. 'That woman is impossible.'

'You mean she's done this before?'

'Where would you like me to start?'

'I see.' He laughed. 'Well, I expect they'll have tracked her down by now. I told them her daughter was living at the gatehouse, and they should ask her where she was.'

'Poor Caroline.'

'My thoughts exactly.' He drained his cup.

'Let me show you around,' Ella said, standing up. 'I might as well, now you're here. Although,' she glanced down at his feet. 'I might have to loan you a pair of Adam's wellies. The fields are a bit muddy, after all that rain.'

'Your husband's?'

'My son's,' she said. 'Lewis wouldn't be seen dead tramping through boggy fields. He's away on a shoot. He's a film producer,' she explained. 'His company is filming up in Edinburgh at the moment. Some crime drama. I can't remember the name. Isn't that awful of me?'

'Sounds exciting.'

'It really isn't.' She smiled and handed him a pair of dark green rubber boots from the rack by the door. 'Just doing a conducted tour,' she called to Sally, in the office. 'Won't be long.'

Hollyfield Stables was a much bigger establishment than

he had initially thought. Not only was it a busy riding school, but it also had amenities for eventing and show jumping, including a well-maintained cross-country course.

'The stud buildings are over there.' She pointed to a row of stables beside a huge black barn. 'We have facilities for visiting mares, and separate paddocks for the boys, obviously.'

He grinned.

'Having Sabrina virtually next door will be a godsend. We don't often have a problem, and Jed is more than capable. That's our stud manager,' she added. 'But honestly, I can't wait for her to move back. When do you think she'll get here?'

'She said two weeks. I'm hoping sooner. She's in Berkshire at the moment.'

They were strolling towards his car as they spoke.

Grant clicked open his door. 'I suppose I'd better get back before anything else happens. Thanks for showing me round.'

'My pleasure.' She stepped to the side. 'Next time, bring your wellies.'

He laughed. 'Noted.'

What a lovely young woman, he thought, as he drove out of the car park and onto the lane. He could see why his daughter liked her. They were similar in many respects; a passion for horses being one of them.

As for her stepmother, well, words failed him.

From what Ella had told him, and from what he had experienced himself, Ursula Lloyd-Duncan was a law unto herself and a force to be reckoned with. She might be a doting grandmother, but aside from that, she was opinionated and outspoken.

He wondered how the bailiffs were getting on.

Chapter Fourteen

'Of course, I had to tell them where you were living,' Caroline said, as she drove her mother home from the chiropodist in town. 'They would have found out one way or the other. It was fortunate you had that appointment to get your feet done, because I knew you wouldn't be there.'

'That's not the point.' Ursula looked cross and implacable. 'What sort of impression does it give if those two so-called ruffians go banging on my door? St Johns is a genteel retirement complex. They don't want bailiffs turning up.'

'Mother, you owe the tax people money.'

'Oh, piffle. It's all a misunderstanding.'

'Which you need to sort out. People get sent to prison for tax evasion. This is serious. You need to do something.'

'Yes, I know, and I will.'

Caroline wasn't convinced. Her mother had perfected the art of putting things off until they reached crisis point. She parked her car on the grass verge opposite the gatehouse and opened the door. 'Come in. I'll make you some lunch. Monty will be pleased to see you.'

Monty was indeed delighted to see Ursula, who had a habit of giving him a variety of tasty snacks and titbits, which had, in Caroline's opinion, contributed to his weight gain.

She was being strict with his diet now, if only to stop Grant from making pointed remarks about fat-bellied dogs and unsuitable food.

'Is a cheese and tomato sandwich, okay?' she called from the small kitchen. She had bought a fresh crusty loaf in town, which the bakery sliced for her. It looked and smelled amazing.

Her mother lounged on the sofa, with her feet propped up on the stool. Monty sat beside her, panting, his pink tongue hanging out.

'Fine.'

She could hear her mother fussing over the spaniel as she buttered the bread and sliced some tomatoes. No wonder he was so spoiled. Lovable though he was, he could definitely benefit from some training.

As she made the sandwiches, she heard a loud rap on the door, which sounded ominously like the bailiffs had returned.

Monty was on guard duty in an instant.

'Don't answer it,' she called, but it was too late. Her mother had followed the dog to the front door and was in the process of opening it.

Caroline wiped her hands on a tea towel and hurried into the sitting room to see her mother holding an enormous bouquet of cellophane wrapped flowers and a large box of chocolates. 'Oh,' she said, her eyes widening.

'Yes, oh.' Her mother laid the flowers on the table and plucked out the small accompanying card. 'Who's been sending you these?'

'That's for me.' She tried to grab it but was too late.

'Sorry. Grant.' Her mother read and then fixed her with one of her probing stares. 'What's that all about?'

'Nothing.' She snatched the card from her and picked up the flowers. 'These are lovely. I'll put them in some water.'

'A man does not send flowers with a note saying "sorry" unless he's done something wrong.'

Caroline pretended she hadn't heard her, as she rummaged in the cupboards to see if she could find a suitable container. She rarely, if ever, received flowers, so a vase was not something she possessed. The water jug would have to do.

They really were quite beautiful, she thought, as she tried to arrange them in a tasteful and artistic manner. The pink, long-stemmed roses were particularly stunning, and the green waxy leaves complimented the white gypsophila perfectly.

'What has he done?' Ursula repeated, poking a pointed finger between her shoulder-blades, 'that he has to be sorry about?'

'Nothing. Now excuse me a moment, mother, while I sort these out. Maybe you could make a cup of tea while you're waiting.'

Caroline had no intention of telling her about Grant's drunken binge, nor the fact that he had slept on her sofa. She wasn't a teenager anymore, and it was none of her business. 'Instead of concerning yourself about Grant Dalton,' she said, 'you need to worry about your debts and how you're going to sort your mess out.'

She finished arranging the flowers, pleased with how lovely they looked in the clear plastic water jug, and carried them into the sitting room to place on the windowsill.

Her mother had resumed her place on the sofa, having finished making the sandwiches and a pot of tea in a huffy and stony silence. Monty sat, drooling and expectant, at her feet.

'Don't give him any cheese.'

'He likes cheese.'

'Mother!'

The dog gobbled down a crust of bread that she had tossed to him.

Caroline hastily removed the luxurious box of chocolates from the table, and put it on top of the bookcase, in case she had ideas about giving him one of those as well. 'Have you thought about what you're going to do?'

'I have, actually.' Her mother swallowed the last morsel of her sandwich and took a sip from her cup of tea. 'You're going to have to contact Marcus.'

'What?' She couldn't believe what she was hearing. 'Why?' Her ex-husband was the last person she wanted to speak to.

'Well, he's a tax inspector. He'll know what to do.'

'Mother, it wouldn't surprise me if he's behind this in the first place. You know how fastidious he is about rules and things.'

'Rubbish. He's family. Well, sort of family,' she added. 'Anyway, I want you to ring him. Or visit him. I don't care which.'

Caroline almost choked on her sandwich. 'Why don't you ring him?'

Her mother gave her one of her most condescending smiles. 'If we're going to accept that I'm senile, and on the verge of dementia, don't you think it would be better coming from you?'

***

The last time Caroline saw her ex-husband, it was in a supermarket carpark. He had been pushing a laden shopping trolley whilst his very pregnant girlfriend waddled beside him. She'd ignored the pair of them and pretended to be engrossed in an important message on her mobile phone, not raising her gaze until she was sure they had gone. She hoped they hadn't seen her.

They would have had the baby by now. She couldn't imagine Marcus as a father. He hated mess, noise, or any kind of disturbance to his orderly routine. A new baby would provide all that, and more.

Serves him right, she thought. Their divorce may have been a mutual agreement, but it still hurt to know he left her for somebody else; and was happy and settled, while she was still on her own, and looking to remain so for the foreseeable future.

She wasn't looking forward to seeing him again, but she knew her mother needed help to sort out her latest financial disaster and, much though it pained her to admit it, Marcus had always excelled at his job.

'Caroline,' he said, in that nasal voice she had grown to hate, when she finally plucked up the courage to ring him. 'This is a surprise.'

'It's mother,' she said.

'Oh.' He sounded curious. 'She hasn't…. er…'

'No. No, she's fine,' Caroline said hurriedly, just in case he was thinking otherwise. 'She's not ill or anything, but she is having a few problems.'

'Indeed.'

'Tax problems.'

'Ah.'

She heard his long, drawn-out sigh, as if he had expected nothing less from his ex- mother-in-law.

'I was wondering if it would be possible to meet you, so I could discuss a few things on her behalf?'

'I can give you an hour,' he said. 'The Black Swan. Six o'clock, after work.'

The fact that he didn't seem surprised by her request made her wonder if he did have anything to do with the investigation into her mother's tax affairs. Or was that her being too suspicious? Marcus may be many things, but she didn't think he would stoop that low.

The Black Swan was an old-fashioned pub, popular with the farming community, in the middle of Ecclesfield, a short walk from her old marital home. It felt strange to be back.

Caroline bought a glass of elderflower cordial and soda and sat at a corner table by the door. She didn't feel confident sitting there on her own, in case she saw any of their old neighbours. When she had moved back in with her mother, she had severed all ties.

She didn't have the time or the inclination to explain why she was back. But she had arrived early because she knew Marcus would not be late. He was a stickler for punctuality.

At exactly six o'clock, she saw him walk in, give a cursory glance round, and then head to the bar. His thinning scalp shone beneath the stark overhead lights, and he looked as though he'd put on some weight since their last encounter, many months ago.

'Marcus.'

He turned and gave her a brief nod. 'Caroline.'

'Let me get you a drink,' she said, standing up.

'No need.' He ordered a lemonade shandy, paid for it in cash, and then came and sat down opposite her.

'How are you?' she asked. He looked well. The extra weight

suited him, although the buttons on his shirt looked as if they were under strain.

'Tired. Sleepless nights, you know.'

She didn't. She took a sip of her drink. 'Boy, or girl?'

'A girl. Isabelle. She's five months now.'

'That's nice. Congratulations.'

For one horrible moment, Caroline thought he was going to get his phone out and show her some photos. Fortunately, and perhaps because of the anxious look on her face, he obviously thought better of it.

'So,' he said, taking a mouthful of his drink. 'What's the problem with Ursula this time? You said she had an issue with her taxes?'

One thing was to be said about Marcus, he wasn't one for small talk. He liked to get straight to the point.

Caroline hadn't thought an hour would be long enough to put him in the picture and reach a solution, but she had forgotten how efficient he could be. She couldn't fault him for that.

'Since she's ignored all correspondence,' he said, 'the next step is the bailiffs and a court order. If it's reached that stage…'

'Which it has.'

'Then it's a good idea if you suggest she has failing mental health. They might be lenient if there's a reasonable excuse, preferably backed up by a doctor. Perhaps she was unaware or misunderstood her legal obligations, or maybe she'd always relied on someone else to file her returns.'

Her mother was renowned for delegating. That went without question. Asking people to do things for her and expecting them to comply was part of her nature. However, regarding bills and invoices, she had a feeling her mother just shoved them in a drawer and forgot about them.

'I think, "misunderstood her legal obligations" just about sums things up,' she said.
'You know what she's like.'

'I'm not likely to forget,' Marcus said with an

unmistakable sneer. He jotted a few notes on a piece of paper.

Caroline tried to make out what he was writing, but his scrawl was barely legible, and she was trying to read it upside down.

'Now then, the most important thing is to ensure she makes some sort of payment, either through a plan like a TTP arrangement. Time to pay,' he explained, writing the letters in thick capitals on another bit of paper and sliding it towards her. 'Or she clears the debt completely, because this won't go away, Caroline. HMRC can pursue this for up to twenty years. The bailiffs don't need her to be at home to seize her assets. They'll get a locksmith to break in and they'll have a court order to say they can do it.'

He folded his arms and leaned back in his chair, watching her with the sort of superior smile she would love to wipe off his face. She was grateful for his advice, and he knew it. The thought infuriated her.

'Your mother is not above the law, even if she thinks she is.'

'Yes. I know that, Marcus. Why do you think I'm here?'

She swallowed the last of her drink and swilled the ice round in the bottom of her empty glass. 'Sorry,' she said. 'I know you're trying to help. It's just, I didn't realise they could enter her property if she wasn't there. I've left her at mine.'

'It makes no difference. They want the money that's owed them.'

'Right.'

'But if she's sold Grey Lodge, that shouldn't be a problem.'

'You'd think.' Caroline recalled the expensive furniture her mother had purchased for her apartment, the deluxe bedding and curtains, a whole new array of kitchen crockery, white goods, pots and pans. Everything, in fact, was brand spanking new. Give her mother money, and she could find endless ways to spend it.

He drained his shandy and stood up. 'I'll see what I can do, but right now I need to go.'

'Of course, Marcus, and thanks, I appreciate you coming.' She rose from her seat, half wondering if she should offer to shake his hand. But he was shrugging his jacket on, and the moment passed.

It felt strange, seeing him again, in the pub that had once been their local. Stranger still, to imagine him as a father. Marcus had never liked children, but his face lit up when he talked about his daughter. Maybe things might have been different if they'd had a child, but somehow, she doubted it. Theirs was a marriage doomed to failure from the start.

Looking back, she realised she had only married him to escape her domineering mother, not because she loved him. The sad thing was, they had wasted so much time making each other unhappy; it was time they would never get back.

At least Marcus was getting on with his life now, and she was pleased and jealous in equal measures. She felt it was too late for her.

On the journey home, she contemplated how she was going to convince people her mother had mental health problems. Part of her thought, it might not be too hard, given the way her mother behaved at times. Irrational and impulsive, being two thoughts that sprang to mind.

She suddenly remembered the gigantic bouquet that had been delivered to her door. The flowers were not cheap garage forecourt ones, and the chocolates were artisan and handmade. She hoped her mother hadn't helped herself to them in her absence. Grant Dalton must have spent a fortune on them.

Well, too right, she thought, swinging the car onto the narrow lane leading to her cottage. It was the least she deserved. Not only for the dismissive way he had treated her, when he'd been a guest at Grey Lodge, but for the way he had expected her to put him up for the night, when he couldn't get back in time to collect the keys.

She'd come across men like him before; men who naturally assumed they could do as they pleased. Her old boss at work had been a prime example, swanning in and out of the office. Expecting her to handle all his appointments and awkward clients. And what thanks had she got for that? Redundancy, or a "re-shuffle", which left her surplus to requirements.

At least Grant Dalton had taken the trouble to buy her chocolates and flowers, by way of an apology, which raised her opinion of him, slightly. Although she was concerned that he might have some sort of alcohol problem. How a qualified vet could drink himself into a stupor and hope to run a new practice was beyond her.

She climbed out of her car and locked the door. The faint strains from the television drifted through the open cottage window. Her mother was making herself at home.

Caroline strode up the garden path, increasing her pace as she neared the front door. She had the horrible feeling Ursula might have helped herself to her chocolates Worse than that, she could well have shared them with the dog.

Chapter Fifteen

Having safely delivered her mother back to her retirement apartment, with strict instructions to phone the number left on a card by the bailiffs, or risk having her door broken in, Caroline headed home to have a re-think.

The meeting with Marcus went better than expected. Though she wasn't sure they could ever be friends again, she found it reassuring to know that he would help her in her time of need. She supposed she would do the same for him, at a pinch. They'd spent many years together, and that had to count for something. But it didn't mean she had to like him.

She reached for the box of chocolates she had placed on the bookcase out of Monty's reach. To her relief, the wrapper remained intact. Not that she wouldn't have shared them with her mother. She just didn't want her gorging on them. Ursula had a sweet tooth, and these were special chocolates.

They nestled in a silk-lined box, fastened with an exquisite red bow. She sampled one, knowing she had tasted nothing so smooth, creamy and decadent in her whole life. Champagne truffle, she read on the accompanying leaflet. An Italian coffee mousse in dark, rich cocoa, topped with grated white cocoa flakes, came a close second. That was enough, she told herself, closing the lid and returning the box to its safe position. These weren't the type of chocolates to be scoffed in one sitting, however much she enjoyed them.

She read the card again. 'Sorry. Grant.' She flipped it over, but the reverse was blank. He was a man of few words. A closed book, her mother said, and it was true. Even though he'd stayed with them for a week, all those months ago, his private life had remained…She thought about it for a moment. Well, private. And when she'd put him up on her sofa for the night, conversation didn't come into it. They were both tired, and he'd already gone by the time she woke in the morning.

She propped the card next to the water jug holding the bouquet. The pink roses gave off the most beautiful perfume, which was proof they were expensive. Normally, she couldn't smell anything when she sniffed the flowers in the supermarket.

Who are you, Grant Dalton, she wondered?

From what she could see, and despite the wedding ring, it seemed he was on his own; a single, professional middle-aged man. Was he a loner or lonely? It was hard to tell. If he was a loner, that could explain his blunt manner (although her mother seemed to think that was the Yorkshire way). If he was lonely, that could be the reason for his drinking.

She'd had a few too many glasses herself when going through her marriage break-up. Maybe that was the reason he moved here, to escape a failed relationship? She knew how that felt; all that bitterness, anger, and sadness. It could explain his unpleasant manner, she supposed. Yes, of course it could.

She breathed in the scent of the roses. It was obvious, when she came to think about it. They might have more in common than she thought. Maybe the time had come for her to find out.

He'd made the first move by sending her flowers. She could follow that up with a visit to say thank you, and to see if he was okay. It was all perfectly reasonable; one neighbour checking in on the other. And there was no time like the present to do it.

She had a quick shower and then dressed with particular care, not especially for him, but for herself. If she looked good, she felt good.

If dogs could speak, Monty might have mentioned it seemed a bit over the top, for an evening dog walk, but he couldn't, and that was an end to it. She put on her smartest black jeans, a floral blouse and an almond-coloured cotton sweater, which she tied artfully over her shoulders. She exchanged her muddy hiking boots for tan leather ankle ones, brushed her hair loose, and used straighteners to add a few artistic curls.

Make-up? Perhaps just a smattering of mascara and blusher, and a tinted lip gloss. Otherwise, it might look too obvious. She peered at her reflection in the dressing-table mirror. Not bad. Not bad at all.

She planned to take Monty for a stroll through the fields and, accidentally on purpose, come out halfway up the drive to Grey Lodge. If his car was there, she would knock, to thank him for the flowers, saying she was just passing and hoped he didn't mind. He might invite her in, and she'd initially refuse (no sense in being too forward) and then she'd say, oh, why not, and they'd get talking, and…

The loud banging on her front door abruptly broke her train of thought, as did the excited yapping of the dog.

'It's only me.'

How was it that her sister had the annoying knack of turning up at completely the wrong moment?

Caroline opened the door.

'Going somewhere nice?' Vanessa tossed her jacket over the back of the settee and flopped down on it as she spoke.

'No.'

'You're all dressed up. Is that new?'

Caroline plucked at the sleeve of her blouse. 'What, this old thing? I don't think so. I'm about to take Monty out.'

'I've just had mother on the phone.'

'And?'

'You didn't tell me the bailiffs had been round.'

'I've only just got home,' she sighed, wandering into the kitchen to put the kettle on. It looked like her dog walk would have to wait. 'She sent me to see Marcus. Did she tell you she hasn't paid her taxes?'

'In passing. She was more worried about damaging her reputation with the other residents in her complex than the debt she owes.'

'That sounds like mother.' Caroline carried a tray with tea and a tin of biscuits into the sitting room and handed her sister a mug. 'Marcus says we have to convince people she's losing the plot, and they might be lenient with her.'

'Thanks.' Vanessa eased open the tin and selected a custard cream. 'How is the miserable man?'

Her sister had never liked her ex-husband. It had been a pretty mutual agreement.

'Remarkably well, actually. He looked happy.'

'What, Marcus did?'

'Hmm.' Caroline nibbled on a biscuit and tried to ignore Monty's beseeching gaze. 'He's got a little girl. She's called Isabelle.'

Vanessa's face softened, and she stroked her stomach absent-mindedly. 'How times change. Who'd have thought it, Marcus Milton, a dad? Anyway, I want to know about the chocolates and flowers from your new neighbour.' She sat up straight again and glanced round the room, her gaze spotting the jug of blooms on the window-sill. 'Ooh, they look nice.'

Caroline sighed. She knew her mother would have enjoyed passing on this bit of juicy gossip, more so than her own problems with the Inland Revenue.

'What's he apologising for?'

She lowered herself onto the stool next to Vanessa. 'If I tell you what happened, you've got to promise you won't tell mother. I don't think she likes Grant very much.'

'I didn't think you liked him, either.'

'Not initially, no, but…'

Vanessa patted the cushions beside her. 'Come on. What's happened to make you change your mind?'

Caroline knew her sister wouldn't be satisfied until she heard the whole story, so she started by telling her how she planned to return the money he left her after he stayed on her sofa for the night and finished by recounting the tale of his drunken state at Grey Lodge.

'I helped him to bed. He was totally incapable. When he

sobered up, I think he must have been grateful I'd kept an eye on him, and that's why he sent me the flowers.'

'Do you fancy him?'

'What? No, of course not,' she lied, because oddly enough she did find him attractive. There was something about him that made her heart beat just that bit faster whenever he looked at her. Which was bizarre, because he hadn't been particularly pleasant to her. Treat them mean, keep them keen; wasn't that the saying?

She knew Vanessa was watching her with a knowing look on her face. 'It's not like that,' she said, plucking at an invisible thread on her trousers. 'I hardly know the man, but I am worried about him. I'm interested in getting to know him better. As a friend,' she added.

'Of course.'

'He is my nearest neighbour.'

Vanessa grinned at her in a manner not dissimilar to the proverbial Cheshire cat.

'Oh, stop it,' she snapped. 'I do not fancy him.'

'Well, I would, if I was single. A knight in shining armour.'

'To you, maybe.' She gathered up the empty mugs and carried them into the kitchen. 'He's a liability as far as I can see. Anyway, I'm enjoying being on my own. I can do what I want, when I want, with no one to boss me around.'

'Or snuggle up to at night?'

'Or snore like a pig and hog the covers.'

Vanessa laughed. 'I think Marcus has put you off men for life.'

'That wouldn't be hard. No, seriously,' she said, coming back into the small sitting room. 'I see nothing wrong with being friendly.'

'I think you're just a teensy-weensy bit attracted to him. He's quite handsome for an older man.'

'I can't say I'd noticed,' Caroline said, although it was one of the first things she had observed. 'And, for your information, I am not.' She picked up the jacket her sister had flung over the back of the settee. 'Isn't it time you were going home?'

'I suppose so.' Vanessa heaved herself up off the settee. 'I was going to ring, but I wanted to see what was going on for myself.'

'Well, I'm sorry you had a wasted journey.'

Vanessa pulled her jacket on. It gaped visibly at the front.

She really was getting rather large, Caroline thought. She hoped she wasn't planning on working full time until the baby was born. 'Do you want me to open the shop for you tomorrow?' she said. 'I don't have anything else on.'

'Would you mind?'

'No, of course not. You have a morning in bed.'

Vanessa nodded and fumbled in her pockets for her keys. 'Thanks. I'd appreciate a lie-in. Jed always wakes me at the crack of dawn, and I never see the point in going back to sleep, when I have to get up an hour later.'

'Yes, well, make the most of it while you can.' She held the car door open and waited until her sister had manoeuvred herself into position. 'And remember, say nothing about Grant to mother.'

She waved until Vanessa's car, newly patched up and with a brand-new exhaust pipe, disappeared down the lane. Right, she thought, reaching for Monty's lead. Time for that dog walk.

Chapter Sixteen

The recent heavy rainfall had left the trees and grass looking lush, though the ground was still boggy underfoot. The clouds had cleared, leaving a vast, blue sky that seemed to stretch forever. It was nearly midsummer, and it would be a while yet, until sunset. Apart from the midges and other biting insects that seemed to be attracted to Caroline, as if she were a gourmet feast, the conditions were perfect for an evening stroll.

Perfect too, for some of the village youngsters, to head to the woods for an impromptu party. Since the closure of the church youth club, following a spate of vandalism, there was nowhere for teenagers to go, and nothing much for them to do, apart from to hang out in the woods.

Caroline heard them before she saw them. By the shrieks and giggles, she gathered it wasn't only the boys. The girls had decided to join in too. The acrid smell of burning wood drifted towards her through the trees.

She clipped Monty's lead on, and hung back, watching the group of youngsters gathering round a campfire, with what looked like cans of beer and bottles of cider being passed around. She could count five, no six of them; four boys and two girls. One of them—a tall lad with a shock of blonde hair hanging forward over his face, which he swept back as he took a swig from a can—caused her to gasp in surprise. She recognised him straight away. It was her nephew, Adam.

Oh, my goodness, he wasn't even sixteen, and he was in the middle of his exams. Vanessa said he brought his school books to study when he was helping her in the shop. Yet, here he was, on private property, round a potentially dangerous camp fire, drinking beer. Or Cider. Or both.

She shrank back behind a tree. She didn't know what to do. Half of her wanted to march up to him and say something. The other half didn't want to humiliate him in front of his friends. It was all show at that age. Especially if girls were involved. She screwed up her eyes to peer closer. They weren't behaving in a ladylike manner. She suspected the dark-haired girl had, had a bit too much to drink. She seemed rather loud. The other girl, smaller, with shorter brown hair, swayed backwards and forwards, dancing in time with the music. She wore skin-tight denim shorts, a baggy shirt, and oversized boots.

Adam walked over and draped one arm round her waist. He leaned towards her, and Caroline thought he was about to kiss her. She closed her eyes. She didn't want to watch.

This was her nephew. Normally a lovely, thoughtful, polite young man. And he was out here, drinking and canoodling in the woods, with a young girl who looked like she'd forgotten to get dressed before she went out. Those shorts were practically indecent.

She glanced down at Monty, who busily sniffed through the undergrowth by her feet. Fortunately, he was pre-occupied with other forest scents, and hadn't noticed the group of teenagers a couple of hundred metres away. She gave a gentle tug on his lead. Maybe she'd head back the way she had come and pretend she hadn't seen them. After all, they were just doing what most teenagers did; hanging out with their mates.

'Oi! This is private property!'

Caroline shrank back against a tree. She would recognise that indignant roar anywhere.

Grant Dalton came marching into the clearing, where the youngsters had set up their campfire. He looked furious.

'Don't you know you're trespassing?'

One youth stood and waved a can of beer at him. 'All right, Grandad. What's your problem? We're only having a bit of fun.'

'Then I suggest you have it somewhere else.' He planted his feet apart and glared at them, his hands on his hips. 'Go on, clear off. This is private land.'

Caroline saw Adam step forward, to say something to his friend, but the youth shook him away, with an irritated flick of his arm.

'What you going to do about it, Grandad?'

Oh dear. This was looking confrontational. Caroline had the horrible feeling Grant wasn't going to back down, that he never backed down. This could all turn nasty. She would have to do something. She looked anxiously around, not sure what she could do, and then she suddenly had a brainwave.

Crouching down, she unclipped Monty's lead. 'Squirrels.' She pointed excitedly towards the thicket of trees.

She knew that if there was one thing the dog hated, it was squirrels. He would take it upon himself to chase anything remotely fluffy tailed from his territory. Since it appeared that he already thought the woods and fields belonged to him (even though they no longer did), any squirrel was fair game. So, when Caroline whispered, and pointed, she could tell he thought he was onto a good thing. With a rapid volley of vicious sounding barks, Monty bounded into the trees, in hot pursuit of his, as yet unseen, foe.

The distraction was enough for the youngsters to grab their things and make a run for it, apparently believing Grant had come armed with a guard dog. In fairness, Monty could sound aggressive when he chased something.

By the time she caught up with him, the teenagers, including her nephew, had scarpered, and Grant was trying to hold Monty at arm's length by his collar, while stamping on the remains of the campfire.

'Thanks,' she said, quickly securing him with the lead. 'He ran off.'

'Doesn't he always.' He kicked aside a smouldering log before glancing across at her. 'Bloody kids. Unbelievable! Did you see them?'

'Um...' She tried to appear non-committal. She wasn't good at lying.

'I can't have them in the woods. You shouldn't be here either.'

Caroline was taken aback for a moment. She'd just saved him from a possible beating by a tipsy, hormone challenged adolescent, and this was all the thanks she was getting.

'Excuse me?'

'Technically, I mean.' He stamped out the last of the glowing embers. 'I didn't mean you couldn't be here. I just meant…Oh, never mind. That came out all wrong.'

I'll say, she thought, bending down to stroke Monty's silky ears. He seemed to have picked up a few stray brambles and twigs in his headlong dash through the undergrowth.

'Grandad indeed,' he muttered.

'I suspect they think anyone over thirty is ancient,' she said. 'Didn't you, at that age?'

'Probably.' He stuffed his hands into the pockets of his jeans. 'I…um…I wanted to thank you. You know, for the other night. Well, both nights, really.'

He looked decidedly sheepish.

'I swear I rarely drink. It was a one-off.'

'You could have killed yourself.' She wiped her leather boot on a clump of damp grass. She had stood in something suspiciously like fox poo, judging by the pungent aroma. It was all she could do to stop Monty throwing himself onto the ground and rolling in it.

'I know. Stupid really.'

'The flowers were lovely, though,' she said. 'Thank you.'

'It was the least I could do.'

She didn't dispute that. 'So,' she said, as she picked her way along the muddy path towards the drive. 'How's it going up at the house? I see the builders have started already.'

'Come and have a look, if you like.'

'What, now? Oh, I couldn't.' She hesitated for a moment, but not long enough for him to withdraw the offer. 'Oh well, maybe a quick look.'

Grant laid the plans out on the pine kitchen table and took an age to explain everything to her; where he planned to have the consulting rooms and operating theatres, what he envisaged for the waiting area, and how he was incorporating the staircase into the space earmarked for the reception desk and office.

The builders had already started with the construction of some of the internal dividing walls, and the carpenter had erected a skeleton framework for new doors and partitions.

'It's a magnificent building,' he added, rolling up the detailed drawings, 'so I'd like to keep to the original structure as much as I can, but obviously there'll need to be some modernisation.'

'Sounds expensive.'

'It is, but…' He paused, and then sighed. 'I'm hoping it will be worth it.'

'Mother says nothing worth having ever comes easy.'

He glanced up, and she caught the merest glint of amusement in his eyes. 'I'd say she was a wise woman, your mother, but experience begs me to differ. No offence.'

'None taken.' She smiled. 'What made you decide to come to Suffolk?'

She could have sworn it was like a shutter being pulled down. One minute, he was enthusiastic, and almost joking with her, the next, his face had changed. His eyes had darkened, and she could see a faint twitch on his cheek.

Yet, it had been a simple question, the sort of question loads of people would ask him, when they heard the trace of a Yorkshire accent. It was clear he wasn't from round here. They would want to know why had he moved to the area?

'I had my reasons,' he said. 'I don't want to go into it right now, if you don't mind.'

'That's fine.'

He folded up the plans. The silence between them was deafening.

Caroline wasn't sure what to do. She knew she'd said

something wrong. He wasn't even looking at her but making a show of finding the creases in the plans, and folding the papers in the correct order. A furrow of wrinkles crossed his brow.

She picked up Monty's lead. 'Actually, I need to be getting back now. I didn't realise how late it was.' She scraped back her chair. 'Thanks for letting me see what you're going to do with the house. I'm sure it will be lovely once it's completed.' She kept her voice light and friendly, as if she hadn't noticed his sudden change of mood.

'No problem.' He stood up. 'Let me see you to the door.'

'That's okay.' She risked a shy smile. (It wasn't returned.) 'I know where to go.'

She followed Monty as he scampered across the tiled floor of the kitchen, his claws clicking on the hard surface. Grant didn't follow them, but turned back to the table to resume packing up the plans. He seemed relieved she was leaving. She heard his steady exhale of breath when she opened the door.

'Bye,' she said.

He did not respond.

'It's a mystery, Monty,' she told the dog, as they walked back down the drive towards her cottage. She glanced over her shoulder, but the front door remained shut. 'I do like a puzzle to solve, but something tells me this one is beyond me. What do you think?'

The spaniel wagged its tail from side to side, as he always did when someone spoke to him, or gave him attention.

'If only we could all be as happy as you.' She patted his head. 'Life would be much simpler for everyone.'

The awkwardness between Grant and her had come out of nowhere, just when she thought they were getting on well. It was evident that something from his past still troubled him, and she was curious to know what it was. More than that, she wanted to help him.

Chapter Seventeen

Caroline didn't expect the tack shop to be busy. Vanessa told her it was usually quiet mid-week, and built up steadily towards the weekend, when people were getting ready for shows, and suddenly needed ribbons, and brushes and saddle soap, and every other necessity that went with the whole equestrian business.

She flicked a duster over the saddles and bridles, paying particular attention to the ones higher up; ones she felt sure her sister, in her condition, wouldn't be able to reach. She was enjoying her time pottering round the shop, sorting through the tack, and tidying the shelves. The boxes of stable boots needed sorting into size order; the rails of hacking and show jackets into small, medium, and large.

This had once been her life, she thought. Preparing for the next gymkhana or jumping competition. Not that she ever won anything, but she was the proud owner of several rosettes, routinely given out to those who took part. Her mother had arranged them in a large glass frame and put it on display for years.

How long was it since she had last ridden a horse? It must have been years ago. Marcus didn't like horses, or dogs, or any other animal for that matter, so riding had come low down on her list of priorities when they married.

But now that she was divorced, maybe it was the right time for her to take it up again? With Hollyfield stables on her doorstep, she'd never get a better opportunity.

She held up a pair of large navy jodhpurs and wondered if the stockroom had them in her size. She'd slimmed down considerably over the past couple of years. All her old clothes, including her riding stuff, had gone to the charity shop or the tip. She felt sure she could fit into a medium now.

The bell above the shop door jangled. Caroline hung the jodhpurs back on the rail and turned to see if she could help whoever had come in. To her surprise, it was Adam.

'Why aren't you in school?' she said.

'I'm revising.' He pointed to the bag, slung over one shoulder. 'Why are you here? And where's Aunty Van? Is she okay?'

The lad looked concerned, and Caroline knew he had a soft spot for her sister. Not so much for her, in truth, but Vanessa had spent more time with him and his sister, Rosie, when they were growing up. They were still growing up now, she reminded herself, although Adam was almost six feet tall, and a young man, not a boy.

'Yes, don't worry. She's fine. She's having a rest, that's all.'

Adam dropped his bag on the floor and kicked it under the counter. 'Are you taking over the shop when she has the baby?'

'No.' Caroline folded up some cotton scarves and tidied them into a neat pile. 'I won't be taking over, but I'll certainly be helping her when she has the baby. She's going to need all the help she can get.'

'Yeah, I know, but I can do that.' He took off his blazer and tossed it over a stool. 'She often leaves me in charge.'

Oh, the arrogance of youth, Caroline thought. He was miffed because he had found her in the shop instead of his favourite, Aunty Van. (Which was a ridiculous name for her sister, but she was stuck with it).

'I know you do,' she said. 'Vanessa thinks very highly of you. But you can't be here all the time. You've got school.'

Adam shrugged. 'In the holidays, then.'

'We'll see.' She sorted through the bags of horse treats, checking they were in date. She was trying to think how to word things. Did she just come out and say that she had seen him in the woods the previous evening, and his friend had shocked her by fronting up to Grant Dalton? Did she mention the alcohol and the fire? What was the best way to tell him she knew what he had been up to? Or was it best to avoid the subject completely until she got the chance to mention it to Ella?

She was no good at this sort of thing. She hadn't been a rebellious teen. Her mother had been so bossy and domineering, she would have been terrified to step out of line. Her escape had been to get married and leave home, and that hadn't been the right solution, either.

Communication is the key. She had read that in a magazine somewhere. Keep the lines of communication open.

She glanced over at her nephew, who sat on the stool behind the counter. He had pushed his blazer into a crumpled heap on the dusty floor. A maths textbook was open in front of him. She didn't think he was studying it, though. Instead, he was doodling on a Thelwell pony notebook that she was sure he hadn't paid for.

Caroline sucked in a deep breath, held it, and exhaled quietly between her teeth. It was a form of mindfulness. It was supposed to make her feel calm and relaxed, as was writing down her thoughts and desires, but she could hardly do that right now.

She coughed and cleared her throat. Go for the jugular, she thought. No messing about.

'Do you often go into the woods at night with your friends?' she asked.

He raised his eyes, though not his head. 'What?'

'At night. With your friends. I saw you, Adam. Last night.'

This time, he did lift his head. He stared straight at her; a curious look on his face.

'You were drinking beer.'

He shrugged nonchalantly, as if it didn't matter. 'Everyone does that.'

'No, Adam. They do not.' She took a step closer. 'Not at sixteen, and not on a school night.'

He slammed his textbook shut and stuffed it into his bag.

'It's none of your business what I do. You're not my mother.'

'No, but I'm sure she'll want to know about this.'

He grabbed his blazer and looked as if he was about to storm out of the shop, but her words seemed to stop him in mid stride. 'She won't mind. She lets me do stuff like that.'

Caroline narrowed her eyes. She knew he was lying. 'I don't think she does.'

He dropped his gaze. 'Look, it was a one off. We were having a break from all the exam stuff, okay?'

'You were trespassing on private property.'

'Oh, do me a favour. A couple of weeks ago, it was Gran's property. We always used to hang out there.'

'I see. So, that means you and your friends are responsible for the broken glass in the woods which, incidentally, cut the pad on Monty's paw; to say nothing of all the rubbish and the fires you left behind. And now you're trying to tell me last night was a one-off?'

Finally, he had the decency to look guilty. 'It wasn't only me,' he muttered.

'I know. I saw.' Caroline stepped closer until she was practically in his face. 'Who is that pleasant young man who fronted up to Grant Dalton with a beer can in his hand? Friend of yours, is he?'

Adam doodled circles on the pad with a blunt pencil. 'Not especially.'

'Not especially,' she repeated.

'No. He's not a friend. He's a….'

'What?'

Adam pressed so hard on the pencil, it snapped. He brushed the bits to one side, and they fell on the floor. 'Look, I don't want you to tell mum. Okay. It won't happen again.'

'Adam, is there something you're not telling me?'

'No. Nothing.' He ripped the page from his pad and crumpled up the piece of paper he had been drawing on. 'Sorry about Monty's paw,' he mumbled. 'I didn't know.'

'Yes, well, it was a while ago now, and he's fully recovered.

But it could have been a lot worse if Mr Dalton hadn't been staying at Grey Lodge when it happened. Your Gran was frantic with worry. She loves that dog.'

Adam didn't look at her. He seemed genuinely upset. Caroline wondered if she'd been a bit harsh on him. She knew he was an animal lover, and he wouldn't have wished Monty any harm. But he needed to realise that his actions had consequences.

She stooped to pick up the broken bits of pencil. It gave her a moment to think, and for him to calm down. 'There's been a delivery of feed,' she said, placing the bits on the counter. 'I don't suppose you could move the bags into the storeroom, while you're here?'

'Yes, sure.' He looked relieved. 'Shall I move the old bags to the front?'

'Good idea.'

He seemed happier now he had something to do. Caroline watched him from the corner of her eye as he sorted out the bags of food and placed them in date order in the stockroom. She couldn't help feeling he'd be better off at home if he was supposed to be revising, but what would she know? She wasn't a parent.

'I'm thinking of taking up riding again,' she said, raising her voice so he could hear her in the next room. 'It's been a while. Who do you think would suit me?' She knew Adam was familiar with all the horses at the stables. Riding had been his passion since he was a small boy. It was hardly surprising, given his background.

'Merlin's a good bet.' He poked his head round the door. 'The grey Connemara. He's forward going, but sensible.'

'Merlin,' she repeated, making a mental note. 'Anyone else?'

Adam re-emerged from the stockroom and brushed the dust from his black school trousers with the flat of his hand. 'Or Captain. Bit smaller, but bomb-proof. He's a good hacking pony. Nothing fazes him.'

'Sounds perfect. Who's your favourite?'

He pulled up the wooden, three-legged stool and sat down, a renewed look of enthusiasm on his face. 'Blackthorn. He's a cross between a thoroughbred and an Irish Draught horse, so he's got speed and stamina.'

'How often do you ride him?'

Adam glanced over at the shop door as the bell above it jangled. 'Not as often as I'd like,' he said, grabbing his bag.

Before Caroline could speak, he shot back to the storeroom, and shut the door behind him.

The older woman, who had come into the shop, was perusing the racks of saddles and bridles, hanging up on the far wall. She had shoulder-length, bobbed brown hair, and wore a lightly padded burgundy gilet, over a cream shirt, and tailored navy trousers. A name tag and photo hung on a ribbon around her neck. As she half turned, Caroline glimpsed her face, and knew she vaguely recognised her from somewhere, but she wasn't sure where. 'Can I help you?' she said.

'No thanks. I'm just looking.'

'Well, shout if you need anything.'

'I will.'

Who was it? She racked her brain. More to the point, why had Adam skedaddled into the back room the moment she'd shown her face?

And then it dawned on her—Mrs Jeffries—she was one of the teachers from the Academy, and a keen eventer. She'd won stacks of cups and rosettes over the years and kept her horse in livery at Hollyfield Stables.

A glance at the clock on the wall behind confirmed her suspicions. It was lunchtime. She must have popped out of school in her break period, and Adam didn't want to be seen by her. Which suggested he shouldn't be here. No wonder he hadn't wanted to study at home, where Ella might find him. He was supposed to be in school.

'Adam,' she called, after the woman had left, with her purchase of a sack of horse carrots and a currycomb. 'Can you come in here a minute?'

He peered warily round the door.

'There's no need to look like that. She's gone. Which leads me to my next question. Why aren't you in school?'

'I told you I've got study leave.'

'So why didn't you want Mrs Jeffries to see you?'

'Duh!' he sighed, tapping the side of his head as if it was obvious. 'Because I'm supposed to be studying.'

'And you can't do that in the comfort of your own home?'

He hesitated, a fraction too long.

'Adam, if there's something that's worrying you.'

'There isn't.'

'Well, excuse me, but I think there is, and I'm going to hazard a guess and say it's something to do with that so-called friend of yours, who isn't "especially" a friend.' She drummed her fingers on the wooden counter as she spoke. She knew Adam was listening, even though he wasn't looking at her, but appeared to be staring at his feet. 'He's probably a bully. One of the school trouble-makers. I expect he has no respect for authority. In fact, from what I saw last night…'

'This has nothing to do with Max Bradshaw.'

'Max Bradshaw.' Caroline repeated. She would remember that name.

He shuffled his feet, as if realising his mistake. 'Look, it's not what you think.'

'Oh, you do not know what I'm thinking,' she said, her voice calm and measured.

It was true. He didn't. He looked bewildered and uncertain.

'You've got yourself mixed up with the cool kids. The ones that think getting drunk and messing about is what life is all about. Fun now, consequences later, and stuff exams, and studying, and hard work, because that's boring. That's for losers. Well, let me tell you something, Adam Trevelyan.' She leaned forward, forcing him to meet her gaze. 'I didn't study. I found school boring. I have no qualifications. Oh, and I can't even ride a horse properly, even though I have a mother who says I can. And, just like you, I was brought up thinking I was better than everybody else, because I lived in a posh house and rode horses and didn't have to work.'

'I don't think I'm better than anybody else,' he muttered.

'That as maybe, but you do need to get your exams, because believe me, you will need them when you're older. There's no two ways about it. You study now, and the fun comes later. Don't make the same mistakes I did. Please, Adam. Don't follow the sheep, who can't see beyond the next cheap thrill. You're better than that.'

He kicked at the wooden skirting board at the foot of the counter.

She could tell he was paying attention to her words, even if he wasn't saying much.

'You've got a few weeks left before the summer holidays, when you can party all you like, knowing you've done your best.'

'Yeah, but…'

'A few weeks, Adam, that's all.'

It probably seemed like an eternity to him. She could remember those days when weeks seemed to last forever. Now, they were hurtling past, much faster than she cared to think about. 'And as for that Max, whatshisname…'

'Bradshaw.'

'Yes, him. Well, he's a real loser. He's got no respect for anyone, not even himself.' Her voice dripped with scorn. 'He thinks he's the big man by threatening an older bloke. Really? What a cool dude he is.'

Adam glanced sideways at her.

'Scared off by a bouncy spaniel. Oh yes, very cool.'

'No one says "cool" anymore, Aunty Caroline.' He finally smiled. 'So, that was Monty? It wasn't some vicious guard dog?'

'No. Though it could have been. Mr Dalton is going to get cameras and security fencing installed all round Grey Lodge, so you and your mates won't be able to tramp through those woods again.'

'Max said it was a German Shepherd. He reckoned it nearly had him.'

'Max,' she said, 'is a liar.' She leaned down to pick up his school bag. 'And I sincerely hope he is not your mate. Now, off you go. You should be able to get there before the end of lunch break.'

He picked up the bag and slung it over one shoulder. 'And you won't tell mum?'

'Not if I don't have to.'

He nodded.

They had reached an agreement, of sorts. Caroline knew she wouldn't say anything to Ella. But she would keep a watchful eye on him, going forward. Adam was a decent lad, and it would be awful to see him led astray and do something he would regret later, by the likes of Max Bradshaw. Peer pressure could be a heady drug. Thankfully, not one she had ever succumbed to. Then again, she'd never had many friends. Her mother had seen to that.

Chapter Eighteen

Things were progressing better than he could have expected. Within days of starting the alterations, Grant was now in possession of a fully self-contained living area on the second floor. The builders had fitted out the new kitchen in one of the back bedrooms, opposite the new lounge, and he'd made the room next to it an office and study area. The family sized bathroom was adjacent to his own bedroom, and three further guest bedrooms.

Sabrina would be free to choose the one she preferred, or she could opt for the attic rooms if she wanted more space and privacy. It had been a while since they had lived under the same roof. It was going to take adjustments on both sides, but he was confident it would work.

The rooms on the ground floor were coming together, just as he had envisaged. The front door opened into the magnificent hall and reception area. Apart from a couple of dividing stud walls, between the consulting rooms and the waiting room, there wasn't much change to the layout. It was at the rear of the building, where the operating theatres would be, that required most of the building work.

His feet crunched over rubble and brick dust when he pushed aside the protective plastic sheeting, and stared around the room that would be the main theatre. It was all coming together. Even the billboard, advertising the practice, had been delivered and was stored in the garage, ready to be erected at the end of the drive. A new phone line had been installed, and adverts for staff were going into the veterinary journals that week.

He was itching to get back into the day to day running of a veterinary practice, using the skills he had trained long and hard to perfect. All this hanging around was doing him no good at all. It would be better when his daughter got there. At least he'd have some company.

He wondered why he hadn't seen Caroline on his daily walk round the estate. A team of workmen were putting up new fencing round the woods, and he half wondered if they had put her off going there with her dog. He meant to tell her that she was welcome to use the grounds, but she had been conspicuous by her absence ever since the night he came across the teenagers and sent them packing. Or, at least, Monty had.

He smiled. He had a soft spot for Springer spaniels, and Grey Lodge was the perfect place to own such a dog, with its acres of fields and woods to explore. Monty must be feeling a bit cramped in the tiny cottage, after having all this space to call his own.

Maybe he should call round and tell her she was free to use it, in exchange for him putting the billboard at the end of her garden. That sounded like a fair deal. Besides, he felt like he should get to know her better, seeing as how she was his nearest neighbour. Not in a romantic sense, of course. He wasn't ready for that, but she seemed like a level-headed woman who enjoyed her independence, and he liked that.

He knew he hadn't been particularly pleasant to her when he stayed in the bed-and-breakfast all those months ago.

'Like a bear with a sore head,' Sabrina told him. *'Dad, you have to be nicer to people if you're going to move there. No one wants to bring their pet to see a belligerent old vet?'*

'Hey, less of the old.'

His daughter was right, though. He had a few bridges to mend, and there was no time like the present to make a start.

He waited until the workmen had finished for the day. It gave him time to heat a chicken pie in the oven and some frozen vegetables in the microwave. He didn't have his wife's skills when it came to preparing a meal.

Helen had been a fantastic cook. She made everything from scratch, using the vegetables they grew in the garden when they were in season. All organic, wholesome food.

Much good it had done her, he thought. "Eat healthy and be healthy" wasn't always the case.

He pushed a bit of chicken breast, smothered in a glutinous sauce, onto his fork. They used to keep hens in the garden for eggs, which had been fine until one night when the foxes got in and killed them all. They'd burrowed under the wire. Helen had been heartbroken. She refused to have any more chickens after that, but the farmer down the road supplied them with more than enough eggs from his own flock.

He would get a cat, he decided. An older one from a rescue centre, preferably a decent mouser. Maybe a dog, once the building work was complete. He knew that Sabrina would want her own horse, now they had a stable and fields again.

She had grown up with a succession of ponies, from Shetlands, to New Forest and finally, a Welsh cob, that she used for hacking out over the Yorkshire moors. Before Helen became ill, she used to join her on Bessie, a sturdy black and white cob, with a thick mane and tail. Grant didn't ride. He didn't share their passion for horses or other large farm animals. Give him a Labradoodle or a Border collie, as opposed to a cow, a goat or a sheep, any day.

He sat by the window, drinking a mug of coffee and staring down the long drive. It was a sunny, bright evening, with only the merest wisp of a cloud in the sky.

Caroline stood in the gatehouse's garden. He could see her getting in some washing that hung on the line. It was the perfect time for him to take a walk down there. He felt guilty that they had parted with some awkwardness the other day, and he wanted to explain. But he wasn't good at small talk. He never had been, and some things were still painful to discuss.

He drained his mug and rinsed it under the tap. It wasn't worth putting the dishwasher on for a handful of dishes. Then he grabbed his keys and left the house.

Monty was delighted to see him. Caroline, less so. He thought he detected a faint reluctance on her part, as she stepped to one side to let him in to the sitting room.

'I hope you don't mind me calling round like this, but there are a few things I'd like to talk over with you. I'm not keeping you from anything, am I?' He bent over to make a fuss of the spaniel, who jumped up at his legs, demanding attention. 'I won't stop if you're busy.'

'I'm not.' She turned towards the kitchen. 'Coffee? Oh Monty, get down.'

She sounded exasperated, Grant thought, pushing the dog off and straightening up. 'No thanks. I've just had one, but don't let me stop you.'

'I'm fine. It keeps me awake.' She perched on the arm of the settee.

She looked tense, he thought. He chose the armchair on the opposite side of the room. 'I haven't seen you out walking for a few days,' he began. 'Is everything all right?'

'With Monty?'

'With you.'

She nodded. 'Yes. Well, yes, and no. I've been working in the tack shop,' she said. 'Monty has to come with me. He's not good at being left. He wrecks things.' She pointed to a chewed-up corner of the settee that had a woollen throw strategically placed over the torn upholstery.

'Does he behave in the shop?'

She finally managed a smile. 'Not always, but he loves being around people. Probably more than I do. He ate a bag of horse treats when I wasn't looking, and if he can get to the doggy rack, he'll help himself to a rope toy or a ball.'

Grant smiled and fondled the spaniel's floppy ears. 'He's not so daft, after all.' He glanced across at her. 'You know, if you're ever stuck, I'd be happy to have him for a few hours. I miss having a dog in the house.'

'Thanks,' she said. 'Some days, I'd willingly give him away, but he's good company.'

'Animals usually are.'

She gave a small laugh, and he smiled. He thought she was relaxing a little. He watched her brush a few of Monty's hairs from the seat of the sofa and then sit down on it, her legs crossed at the knee.

'How's the building work going?'

'Good. Yep. It's going well, I think. Messy, but that's to be expected.'

'I see you're getting new fencing put up.'

He nodded. 'Yes, and that's what I wanted to talk to you about. Don't let it put you off. You're more than welcome to use the woods for Monty's exercise. It must be hard for him. He doesn't understand why he's here and not up there in the big house.'

'Thanks. That's very kind of you.' She gave a sigh. 'It's not much fun taking him along the lane. Sometimes drivers whizz round that bend so fast, you take your life in your hands walking along it.'

'I should have told you earlier,' he said. 'I was wondering if that was the reason I hadn't seen you out and about.'

'Well, you did say it was private property,' she reminded him.

'To those oiks, not you.'

'Have they been back?'

'No, not as far as I can see.' He had made a point of going through the woods most evenings, just to make sure, but the teenagers had stayed away. 'I reckon Monty excelled himself that day.'

She smiled. 'That's a first. Are you sure I can't get you something to drink? I've got some red wine, if you'd prefer that to tea or coffee.'

'Actually, yes, I'd like that very much. A small glass,' he added hastily. He had been honest when he said he rarely drank. He was a man who liked to be in control of things, and alcohol had a nasty habit of unravelling his best intentions.

Caroline fetched a bottle of red and an opener from the

kitchen and handed it to him. 'Would you mind?' she said. 'I'll just get some glasses.'

They ended up sitting in the kitchen, on either side of the counter above Monty's basket. It made sense, as the dog's tail was at the right height to knock everything off the small coffee table in the lounge with one sweep.

'I thought this place was derelict when I first saw it all those months ago,' he said.

'It was.'

He glanced round the small kitchen. 'Did you do all this?'

She nodded. 'With help, of course, but I did what I could.' She topped up his glass.

He should have refused, but he was enjoying sitting and chatting with her. He'd been stuck on his own for days, with only the workmen for company, and the noise of their banging and drilling and hammering wasn't conducive to normal conversation.

'It's lovely. Perfect for someone on their own.' He hesitated, glancing down at her fingers, curled round the stem of her wineglass and wondering if he'd presumed too much. Maybe she wasn't on her own, and there was a boyfriend lurking somewhere. She wasn't wearing any rings, engagement or otherwise. 'You are on your own?' he said.

'I'm divorced, if that's what you mean,' she said. 'And I have Monty. What about you?'

'No pets. Not yet, anyway. I thought I might get a cat.'

He knew he was evading the question, but he didn't feel ready to talk about his personal life. One day, maybe, but not today. He wanted to keep things light and informal. They hadn't got off to the best possible start, and he would prefer it if they could be friends. It made sense, seeing as how they were living a stone's throw away from each other. She'd come to his rescue several times over the past couple of weeks and asked for nothing in return. He admired her for that.

'You want to talk to my step-sister, over at Hollyfield Stables? I'm sure Adam—he's my nephew—said one of their cats had a litter of kittens.'

'I was thinking more of an older cat. One that knows a thing or two about catching mice.' He took a drink from his glass. The wine was a smooth Merlot, he enjoyed it immensely. 'I was over at Hollyfield stables the other day,' he said. 'I was impressed with the set-up. And the owner,' he added. 'I didn't realise you were related.'

'Ella's father married my mother,' she told him. 'It was a long time ago. When he died, she married Michael Lloyd-Duncan, and that's how she ended up at Grey Lodge, which was his home. He was a solicitor,' she added. 'He was old and rich. Mother seemed to like older, wealthy men. But then, he died, and she found out he wasn't so rich after all.'

'You're painting a poor picture of your mother,' he said.

She smiled. 'It does sound bad, but I think she was genuinely happy with Michael. I didn't know him that well. I was married and living in Ecclesfield by then.'

'So, you moved back here after your divorce?'

'Yes, with no idea she was going to turn Grey Lodge into a Bed and Breakfast business, let alone sell it,' she said.

He gave her a rueful smile. 'Sorry about that.'

'It was probably for the best. I think I'm a bit too old to be living with my mother and tied to her apron strings. I'm pleased at what I've done with this place. I feel like it's something for me. I can be independent for the first time in my life. Well, I can, once I get a proper job,' she added.

'I thought you said you were working at the tack shop.'

'Only because Vanessa is pregnant.' She topped up his glass with the last of the bottle. 'She's my sister, so I'm helping her while I can.'

'And after that?'

She shrugged. 'Who knows?'

He stroked his chin, thoughtfully. She seemed to have coped with so many changes in her life and come out on top. All credit to her. He hoped he could do the same.

For the first time in days, he felt mellow and relaxed. It

was a beautiful evening in early summer. The work on the house was progressing well, and he could see a future ahead of him that, a few short months ago, had seemed like a pipe dream.

He bent down to stroke the spaniel's head. Monty sat by his feet, gazing up at him, with a deep and soulful look in his dark brown eyes. 'I guess he hasn't realised I'm a vet, yet,' he said.

'Monty likes everyone, even vets.' She picked up the empty glasses, to carry them to the sink. As she did so, she bumped against his arm. 'Oops, sorry,' she said, stumbling forwards.

He reached out and grabbed hold of her with both hands. 'Steady.'

For a second, they stared at each other. A brief, sudden, and totally unexpected flicker of something flooded through him. A feeling he hadn't felt in a long time.

Shocked, he released his grip.

Her cheeks flushed pink. 'Sorry,' she said, regaining her balance. 'That wine has made me a bit tipsy.'

She hurried to the sink and turned on the taps. Her back was towards him.

'I'd better go,' he said, mortified. 'I've taken up far too much of your time.'

She didn't turn round, busy plunging the glasses into a basin of foaming suds. 'No. It's fine, but I do have to be up early in the morning, and it's getting late.'

'Yes, of course. I'm sorry.'

He hesitated by the front door, one hand resting on the wooden frame. She didn't seem to have noticed his discomfort, and for that, he was grateful. 'Do you want to drop Monty off with me tomorrow if you're going to work?'

She glanced back over her shoulder. 'If you're sure you don't mind. That would be really helpful.'

'Good.' He lowered his gaze. 'Thanks for the drink. I'll see you in the morning. You too, Monty,' he added, stroking the spaniel who had come to the door. He closed it firmly behind him and let out the breath he had been holding for what seemed like ages.

Idiot! He thought, as he marched back up the gravelled drive. It was too soon. It was unexpected, and he didn't want to feel like this. He should never have drunk more than that first glass of wine.

When he reached the heavy oak door of Grey Lodge, he unlocked it, walked inside, and slammed it shut behind him, with a hard and resounding thud.

Chapter Nineteen

For the first time since moving into the cottage, Caroline had a sleepless night. She could have blamed the wine, but she knew it wasn't that which caused her to toss and turn, and eventually get up in the small hours to make herself a mug of tea. It was Grant Dalton. She found him increasingly attractive. She couldn't help herself.

The more she got to know him, the more she liked him, and she got the impression that the feeling was mutual. But when he'd grabbed her to stop her from overbalancing, she had seen something in his face; something that shocked him.

She felt it, too. That unmistakable quiver of physical longing.

But then, he'd jerked away with a fleeting look of horror on his face, and a wall had sprung up between them again.

Why?

What had she done wrong to make him act as if he were embarrassed and ashamed? Was he still married? And if he was, where was his wife?

Nightmare visions of a mad woman shut up in the attic had disturbed her dreams. Grant Dalton had the same sardonic manner as Mr Rochester, a character she had read about in a book. The heroine, Jane Eyre, had been devastated to discover he was already married, and his wife was insane and locked up in the upper floors of his mansion; a house not dissimilar to Grey Lodge.

Waking up gasping, and unable to go back to sleep, she gave up trying, and got out of bed; the memory of her bad dream still fresh in her mind.

She made a mug of tea and a slice of toast as she considered it. The sun streamed through a chink in the blinds and the air felt warm already, even though it was still early.

Monty snoozed in his basket. He'd given up begging for food, since she rarely tossed him any treats when eating, but she was aware of him watching her through one half-closed eye, just in case she dropped something.

It was a nightmare, that was all, she told herself. Caused by a vivid imagination and too much red wine. Grant didn't have an insane wife locked in his attic. That was a ridiculous idea.

Nevertheless, he wore a wedding ring, and she would never contemplate an affair with a married man. She'd seen the hurt it could cause. However, if he wasn't married, if he had been separated or divorced, well, that would change things.

She needed to find out.

The trouble was, short of asking him outright, which she wouldn't do as he'd already shown a reluctance to talk about his personal life, she didn't know how to.

Her mother was not very forthcoming, when she rang her, a little after seven o'clock, that morning, on the pretext of asking if the bailiffs had been round to her apartment again. (Fortunately, they hadn't, but the day was still young)

'How should I know if he's married?' she snapped. Her irritation at being woken so early wasn't lost on Caroline. 'He's got a daughter who's a vet, so I'm presuming there's a wife somewhere. Why do you want to know?'

'I just wondered,' she said, trying to sound as if she didn't care one way or the other. 'I take it you're going to contact the Inland Revenue today?'

'Yes, but not at this ungodly hour.'

She heard the sound of a stifled yawn.

'Sorry. I didn't mean to wake you, but I'm going over to the tack shop to help Vanessa, and I wanted to check you were okay first.' She twirled a strand of hair round her finger. She didn't know Grant had a daughter. This was news to her. What else had her mother not told her?

'There are no doors broken down, if that's what you mean.'

'Well, that's good, isn't it?'

Her mother sighed. 'Darling, I'm still in bed. Can we have this conversation another time? I'm half asleep.'

You and me both, Caroline thought. She glanced at the clock on the kitchen wall and realised it was a bit early. Since giving up the bed-and-breakfast business, her mother had been enjoying the luxury of long lie-ins. Being disturbed at this hour didn't suit her.

'Fine,' she said. 'I'll call back later, but ring me at the shop if you hear anything from the bailiffs. You can always give them my number. We need to get this sorted quickly. You don't want any scandal,' she added, knowing that was the one thing which would stir her mother into action. Appearances mattered to her. More than feelings, usually.

Caroline had a cool shower, hoping it might wake her up a bit, but she was still yawning as she got dressed. The rumble and clatter of the builder's vans as they drove up the drive towards Grey Lodge woke Monty up. He rushed to the window and jumped onto the settee to look out at them, barking furiously.

'You'd better get used to them,' she told him, as she reached for his lead. 'They won't be leaving anytime soon.'

The grass was wet with dew, but the air smelled clean and fresh, and there was the lightest of breezes. It was a beautiful morning, which lifted Caroline's spirits, as she followed the dog over the field. Like her mother, she wasn't good on little or no sleep.

She planned to give Monty a long walk before she dropped him off with Grant. The spaniel had loads of energy, and she hoped to tire him out, so he was less boisterous. She suspected Grant wasn't keen on badly behaved dogs.

The path through the woods was dry for once, and she walked briskly, letting Monty run free to sniff and scamper through the trees. The rubbish had been cleared away around the blackened oak tree, and she could clearly see the new fencing and 'Keep Out' signs. It wouldn't stop anyone who was determined to get in to the woods, but it was better than nothing. She was pretty sure Monty's aggressive sounding barking would deter them more.

It was almost eight thirty, before she headed back across the field, clipped the lead on Monty, and walked him up the drive. Grant had parked his car outside the front door, which was wide open. Someone had laid dust sheets on the tiled floor of the hall. She could hear banging and drilling, and the loud, tinny sound of a radio playing.

She couldn't help feeling apprehensive as she rang the bell and waited for him to come to the door. It was his suggestion that she drop Monty off, but it didn't seem right to walk in unannounced. Purely because of the tension she had detected the previous day, when everything had been going so well. It was like he blew hot and cold, and she wasn't sure where she stood, or what that meant.

She pressed the bell again. With all the builder's noise, she wondered if he'd heard it the first time. Edging forwards a couple of steps, she peered through the open front door. 'Hello? Grant?'

'Coming.'

He hurried down the stairs, rubbing his face and neck with a damp towel. His feet were bare, and she noticed that his hair looked wet.

'Sorry, I was in the shower.' He gave her a rueful smile. 'Have you been waiting long?'

'No. Just a minute or two.' She felt her cheeks redden, and stooped down to stroke Monty's silky head, hoping he hadn't noticed. 'I should have let you know when I was coming. Are you sure you're all right to have him?'

Grant was towelling his hair, and she straightened up, glad he was no longer staring at her. 'Yes, of course. You'll be all right here, won't you, boy?' He crouched down to greet the spaniel.

'Thanks. I'd better go.' She backed towards the door as she spoke. Monty didn't seem in the least bit concerned about being left at the big house. He was lying on his back, letting Grant rub his tummy.

'No problem.' He glanced sideways up at her. 'Go on. Go. He'll be fine.'

She placed the lead on the mat by the door and caught the scent of his shower gel. Something fresh and citrusy. It smelt divine. 'I'll see you later, then.'

'Yes, of course, but don't rush. I'm here all day.' He jerked his head over his shoulder. 'Got to keep an eye on this lot.'

She could hear someone whistling tunelessly amidst the hammering and drilling that came from the back rooms. 'Rather you than me.'

When the workmen had been doing up the gatehouse, she'd escaped to Grey Lodge for some peace. She half wondered if she should offer Grant the use of her cottage, whilst there was so much noise going on, but decided against it. He didn't seem bothered. Besides, he could always go for a walk if he needed a break from the constant racket. He had acres of grounds to explore. The woods were only a small part of the estate. Apart from the extensive lawns, there were several paddocks, which her mother had let Ella use for extra grazing. She wondered if Grant might do the same, at least until he had the practice up and running. Maybe she'd suggest it to him.

By the time she arrived at the tack shop, Vanessa was already there. She found her in the storeroom, unpacking a large carton of children's riding hats.

'You shouldn't be doing that. Here, let me do it.' She hustled her to one side, steering her towards a chair. 'All that bending and lifting won't do you any good.'

'I know.'

Caroline shot her a worried glance. Something about her sister's tone of voice seemed off. 'What's wrong?'

'I'm fed up with being pregnant, if you must know.' She sat down heavily. 'I'm fed up of being fat, and feeling cumbersome and awkward. I'm fed-up of suffering half the night with heartburn. I can't sleep without three pillows propping me up, and when I do sleep, the baby doesn't.' She rested her hands on her bump. 'And it seems to be going on forever.'

Caroline gave her a sympathetic smile. 'It won't be for much longer.'

'I know, and I should be grateful all is fine, considering I'm a geriatric mother.'

She said this last bit with emphasis on the word geriatric, and Caroline couldn't fail to notice the sarcasm in her words.

'But I've had enough of it now. I just want it to be over.'

'And it will be. A few more weeks, that's all.' She rested a consoling hand on her shoulder but withdrew it when Vanessa gave her a curious look. 'What?'

'You, all touchy-feely. That's not like you.'

'I can be sensitive to others; I'll have you know.'

'Not usually.'

She pulled a face. 'Anyway, you sit there, have a rest, and I'll put the kettle on.'

'I think I'd rather go home.'

Caroline glanced back at her. Vanessa did look exhausted. Her face was puffy, and she had dark shadows under her eyes. 'Actually, that's not a bad idea. You need to get all the rest you can at this stage. Go on, off you go. I can manage here.'

Relief flooded her sister's face. 'Are you sure?'

'Yes, of course. If there's something I can't deal with, I'll give you a ring.'

Vanessa hauled herself up by leaning on the counter to get her balance. 'Thanks. I'm beginning to think it's getting close to the time when I need to give up work.'

'Well, it's certainly something you should be considering. Don't worry about the shop,' she added, giving her a gentle nudge. 'You need to think about your health, and your baby's health. Everything else can wait.'

'When did you become all concerned?'

Caroline pulled a face. But her sister's words rang true. She knew she was thinking of others more than herself. It was since she had moved out of Grey Lodge, and found herself on her own, for the first time in her life. That's when people's feelings mattered to her.

Maybe it was because she was alone, that she had matured. She didn't know. But she was concerned about Grant and how troubled he seemed; about Adam and if he was mixing with the wrong crowd; about Vanessa, and how she was managing while heavily pregnant. She was even worried about her mother, and if she was about to be taken to court.

With all of them, she liked the feeling that she could be useful; that she could help, while expecting nothing in return. She was changing, she realised, from the spoilt and entitled person she used to be, and that wasn't a bad thing.

It had taken her almost forty years to get there.

***

Grant couldn't see himself changing anytime soon. He liked Caroline, but he didn't want a relationship with her. Not with her, not with anyone. They had a certain chemistry together. That much was undeniable. He had felt it the moment he grabbed her to stop her from falling. The shock had been intense. The sudden rush of desire, incomprehensible.

He was utterly ashamed of himself. How could he think of anyone else after what had happened to Helen? The guilt that he'd even felt that way was beyond him, after the anguish, and the total despair he had gone through.

Well, he had no intention of putting himself through that heartbreak again. He wouldn't allow it to happen. He would throw himself into his work and forget any thoughts of a relationship with Caroline.

Work had kept him sane in the time since he lost Helen, and work was what would see him through this unfortunate distraction. He must stay focused. Concentrate on the job at hand.

To that end, he spent the day clearing out the old stable block. Monty was the best kind of company, rooting his way through the straw and rubbish in search of mice or rats, and snoozing on an old blanket, while he swept the place clean and whitewashed the walls.

In between work, Grant practised a few dog-training lessons, surprised at how keen the spaniel was to learn new tricks. He had a brain, somewhere between those floppy ears. He needed to be taught how to use it.

The apple orchard was the perfect place to practise recall. Brick walls enclosed it on three sides, and a wire fence, to keep the deer out, on the other. Armed with a supply of cheese and ham, and a cold sausage, Grant gave it his best shot. In an enclosed space, the dog was perfect. Out in the fields, with the distraction of rabbits, or other dogs, it might be a different story. But overall, he felt satisfied that Monty was listening to his commands and enjoying the challenge.

'We'll get you trained yet,' he murmured, slipping him the last of the treats. Monty acted as if Grant was his new best friend, running obediently to his side as they made their way back to the house.

The workmen were loading their tools into the vans. Grant would wait until they departed before having a thorough look around. Judging by the amount of noise they made, he assumed they were on schedule.

They had left the front door propped open while they shifted their stuff.

He decided Monty wasn't likely to run away, not while treats might be in the offing, so he didn't close it. He went into the downstairs kitchen to get them both a cold drink.

This would be the staff room once the alterations were complete. Unlike the staff room at his old practice, which contained a sink, microwave, fridge, kettle and not much else, this one would have everything, from chairs and the solid dining table, to all the facilities for cooking and relaxing, essential for anyone spending the night on duty.

The adjoining small sitting room would have a sofa bed, television, and comfortable chairs, and the utility room would be for the washing and drying of animal bedding and scrubs only. The kitchen upstairs would handle everything else.

'Here you are, boy.' He placed a bowl of water on the floor.

Monty lapped it up eagerly, his long floppy ears trailing in the dish. He then lifted his head and shook them, scattering droplets all over the tiled floor, before settling down on a rug in front of the Aga.

Talk about making himself at home. In a matter of minutes, Monty had closed his eyes and fallen sound asleep.

The dog wasn't the only one feeling exhausted after the day's exertions. Grant felt muscles aching that he never knew existed. He poured himself a large glass of water and sat down at the table. It was nearing half-past five, and he expected Caroline to turn up fairly soon. He wouldn't invite her in. That was just asking for trouble. No, he'd tell her he had to go out or make some other excuse. Small talk on the doorstep would be the best way forwards. He didn't want her getting the wrong idea.

On reflection, he decided it had been his own fault, what with buying her chocolates, flowers, and then sharing a bottle of wine with her. But he had been lonely, and she was interesting company. Too interesting, perhaps. It would be different when his daughter got here. In the meantime, he would have to nip this in the bud before he did something he would regret.

Sabrina rang him at almost the same moment he was thinking of calling her. Talk about weird coincidences. He answered his phone, smiling when he heard her cheerful voice.

'Hi Dad. How's it all going?'

'Good,' he said. 'The second floor is ready. They've fitted the new kitchen and you've got the pick of several rooms. Or the attic, if you'd prefer. When do you think you'll get here?' Soon, he hoped, keeping his fingers crossed.

He drained his glass of water and listened to her excited chatter about some animals she had treated, including an injured badger that a motorist had brought in. He'd put it in the boot of his car, and it had taken three of them to extract it with gauntlets. Badgers, she informed him, especially injured ones, could be quite vicious when cornered.

He laughed. He could have told her that.

'Anyway, I've finished my stint in Berkshire. I'm moving out of my accommodation at the weekend. So, all being well, I should be with you on Saturday afternoon.'

'This Saturday?'

'Yep.'

Grant gave a sigh of relief. 'Thank God for that.' He stood up and paced to the window, as he spoke, glancing down the drive as he did so. The builders had gone, and there was no sign of Caroline. 'You've no idea how lonely it's been without you. There's so much going on, and no one to share it with.'

'Dad, I'm only at the end of the phone.'

'I know, but it's not the same as having you here with me. I've got so many plans and ideas, and I need your womanly expertise to cast an eye over them for me. I've been clearing out the stables today.'

'That sounds promising.'

'You wait till you see them.' He rubbed a hand over his bristled jaw. He hadn't managed to fit in a shave for the past couple of days. He'd need to tidy himself up before his daughter arrived.

'I can't wait,' she said. 'I'll ring you when I'm leaving, but I'm thinking it'll probably be mid-afternoon before I get to you.'

'That's great. I can't tell you how much I've missed you.'

She laughed. 'Dad. I'll remind you of that when you complain I'm getting under your feet and interfering with things.'

'As if,' he said. Though what she said had a grain of truth in it. They were similar in many ways. Both were ambitious and single-minded, and both liked things done a certain way; usually in their own way. They were bound to get on each other's nerves from time to time. It would be interesting to see how things panned out. But, in the meantime, he couldn't wait to see her. 'Love you, darling,' he said. 'I'll see you on Saturday.'

He placed the phone on the table and glanced at his watch. It was after six.

Where on earth had Caroline got to?

Chapter Twenty

Caroline stood waiting by the oak front door and had overheard every word of his one-sided conversation. She hadn't meant to eavesdrop, but the door had been propped open, allowing her to hear him talking. At first, she thought it was with one of the builders, and she was about to knock, when she heard him say, 'You've no idea how lonely it's been without you.'

Then her ears pricked up in earnest. Her stomach churned as she took a step into the hallway.

'I can't tell you how much I've missed you.'

Caroline rested a hand to steady herself. She felt like someone had thumped her in the chest and taken her breath away.

'Love you, darling.'

Oh God. He really was married. She felt her legs go weak. Well, of course he was married. It was obvious. He hadn't tried to hide it. For goodness' sake, he wore a gold wedding ring.

She sucked in a deep and calming breath. She'd been reading too many romantic love stories, and it wasn't doing her any good whatsoever. Straightening up, she cemented a smile on her face, and rapped loudly on the half-open door.

Monty came bounding towards her from what had once been her mother's kitchen, his tail wagging joyously, closely followed by Grant Dalton, his mobile phone still in his hand.

'Sorry I'm on the drag,' she said, stooping down to stroke the dog. Her hands were trembling and she couldn't look him in the eye, guilty that she had overheard his phone call. Monty provided a convenient and diversionary tactic. 'Has he been good?'

'Very good, surprisingly,' he said. 'He's been helping me clear out the old stables. Apologies for the dirt and cobwebs. It was a bit messy in there.'

That explained his dishevelled appearance, she thought. His jeans were filthy, and he had streaks of what looked like white paint on the sleeves of his checked shirt. His brown loafers had splatters of it, and she could see some in his hair.

She'd always liked a man who could get his hands dirty. Marcus had been useless at anything remotely related to DIY. He hadn't enjoyed paying tradesmen, either, so consequently, nothing much had been fixed unless she attempted to do it herself, with varying degrees of success.

It was only after she moved into her little cottage that she realised she was more capable than she thought. She actually enjoyed decorating and fixing minor problems, like a wonky shelf or a blown lightbulb. More than that, she took pride in her achievements. It was immensely satisfying to sit back and realise how much she had done over the past few months, knowing that most of it was her own hard work.

'Thanks for having him,' she said, catching hold of Monty's collar, before he high-tailed it off down the drive. 'It was a great help.'

'No problem. If you're working tomorrow, you're welcome to drop him off again. In fact, I can do any day this week, apart from Saturday.'

She glanced sideways up at him. Monty was wriggling and trying to pull free from her grip. 'It's fine. I can take him to the shop with me. You must have loads to do.'

He smiled. 'True, but he wasn't any trouble. I wouldn't offer if I didn't want him here.' He handed her Monty's lead. 'We get on fine.'

She clipped on the dog's lead and straightened up. 'Well,' she hesitated a moment. 'It would make things easier.'

'Good. That's sorted.' He ruffled Monty's ears as he spoke. 'What time do you need to leave?'

'Vanessa likes the shop to be open by ten.'

'Okay, well, drop him off on your way out.' He leaned sideways against the door-frame, with his arms folded in front of him.

Caroline realised he wasn't going to invite her in. That much was apparent. After what she had overheard, she didn't want to go in anyway. The trouble was, she couldn't help finding him attractive. His rugged and unshaven appearance stirred up all sorts of feelings that she didn't want to dwell on. He was married, and that was an end to it. Grant Dalton was out of bounds. But even so, it didn't stop her from fancying him.

She tried to appear casual as she walked away, saying, 'Thanks again,' and acting as if she was in a hurry to get home. 'See you tomorrow.'

He gave her a last wave, which she watched from the corner of her eye, before he went back into the house and closed the door.

'Well, Monty. That's the end of that. Come on. It's just you and me now.'

**

With Vanessa out of action for a few days, having been told to rest by the mid-wife on account of her high blood pressure, Caroline found she was well and truly left in charge of the tack shop. It was fortunate that Grant seemed so keen to look after Monty, as it meant she could concentrate on the customers, and not on what her daft spaniel was doing.

She'd never been one for small talk in the past but chatting to the people who came into the shop made her see that it wasn't so hard after all. More than that, she enjoyed asking them about their horses and ponies and recommending products and services they might like.

When she'd casually mentioned to one young woman that she was Robert Johnson's stepdaughter—yes, the famous show-jumper Robert Johnson—it had started a whole new conversation about jumping and eventing, that made her desperate to get back in the saddle again. Why had she left it so long?

Marcus, she realised, who had liked nothing remotely equestrian, and poured scorn on those who did, was the one who had stopped her riding.

'You're not a teenager anymore,' he said. 'You're a married woman, and I don't like to think of you getting hurt. What's the point in going round in circles trying to persuade a horse to jump over a few poles, and risking life and limb to do it? It's a bloody waste of time, if you ask me.'

At the time, she had been flattered that he was so concerned about her welfare. But now, she realised, her ex-husband had wanted her to concentrate on him. She suspected he was frightened of horses as well, but, of course, he would never admit as much.

Well, he was out of the picture now, and she could do what she liked.

Before she lost her enthusiasm, she took advantage of a lull between customers and rang Ella to see if she could go on one of the evening hacks that Adam had told her about.

There was no sign of surprise in her step-sister's voice. In fact, she sounded delighted that Caroline was thinking of taking up riding again.

'I've got one going out on Saturday at 6.30,' she told her. 'And I know there are some spare places, because I'm escorting it. Shall I put you down for that one?'

'Yes, please,' she said, and quickly, before she changed her mind. 'Adam suggested I might like Merlin, if he's available.'

'Merlin,' Ella repeated.

Caroline got the impression she was writing the name down.

'Yep, He'd be an ideal one to start with. I'll see what I can do.'

'Thanks, Ella.'

There—she had got it sorted. Now, she had to find herself something suitable to wear, and with a whole tack shop at her disposal, how hard could it be?

By the end of the day, she had found a pair of navy

jodhpurs in her size, a hat, gloves and a pair of leather ankle riding boots. Giving herself the bonus of a staff discount brought the price down to a slightly less eye-watering amount, but it was still a lot to spend for an evening hack. It would be worth it if she enjoyed it and persevered. If she hated it, well, it was just another mistake she had made in her life. One more to add to the list, she thought.

At least she had discovered the truth about Grant Dalton before she got herself in too deep and made a fool of herself. It was obvious why he had been upset and drunk too much. For some reason, his wife hadn't been able to make the move into Grey Lodge at the same time as him. It could be work commitments, or family troubles perhaps, and he'd been lonely without her. No wonder he'd been so keen to look after Monty.

Now it looked like his wife was on her way and all would be well again. She had been worrying needlessly about him. It was time she turned her attention to other matters. Like finding someone else to keep an eye on the dog while she worked.

***

'No, no, absolutely not,' Vanessa said, when she suggested she might like Monty's company for the last few weeks of her pregnancy. 'That dog is a liability. I'm supposed to be resting, not looking after a scatty spaniel.'

'Well, I can't expect Grant to have him once his wife arrives. I'm sure he only offered because he was lonely.'

She'd popped round after work on the off chance that her sister might be willing to compromise, seeing as how she was running her business for her, but Vanessa would not be swayed.

'You could always ask Ella. I'm sure Adam and Rosie would love to have a dog in the house again.'

'Maybe,' she said, though she doubted it, knowing that one of their cats had a litter of kittens. That would be too much for Monty to cope with. On the other hand, cats always seemed to come up trumps when it came to ruling a household with dogs in it. A mother cat might be just the thing to teach him some manners.

'I could ask her, I suppose. I'm seeing Ella on Saturday night,' she said, swirling the tea bags round in the teapot and peering in to see if they looked stewed enough. Her sister preferred a strong cup of tea.

Vanessa was lying on the sofa, with her feet propped up on a round, tapestry-covered footstool. Her ankles, Caroline observed, did look rather swollen.

'I'm going on a hack.'

'What, as in riding?'

'Yes.' She placed the steaming cup on a table beside her.

'Really?'

'Yes,' she repeated, slightly annoyed that her sister sounded so amazed. 'I know it's been a while since I last rode, but I realised, after being in the shop and talking to customers, that I missed it. I don't have Marcus telling me what to do, or mother, for that matter, and I can do what I want, so I'm doing it.'

'Get you,' Vanessa said, looking suitably impressed.

'Yes, well, it's keeping you in profits.' She produced the carrier bag of items she had bought from the shop to show her. 'I've asked Ella if I can ride Merlin. That was Adam's suggestion. And while we're on the subject of Adam, I've got to admit, I'm a bit worried about him.'

She told Vanessa about the incident in the woods, and the fact that their nephew had been bunking off school, drinking alcohol and mixing with those she considered were unsuitable friends.

'That doesn't sound like Adam.' Her sister looked worried. 'He's normally a sensible lad.'

'It surprised me as well. I don't know if I should say anything to Ella. I told him I wouldn't.'

'Then don't.'

'But what if something happens?'

'Like what?'

Caroline shrugged. 'I don't know. I honestly don't. But that Max Bradshaw he was hanging around with seemed like a nasty piece of work. I was hoping Adam would see that for himself.'

'I'm sure he will, given time. He's not daft. We'll get him to do some more shifts in the shop. That'll keep him out of trouble over the holidays.'

'It's not the holidays I'm worried about,' Caroline said, finishing her tea. 'Anyway, I'd better go. Grant will be expecting me to collect Monty, and I've been ages.'

She left the day's taking with Vanessa, keeping only a small float to take back to the shop in the morning. Adam normally helped on a Saturday and she was holding him to that, because she knew she would have the dog with her for the day.

Grant had made it clear that he wouldn't be available on Saturday, and Caroline suspected she knew why. If he was planning a joyful reunion with his wife, she wanted to be well away from the place. She should have felt happy for him, and she did, to a point. But she couldn't deny her own feelings, either. Trust her to fall for someone she couldn't have.

Another reason to distract herself with an evening hack, she thought, and with any luck, she could persuade Adam to join her.

Chapter Twenty-One

The red Fiesta parked outside Grant's front door was the first thing Caroline noticed when she arrived home from work on Saturday.

His wife has arrived, she thought glumly, as she bundled Monty out of the car. She wondered what she was like and then tried to blank the thought from her mind. It didn't matter what she was like. The woman existed, and that was the end of it.

She clipped on Monty's lead. She had enough time to take him for a quick walk before changing and heading back to Hollyfields for the evening hack. Once she'd walked and fed him, he would be fine for a few hours. He normally settled down and went to sleep after a run round the fields.

She didn't have time to prepare anything for herself so grabbed a couple of biscuits and a cup of tea while she changed into her new riding clothes.

It felt strange to be wearing jodhpurs again. She had forgotten how comfy they were. Figure hugging, but stretchy in all the right places. They would be perfect to wear at work. She tied her hair back, pulled on a light fleece, and was ready to go.

As she climbed back into her car, she glanced up the long drive, but there was no sign of anybody at Grey Lodge, even though both cars were parked side by side. She felt a wistful pang of longing as she thrust the car into gear and headed off down the lane.

Adam had declined the offer to join her on the hack. He was meeting some of his mates from the village after work. They were going to a party.

'Not in the woods.' She raised an eyebrow at him.

'No, at a friend's house.'

'Which friend?'

He'd pushed his hair back over his forehead with an irritated sweep of his fingers, looking like a carbon copy of his father as he did so. 'It's not Max, if that's what you're thinking.'

'I wasn't,' she lied. It was exactly what she was thinking.

'You won't know her. She's new to the school. Jessica Marchant.'

Caroline considered this for a moment. 'Is her father the new doctor that's started at the medical centre?' She was sure Vanessa had told her about a Dr Marchant, when she'd been for her last check-up.

Adam nodded as he swept the floor of the tack room with a long-handled brush. 'She's having a housewarming party, or at least, her parents are, and they've told her she can ask some of her school friends.'

Well, that sounded feasible, if it was the truth, she thought. Though, she couldn't help feeling disappointed, he wouldn't be joining her on the ride. She could have done with some moral support.

Despite everything that had happened, he was a helpful lad, and she could see why her sister held him in such high regard. Not least, because of the way he had sorted out the mystery surrounding Jed when he first arrived at the stables, masquerading as Hank, an all-American cowboy. Adam had been fourteen at the time. His quick thinking had saved his mother and Vanessa from what could have been a tricky situation.

'If you go again,' he told her, I'll definitely be up for it. I might ask Jessica along. She says she loves horses.'

'Can she ride, though?'

He grinned. 'She says she can.'

'Bit of a plus point, then; you living at a riding-school?'

Adam put the broom back in the storeroom and picked up his jacket. 'That's not the only reason she likes me. See you next week, Aunty Caroline. Have fun.'

She pulled into the car park at Hollyfield stables and wondered if she had time to pop over to the Groom's Cottage for a quick word with Vanessa. But before she had the chance to do so, she saw Ella coming out from the stable block, leading a grey horse, which she presumed was Merlin. The Connemara gelding was bigger than she expected. Thank goodness for mounting blocks, she thought. Otherwise, she doubted whether she would get on it.

Her stepsister saw her and gave her a welcoming wave. 'Perfect timing.'

'If that's Merlin, he's huge.' Caroline walked towards her, fastening the strap of her riding hat under her chin.

'He's a gentle giant.' Ella smiled. 'Shall I lead him to the mounting block for you?'

'Yes, please.' Caroline pulled on her riding gloves. They felt stiff. She felt stiff. Oh dear, maybe this wasn't such a sensible idea.

'How long has it been?' Ella asked, as she held the horse steady for Caroline to climb on board. The horse's back seemed way too broad and high. She didn't know if her hips would stretch that far.

'Years,' she said. 'Well, at least two, maybe three. I can't remember. It seems ages.' She lowered herself onto the saddle, and wiggled her feet, trying to find the stirrups. 'Marcus wasn't keen for me to ride. He said it was too dangerous.'

Ella smiled. 'So is driving a car. But this is a lot more fun.'

Caroline decided to reserve judgement on that. She gathered up the reins, pleased that she remembered how to hold them. 'Thumbs to the sky, heels to the floor,' was a mantra that popped into her head from nowhere. Her mother used to shout it out from the side-lines.

'If you want to walk him round the sand school while I get the other riders sorted, feel free. It'll give you a chance to get used to him before we head out.'

This seemed like a practical suggestion. Apart from

anything else, it would give her time to find her balance and get used to the gentle swaying motion of the horse.

The familiar warm, horsey smell wafted up from Merlin's shaggy, white mane. Caroline breathed it in and relaxed. This was fine. She could do this.

It took a couple of slow, plodding circuits of the arena before she felt the stiffness in her hips and knees lessen.

From the corner of her eye, she saw the other participants assembling by the mounting block. They all looked a lot younger than her, apart from a woman in a faded tweed hacking jacket, who had grey hair. She counted five of them, six including Ella. One of the stable girls held the horses while Ella helped them mount. Fortunately, most of them, including the older woman, looked like novice riders.

Caroline felt the tension ease from her shoulders as she settled into the rhythmic movement of the horse. It was all coming back to her; the way to sit and hold the reins, the way to position her feet in the stirrups, everything, in fact, that she thought she had forgotten.

Ella mounted a flighty looking chestnut thoroughbred, and told the group to follow her into the sand school, where they would do some warming up exercises, before heading out for the countryside hack.

Much of this involved riding without stirrups, which caused Caroline a moment of panic, but it wasn't long before she was doing the same as everyone else and enjoying the moment.

Adam had been right. Merlin was a joy to ride. She could feel her confidence growing by the second, and was more than happy, when Ella announced it was time to head out onto the sandy track around the cross-country course.

'Caroline, are you happy to lead, and I'll follow on at the back?' Ella asked, as she leaned sideways and forward over her horse's neck to open the gate for them. 'You're the one with most experience, and I know you're familiar with the course.'

'Me?' She glanced over her shoulder, wondering if the other older woman was called Caroline, too. Apparently, she wasn't. Ella expected her to lead. She felt a sudden surge of unexpected pride. 'No problem,' she said, and with a soft nudge of her legs, she pushed Merlin towards the gate.

It was a mild and tranquil evening, with only the merest hint of a breeze. The track wound away from the stables and ran round the whole area of paddocks and fields, and through a small wood with a stream to splash through, up a gentle incline, and down towards a shallow lake, before following the line of the hedge back towards the sand school.

Caroline felt content and happy as they walked, and then trotted, and walked again, all following Ella's instructions. The horses behaved impeccably, and everyone was having a fun time. It could not have been a more perfect evening, until a large pheasant, startled from its resting place under the hedge, suddenly took flight in fear, flapping its wings and shrieking as only a startled pheasant can do. It soared up in front of the lead horse, which, unfortunately, happened to be Caroline's supposedly sensible and bomb-proof mount.

Many people regarded Merlin as a calm and easy ride, but even the most well-behaved horse was a flight animal at heart. He shied to the side, and then took off down the track like a runner in a sprint race, going from zero to top speed in seconds.

Caroline wasn't sure who received the bigger shock; her or the horse. It took her a few panicked seconds to snatch up the loose reins and regain her balance, before she could think about trying to stop him.

His hooves thundered over the ground, churning up clouds of dust. The air whizzed past her.

It was terrifying, and exhilarating, and… and wonderful.

She leaned forward in her seat, meeting the challenge head on, and gently, ever so gently, brought him back under control, first to a steady canter, and then a trot. She turned him in ever decreasing circles, and gradually slowed him to a walk and then a halt.

She stroked and patted his neck. 'Good boy,' she said. 'It was only a bird. Nothing to worry about. Let's go back and join the others.'

It was fortunate that Merlin had taken the brunt of the scare. The other horses, though unsettled at the grey gelding's dash for freedom, were content to snort and prance on the spot, until Ella had them all safely gathered in a circle, while they waited for Caroline to return.

She plodded Merlin over the rise of the hill, and smiled as she approached them.

'That was great,' she said.

'Not really,' Ella said. 'But well done, Caroline. I don't know if I could have handled that so well.'

'Thanks,' she said, her cheeks flushed with pride. She could hardly believe she had done it. What's more, she had loved every minute. Well, not the initial fright, admittedly, but after that, it had been amazing. The speed, the motion, the sheer exuberance of the moment—it was indescribable—and she felt like she was buzzing all over with excitement.

To say nothing of the second when she'd felt Merlin come back under her control and respond to her movements. And now look at him. As calm and docile as could be, almost as if nothing untoward had happened. She stroked his neck.

'Right then,' Ella said, turning her horse to face the group of assembled riders. 'How are you all feeling? Does anyone want to try a canter when we reach the bottom meadow?'

The younger riders seemed keen to give it a go.

The older woman shook her head. 'I'd rather not,' she said.

'That's fine. You stay with Caroline, and I'll take the others on ahead.' Ella glanced at her, as if seeking her approval. 'Are you okay to do that?'

She nodded, feeling flattered that her stepsister trusted her with one of her paying clients. Besides, Merlin could probably do with the rest. A slow walk would cool him down.

She turned him so that he was alongside the piebald cob. 'Have you been coming here long?' she asked the woman, who looked nervous as the other horses trotted off in front of them.

'A few weeks.' Her fingers tightened on the reins. 'My

daughter has a pony, but she's going off to University in the Autumn, and wants me to look after her while she's away.' She sighed. 'I haven't ridden a horse since I was a teenager. I'm afraid I'm not so brave as I was in those days.'

'You and me both,' Caroline agreed. 'But there's no harm in being cautious.'

The horses moved off, side by side.

'Have you been riding long?' The woman cast her a sideways glance.

'Not for years,' she said. 'But I used to ride. Ella is my stepsister.'

'Ah, that explains how you were able to get him back under control so quickly.'

Caroline felt that same sense of pride she had felt earlier. It had been a complete fluke, of course; that, and the fact the horse was usually well mannered, but, at the end of the day, she had managed to stop him.

'She's such an excellent instructor. Very patient and kind. Nothing is too much trouble for her, even for an older rider, like me. I'm Mary, by the way.'

'Caroline,' she said. 'You can't be that old.'

'I'm fifty-six next year.'

Goodness, she thought. And here was her, thinking she might be too old at almost forty to get back in the saddle. 'Fancy a short trot?'

Mary smiled. 'I'm game if you are.'

Caroline could not remember when she had enjoyed a ride so much. In the past, it had all been about competing and trying to win rosettes, and making a name for herself, even though she knew she would never be that good. But this had been a ride for pure pleasure, and she loved it. Especially in the company of other people. So much so that she signed up for the following week without a moment's hesitation.

'You did really well,' Ella said. 'Especially when Merlin took off like that.'

'Thanks.' She took off her riding hat and shook her hair loose. Her head felt hot and sweaty. 'I loved it. Well, not that part, obviously, but it was great fun. You can tell Adam that. He said he might join me next week with the new girl from school. Jessica, I think he said her name was.'

'Ah, the elusive Jess.'

Caroline tilted her head to one side. 'Have you met her?'

'No, not yet.' Ella smiled. 'But all he does is talk about her. I think he's smitten.'

Her nephew wasn't the only one. She pushed that thought to the back of her mind.

'Same horse, next week?' Ella asked, jotting her name down in the diary.

'Yes, please.'

'I can't promise, but I'll see what I can do.'

Caroline watched her writing Merlin's name next to hers in the book. She hoped she could have him again. He'd been a joy to ride.

'I meant to ask,' Ella added. 'How are you getting on at the cottage? Does it feel strange, living there on your own? Have you settled in okay?'

She nodded. 'I love it, and I've got Monty to keep me company. Mother couldn't take him to her retirement apartment. He's a bit of a handful because he's not good at being left on his own, but Grant has been taking him for a few hours when I'm at the tack shop. I don't suppose he'll be so keen now that his wife's arrived at Grey Lodge. Actually, that's something I wanted to ask you…'

'His wife?' Ella straightened up and laid the pencil to one side. 'Grant Dalton doesn't have a wife.'

'What?'

'He's a widower. You must be thinking of Sabrina, his daughter. She's moving in with him today. It was Sabrina who persuaded him to set up the new vet practice. She's an equine vet. Well, that and other farm animals, and…'

Ella's words were lost on Caroline. She had been so

shocked when she heard Grant didn't have a wife, that everything else went straight over the top of her head. He wasn't married. It was all she could think of.

'It's been about two years…' Ella was saying. 'Sabrina thought it would be better if he got away and left the memories behind. She's going to join him once she's honoured her commitments to other veterinary practices…'

'He's a widower,' she said aloud. Her mind racing. That's why he was so troubled He was grieving.

'Caroline? Are you all right?'

'What? Oh, yes.' She glanced back at her stepsister, who gave her a puzzled look. 'Yes. I'm fine.' She tucked her riding hat under her arm. 'I had no idea. He never said.'

'Probably didn't want to mention it. Sabrina said he's been depressed, understandably, and she's hoping this new start will help him move on with his life. She's been really worried about him.' Ella closed the diary. 'Right, well, you're in the book for next week, although you might change your mind when you find how stiff you are tomorrow.' She smiled. 'I recommend a long, hot, soak in the bath when you get home.'

'Good idea,' Caroline said. 'And, thanks, Ella.'

'What for?'

'Oh. You know. Everything.'

Chapter Twenty-Two

The residents of St John's retirement apartments enjoyed a slow and relaxed pace of life. Each flat, with its communal gardens (which were carefully maintained to a high standard, with fragrant and colourful flower beds and manicured lawns), came complete with economic insulation and solar panels. Retirement living was supposed to provide a stress-free and comfortable experience.

Ursula was finding it far from that. She disliked the lack of space and the privacy she had enjoyed at Grey Lodge. Her lounge room, with a balcony and splendid views over the river, was small, and the bedroom, even smaller. Compact, was the description in the brochure. Tiny, was Ursula's interpretation of it. She had no room to store her clothes, shoes, or belongings. In fact, she still had a load of boxes in storage, to be unpacked and no doubt discarded to charity at a later date.

Her attempts at being superior to her fellow residents had fallen on deaf ears, since she was obliged to share the place with people like Petunia Fitzgerald, whom she had crossed swords with many times over the years. Petunia had been delighted to tell everyone at the weekly coffee morning, that she was sure she had seen bailiffs banging on Ursula's door. A fact she hurriedly dismissed as a misunderstanding.

Having Marcus turn up at ten o'clock in the morning, in his dark suit and tie, and carrying a black briefcase, was more fuel for the gossip-mongers.

Ursula flung the door open, and practically dragged him inside before they could speculate any further.

'Darling,' she announced loudly, for the benefit of any

onlookers. 'How lovely to see you!'

If Marcus looked surprised, she could hardly blame him for that. He had never been her favourite person, and the feeling was reciprocal. But right now, he was her one and only lifeline.

He perched on the edge of his seat, the briefcase open on his lap, as she hurried into the galley kitchen to put the kettle on.

'Black or white? I can never remember?' she said.

'White. One sugar.'

Her hands shook as she levered out a spoonful of instant coffee into a floral mug.

Marcus coughed and cleared his throat. 'I've been looking in to your case,' he said, shuffling a few papers round. 'It's not good. If you don't clear the outstanding debt immediately, I can see you looking at a custodial sentence. The Inland Revenue is well within its rights to pursue this. And they will, I can promise you that.'

'Oh, but Marcus… Marcus, my dear.' She placed the tray of coffee and a plateful of biscuits on the table beside his seat. Chocolate biscuits, bought in specially, in case she had guests. 'As I explained to Caroline, it was an oversight on my part. A genuine mistake….'

'I'm going to push the senility factor,' he said bluntly. 'It helps that you're living here. I can use that in my argument.'

Ursula chewed on her bottom lip.

'But I need payment today. Now, in fact.' He produced a card machine from his case. 'I take it you have Wi-Fi?'

'Well, yes, but Marcus…'

'When you're ready.'

Goodness, this wasn't like the weedy little man her daughter had once married. She thought she might be able to persuade him to waive some of the charges, or at least plead leniency on her behalf, but he had a look of steely determination on his face that she had never seen before.

She fumbled in her handbag for her purse and card.

'All of it would be preferable,' he said.

Ursula did a quick mental calculation. The bill ran

into thousands. She didn't think her bank would honour the transaction, even though the money was in her account from the proceeds of the house sale. They'd think she was an old lady being ripped off by a con-man. Marcus looked suspiciously like one, with his narrowed squinty eyes and supercilious expression.

He removed a small laptop from his case. 'You can do a bank transfer, if that's easier.'

'Marcus, there's really no need for that tone of voice.'

'Isn't there?' he responded coldly. 'You've been trying to swindle the Inland Revenue, Mrs Lloyd-Duncan, and you're not immune to prosecution. I'm here to help you, though I admit it goes against the grain.'

Ursula gritted her teeth. That would be right. Fastidious little man that he was. She never had liked him, but she supposed she'd better do as he said.

With the bank transfer completed and authorised, he gathered up his laptop and papers and placed them all in his briefcase, which he closed and locked.

'I intend to make a plea on your behalf, for mitigating circumstances; age and infirmity being one of them. Now that the payment has been made, and in full, I hope there will be no further action. You do realise that if you'd paid this at the time, none of this unpleasantness would have happened?'

'Yes, I know that, Marcus, but I forgot. It was a genuine mistake. I wasn't trying to fiddle anyone.'

'That's what they all say,' he muttered, half under his breath. 'So, let this be a warning to you.'

He stood up, and Ursula almost imagined him clicking his heels together as he did so. 'They'll be keeping a close watch on your affairs from now on. I believe you gifted the Gatehouse to Caroline. That, in itself, has tax implications. For her sake, if not for yours, I wish you a long and happy retirement.'

It pained her to have to thank him, but she did so under duress. It was worth it, if only to get one up on Petunia Fitzgerald, who had been lording it around the place and spreading malicious rumours, none of which were true.

Ursula stood in the doorway, a forced smile on her lips, as she saw her former son-in-law off the premises. She hoped Petunia was in earshot.

'Goodbye Marcus. It's been such a pleasure, as always.'

He did not respond, but marched, with military precision, along the corridor and out of the main entrance. He did not look back.

Arrogant little prat, she thought, as she slammed the door behind her. She was several thousand pounds poorer, and no longer in debt. It was her own fault. In hindsight, she should have sorted it out earlier, perhaps by taking Caroline up on her offer to buy the gatehouse from her. It would have given her the ready cash she so desperately needed at the time. But it was too late for regrets. The matter was dealt with now, and with any luck, she might never see her former son-in-law ever again.

She wondered if it was too early for a gin and tonic.

Chapter Twenty-three

Caroline could not believe how much she ached as she struggled to get out of bed the following morning. Everything, from her shoulders to her knees, hurt. Her ankles were stiff from the way she had placed them in the stirrups, with her heels pointing down. Not a natural position at the best of times.

She perched on the edge of the mattress, twirling her feet one way and then the other. If she felt bad, she could only hazard a guess at how Mary, sixteen years her senior felt.

Monty leapt out of his basket and ran to greet her, as she limped her way in to the kitchen. She opened the blinds and gazed out at a bright and sunny morning as she held the kettle under the tap. A breeze stirred the tops of the trees. The forecast predicted wind, and the outside was looking fairly gusty.

It would be a great day to get the washing done. Once she loosened up a bit, she would strip the bed and wash the sheets, but, for the moment, she was content to do some gentle stretching exercises while she waited for the kettle to boil.

She fed Monty and let him into the enclosed front garden, after checking the gate was secure. He had been known to push it open with his nose and hare off in search of rabbits. Standing there, in her white towelling dressing gown, she took the opportunity to peer up the drive.

The two cars remained parked, side by side, outside Grey Lodge. Grant's black BMW, and the red one which she now knew, belonged to his daughter. She wondered if she should wander up there later, with the dog, but decided it was too soon. His daughter would want to get settled in first, before the neighbours started knocking. But maybe she might bake a cake and drop it off in the afternoon. It would be a kind gesture to welcome her to the area. Where was the harm in that?

The truth was, she couldn't wait to see Grant again, now that she knew he didn't have a wife lurking in the background. She felt there could be something between them. There was definitely a mutual attraction there. She could sense it and knew she hadn't imagined it. But grief was a hard barrier to overcome. It would take patience, and time. The trouble was, she didn't know if she could be patient. And she didn't want to scare him off by being too keen.

'You're the perfect go-between,' she said, stroking Monty's head. He jumped up to rest his paws on the top of the white wooden gate, as if he too, wanted to look up the drive. 'We'll go for a walk later, okay? I can't promise we'll see him, but you never know. We just might.'

The spaniel trotted after her, his tail wagging, as she went back inside the cottage to get dressed.

Keeping busy was the best solution she could come up with, to stop herself from thinking about Grant. If she was busy, she didn't have time to think. The tack shop was closed on a Sunday, so she had the entire day to herself. Vanessa would be at home with Jed, and she didn't want to disturb them. It was rare for them to find precious time together. His job at the stud wasn't a nine-to-five position. And visiting her mother was way down on her list of things she wanted to do.

So, she would clean the cottage, sort out the washing and do all the jobs she had missed doing during the week. Then, she'd take Monty for a long walk through the woods, and if she had time later, she might bake that cake.

The wind strengthened as the morning progressed. Caroline found it hard to peg out the sheets, and half wondered if it was safe to do so, or whether they would end up flapping across the fields, torn free by a sudden stormy gust. A walk through the woods did not seem like a sensible idea. She would take Monty down the lane instead. At least with the hedges, it might be a bit more sheltered, and there wasn't much in the way of traffic on a Sunday.

The red Fiesta passed her as she came out of the front garden with Monty on the end of his lead. She glimpsed a dark-haired woman in a cream blouse, and she raised her hand in a wave, but the woman didn't see her. She was peering left and right at the end of the drive and looking for oncoming traffic. The back windows had tinted glass in them, but Caroline was pretty certain the woman was on her own. It had to be Sabrina, Grant's daughter. She glanced back up the drive towards the house. Should she go up there now? Grant would be alone. What excuse could she give? Maybe she could persuade Monty to run off. Normally, he needed little persuasion.

She looked down at the spaniel, who was snuffling and sniffing his way round the edge of the verge. For once, he seemed keen to stay by her side. He hadn't tugged on the lead once. The wind ruffled his fur the wrong way, and he looked up at her as if she was to blame. She crouched down to stroke his head.

'You're right. It is a bit breezy,' she said. 'Maybe we won't stay out too long.'

They managed a quick circuit of the fields, before Caroline decided she'd had enough of the wind whipping her hair into her eyes, and headed back to the cottage. She didn't fancy turning up on Grant's doorstep looking all windswept and dishevelled. Maybe she'd save that visit for later, once the gales had died down.

Monty seemed more than happy to settle down in his basket for a snooze.

She was in the bedroom, replacing the duvet cover, which was being stubborn and tangling up on itself, when her phone rang. It was Vanessa.

'Are you at home?'

'I am now,' she said. 'It's blowing a gale out there.'

'I know. Jed had to go to the stables and help Ella. Apparently, there's some loose felt on the roof and it's flapping and frightening the horses. Did you want some company? I thought I might drive over.'

'Yes, okay,' Caroline said. That would put paid to her plans to bake a cake and take it to Grant and his daughter, but she could do that another day. Patience, she told herself, was the key.

It was only a short drive from the stables, and Vanessa arrived by the time she had managed to straighten the bedding and plump up the pillows.

'Did you know Marcus had been to see Mother?' her sister said, as she made herself comfortable on the settee with a loud 'oomph' sound.

'No.' Caroline pushed the foot stool towards her, and scooped the hairy dog throws from the cushions, leaving them in a heap on to the floor. 'When?'

'Yesterday morning, apparently.'

'She never said.'

'Have you spoken to her?'

'Well, no,' Caroline admitted, 'but I'm surprised she didn't tell me.'

'She rang me last night. She said she'd tried to get hold of you, but you didn't answer.'

That would have been when she was on the hack, she realised. She'd switched her phone off, for obvious reasons, and hadn't checked to see if she had any missed calls.

'I was out riding,' she said. 'I went on that evening hack I told you about. More of that later, but tell me what happened with Marcus?'

Vanessa smiled. 'He made sure she paid off her debts, and he's going to put in a good word for her. So, he says. I can't say mother was pleased, but hopefully that's an end to it.'

'Let's hope so,' she said. 'Marcus likes to do the right thing.'

'Yes, well, I don't think mother saw it like that, but whatever you said to him, it seems to have paid off. Oh!' Vanessa gave a short gasp.

'What is it?'

'Nothing. Just a twinge. I think I twisted something getting out of the car.'

'Should you be driving at all?' Caroline viewed her sister's round stomach with a degree of concern and wondered how she managed to reach the steering wheel. She must have her seat pushed back as far as it could go.

'I'm fine.' Vanessa shifted her position on the settee slightly. 'You've no idea how hard it is to get comfortable these days. I feel like there's always some little niggle. Anyway, tell me about your ride. How was it?'

'Amazing.' She sat down on the seat by the window. 'Honestly, I'd forgotten how exhilarating it could be. We went round the cross-country course. Not the jumps, obviously,' she added. 'There were six of us, including Ella, and we started off in the sand school, and then we went out on the track. I rode Merlin, the big grey that Adam talked about…'

'Oh!' Vanessa gasped again and clutched her stomach. Her face looked alarmed.

Caroline stood up. 'Are you okay, Vanessa?'

'I don't know.' Her bottom lip trembled. 'Am I?' She winced.

'You don't think… no, you couldn't be…' She didn't need to say it out loud. It was what they were both thinking.

'It's too soon,' Vanessa said.

'Baby might not think so.' Caroline reached for her phone. 'I'll call Jed.'

Vanessa nodded, a pained expression on her face.

'He's not answering.' She wandered round the room, the phone clamped to her ear. 'I'll have to leave him a message. Jed, it's Caroline. Vanessa's with me, but I think she might be going into labour. Can you get here as soon as you can? Ring me back.'

'I can't be in labour,' Vanessa said. 'I'm sure it's nothing… Oh.' She held her breath for a moment. 'Then again.'

'Right. Well, first babies take ages, so there's no need to panic,' she said, though she felt like doing exactly that. 'Do I ring the hospital, or the mid-wife? What's the procedure?'

'I don't know,' Vanessa said. 'The hospital, maybe?'

'Okay. Okay, I'll do that. Do you know the number? No, okay.' She was pacing the room, her thoughts racing. 'I can find it.' She scrolled down her phone. 'Got it. Maternity. Here we go. Yes. It's ringing.'

Vanessa watched her every move, as if grateful she was taking charge because she knew what she was doing, even if she didn't.

'Hello? Yes, it's my sister. I think she's in labour, but she's not due for another few weeks. Vanessa Harrison. Yes. No. Yes.'

Vanessa mouthed, "What?" at her, but she shushed her with a shake of her finger.

'How far apart are the pains?'

'I don't know.'

'You have to time them.' She pointed at the clock on the wall. 'Yes, thank you. Yes, okay. Thanks for your help.' She gave Vanessa what she hoped was a reassuring smile. 'She says there's no need to worry. It can take hours at this stage, so make yourself comfortable. Oh, and have you got a bag packed?'

'No. I didn't think there was any need at this stage.'

Caroline glanced at her phone, but there was still no response from Jed. 'Right,' she said. 'Here's what we'll do. I'll run you back home in my car, and you can pack a bag to take to the hospital. Then, if Jed hasn't turned up, I'll take you there.'

'But I want him with me.'

'I know, and he will be,' she assured her. 'You've got loads of time.'

Vanessa didn't look convinced.

Caroline grabbed her bag, jacket, phone, and keys. She tossed a handful of biscuits into Monty's bowl and then helped her sister to the car.

It was blowing a gale outside, and she half wondered if she had time to fetch in her sheets but decided against it. First things first, and getting her sister sorted was her chief priority. Vanessa was not looking very comfortable.

She eased the car slowly off the grass verge, to avoid any sudden jolts, and headed for the lane. Half a mile down the road, she could see that a fallen tree had completely blocked it. The main trunk straddled the hedge, but the rest had come down on the tarmac, rendering the road impassable.

'Oh, blast,' she said, slowing the car to a halt. She would have to reverse back up the road until she could find somewhere to turn around.

The small car was being buffeted by the gusty wind. Bits of branches, straw, and other debris were being blown down the road.

'I don't think they forecast it this bad,' she muttered, backing the car into a field entrance, and narrowly avoiding the metal five-bar gate.

'They said strong winds,' Vanessa said, helpfully.

'We'll need to go via Ridgeway.'

The situation there appeared even worse. An electricity pole had come down, and engineers were attempting to fix it. The live cable sparked off the ground, and work vans and a cherry-picker blocked the lane.

'This is hopeless,' she said. 'We'll need to go back to the cottage until they clear the road.'

The look of alarm on Vanessa's face wasn't helping matters, she thought, as she turned back the way they had come.

'Try to get hold of Jed again,' she said. 'Or, failing that, ring Ella. She can come over the fields in the Range Rover if she has to. Don't worry. Everything's going to be fine.'

Or at least, she hoped it was.

Monty was delighted to see them return to the cottage and acted as if they had been gone for a day, though it had only been fifteen minutes. He scampered round the small lounge with a stuffed toy in his mouth, tail wagging like mad. The biscuits she had left in his bowl were long gone.

Vanessa lowered herself onto the settee again, clutching her back, a pained expression on her face. 'I can't get hold of anyone,' she groaned. 'Everything goes straight to voicemail.'

'Try Sally, in the office.'

After trying for a moment, she shook her head. 'It's Sunday. She won't be there. All I'm getting is the answering machine.'

'Blast.'

Vanessa winced.

Caroline suspected the contractions were getting a lot closer together than she would have liked, given the circumstances. Her sister wasn't the only one getting worried.

'Monty, get down,' she said, pushing the exuberant spaniel to one side as he tried to leap onto her knee. 'Vanessa doesn't need you jumping all over her.' What Vanessa needed was a packed bag of essentials, a road that wasn't blocked, and a straightforward run to the hospital with her husband, none of which seemed likely to happen anytime soon.

'I'm going to get Grant,' she said, suddenly thinking that if they couldn't get hold of a doctor, surely a vet might be the next best thing. At least he had some medical training, unlike her, who knew nothing about babies or childbirth, other than what she had seen on television, and she was sure most of that was highly dramatized.

'Don't leave me,' Vanessa said, panic-stricken.

Caroline hesitated by the door. 'I'll be five minutes, tops. I promise you. I've got my phone. You keep trying Jed, or Adam, or anyone else you can think of.'

She ran up the gravelled drive towards Grey Lodge, her hair whipping round her face. The wind seemed to be getting worse. Panting, she ran up the stone steps and banged for all she was worth on the heavy oak door.

Grant had apparently been painting. He opened the door with a paintbrush in one hand and a smear of cream paint down the front of his faded jeans.

'Caroline? What is it? What's wrong?'

'It's my sister,' she gasped, her breath coming in great gulping pants. 'She's in labour, and the roads are blocked. We can't get hold of her husband. Grant, I don't know what to do.'

'Where is she?' He was staring over her shoulder, as if he half expected to see Vanessa wandering up the drive after her.

'At the cottage.' She grabbed at his sleeve. 'Please, Grant. I'm scared.'

Her words seemed to stir him into action. 'Okay. You go back to her and I'll follow you. I won't be a minute. I'll just get cleaned up and I'll grab my bag.'

She nodded. 'Okay. Thanks.'

She ran back the way she had come, her chest heaving with the unexpected exertion. All thoughts of stiffness and aching muscles had disappeared.

She was starting to get a bad feeling about this. If they were cut off by blocked roads, and Vanessa really was in labour, what on earth were they going to do? She had visions of boiling up pans of water and finding clean towels and, oh my goodness, witnessing the birth, and she wasn't sure she could do that. But what if she had no choice?

Vanessa was stood by the window, her hands resting on the windowsill, when she burst back into the cottage. Caroline could see a trickle of tears running down her cheeks.

'It's okay. I'm back,' she said, 'and Grant's on his way.'

'I can't get hold of anyone.' Vanessa sniffed and wiped her face with the back of her hand. 'I've left messages. Where is everyone?'

'Probably battening down the hatches. That wind is awful out there. Look, it's going to be okay.'

'You don't know that.' Vanessa sighed, and clutched the edge of the windowsill tighter. 'This shouldn't be happening now. It's too early.' A long, drawn-out breath escaped her lips.

Caroline wondered if she should call for an ambulance, but with the roads blocked, there was no way that was going to get through in a hurry, either.

Monty barked, and ran to the door, just as Grant strode in, carrying his black vet bag. The paint smeared jeans had been changed into a dark navy pair, and he had pulled on a clean, checked shirt, but smudges of cream paint were splattered over his face and hair.

'You must be Vanessa,' he said. 'Didn't I move your car for you? Yes, I thought it was you. Hello, again.'

'Hello.'

He placed his bag at his feet and gave her a reassuring smile. 'Now then, how far apart are your contractions?'

Vanessa sucked in a breath. 'I've tried to count. They're not regular, though. Probably every ten minutes or so.'

'Hmm.' He stroked his bristled chin, his head tilted slightly to one side. 'And it's a first baby, yes?'

Caroline nodded in unison with her sister.

'Well, they're renowned for taking their time. I wouldn't panic too much.'

'That's what the hospital said.'

He nodded and looked thoughtful. He glanced over his shoulder at Caroline. 'Maybe you could put the kettle on.'

He was being serious. She gaped at him. 'Do I need to put out some clean towels or sheets? Maybe a pan of hot water?'

'I was thinking more of a cup of tea,' he said, smiling. 'I'm parched. I don't know about you. All this painting has given me a raging thirst. I was just about to make a cup when you banged on the door.'

The tension palpably dropped from the room. Even Vanessa managed a wan smile. If Grant was talking about making pots of tea, there was no reason to feel alarmed. Maybe everything was okay, and she was over-reacting. They both were.

She headed to the kitchen, with Monty scampering by her heels. Her phone rang as she was about to fill the kettle. At last, she thought, seeing Jed's name flash up on the screen.

'Caroline, what's happening? Is Vanessa okay?'

'Yes, but the road's blocked,' she said. 'There's a tree down on the Burningstone Road, and an electricity wire heading to Ridgeway. We were trying to get back to pick up her things.'

'Is she in labour?' She heard the quiver of excitement in his voice.

'We think so.'

'I'm going to be a dad?'

'Well, obviously,' she said. 'Jed, you need to get here. Can you grab some stuff and come over the fields? It's the only way,' she added.

'I'm on it.'

The phone went dead, and she smiled.

'Good news?' Grant peered his head round the kitchen door.

'It's Jed,' she said. 'Her husband. He's on his way.'

'Excellent.' He grinned. 'I'm not sure I'd be much good as a midwife, but don't tell your sister I said that.'

She switched the kettle on and reached for some mugs. 'You sounded pretty confident to me.'

'It goes with the territory. When you don't know the answer, you play for time. Stops clients worrying there's something seriously wrong.'

She shot him a worried look. 'You're not saying…'

'No, no. I'm sure Vanessa's fine. But those initial twinges can cause first time mums to panic and think the birth is imminent. It rarely is.'

She couldn't help thinking that he was the ideal person to turn to in an emergency. He seemed so calm and laid back.

'Here, let me,' he said, taking the mugs from her. 'You go tell your sister the good news.'

Grant may have decided that the situation was under control, but Caroline wasn't so sure. Vanessa looked pretty uncomfortable to her, as she alternated between pacing round the room and resting by the windowsill, her arms outstretched to support her.

Broken bits of twig and leaves rustled against the glass. The hedges were leaning at an angle as the wind gusted across them. A stray carrier bag fluttered upwards and circled, before sweeping away over the treetops like a broken kite.

In the distance, she could see Jed driving the Land Rover across the field. He stopped and jumped out to open the gate, then climbed back in and continued heading towards the cottage, the huge wheels churning a rutted track through the grass. A moment later, and he drew up outside and clambered out.

'He's here,' she said, squeezing her sister's hand. The relief at seeing her brother-in-law, who had obviously come straight from the stables, was overwhelming. He still wore his green overalls, and there was a definite scent of horses on him, but none of that mattered. He was here, and with his powerful four by four, he could drive cross country, to get to the hospital, if need be.

'You pick your moments,' he said, pulling Vanessa into his arms and planting a kiss on the top of her head. 'Come on, let's get you into the car.'

Jed had left the engine running and the door open, and it took them only a matter of minutes to get Vanessa safely seated in the front passenger seat. He had tossed a hastily packed bag onto the bed of the truck.

Caroline resolved to sort out a few more personal items, and follow, once the road was clear. She was certain Jed wouldn't have packed half the stuff Vanessa might need.

'Good luck,' she called, waving them off. Her heart was thumping fit to burst. 'Let me know when you get to the hospital.'

Jed gave her the thumbs-up as he manoeuvred the car through the gate and into the field. And then they were gone, disappearing into the distance in a cloud of dust.

She let out the breath she had been holding for what seemed like forever.

'Now, can we have that cup of tea?' Grant said, coming to stand behind her.

She turned and found herself blushing, no matter how hard she tried to stop herself.

'Tea. Yes. Tea. Good idea.' She dropped her gaze, but jerked her head up as he gave her a reassuring pat on the shoulder.

'You did well,' he said. 'Calm in a crisis. That's what I like to see.'

'I really wasn't.'

'No, but you didn't let it show.' He gave her a long and considering look. 'You'd make a good vet nurse.'

'I don't think so.'

He shrugged. 'Believe me, I've seen a lot worse. I still remember how you held Monty when he cut his paw in the woods. You were a natural.'

'It was a one-off,' she said, turning away. 'Besides, Monty trusts me.'

The dog in question stared up at her with hopeful brown eyes, his tail swishing backwards and forwards on the tiled floor, having heard the mention of his name.

'Animals are usually a sound judge of character,' he said. 'I like to think I'm not so bad myself. Come on, get that kettle on. I'm dehydrating here.'

Chapter Twenty-Four

Grant insisted on waiting with her at the cottage until they heard from Jed. He argued that going back to the house was pointless until he was satisfied that all was well because he would only worry and besides; he deserved a break from decorating.

Caroline was glad of his company. She had never felt more on edge. Her hands trembled as she made them both a mug of tea, and she couldn't decide whether it was delayed shock, heightened adrenalin, or Grant's close proximity.

The kitchen was small enough at the best of times, and as he investigated the biscuit tin, she couldn't help brushing alongside him. It was having a strange effect on her composure. She placed the mugs on a tray and carried them into the lounge, where there was more room. She set it down on the windowsill, out of Monty's reach.

'Was that your daughter I saw leaving earlier today?' she said. 'In the red Fiesta.'

Grant nodded. He had just taken a bite out of a digestive biscuit. 'Sabrina, yes,' he mumbled, his mouth full. He waited a moment and swallowed before continuing. 'She arrived yesterday, with more luggage than I care to think about, and she's got a man with a van delivering a load more tomorrow.'

'Ella tells me she's also a vet.'

'She is.' He finished the last of his biscuit. 'She's been qualified a couple of years, but she wants to specialise in equine veterinary medicine. Rather her than me,' he added, with a rueful smile.

Caroline couldn't help wishing he had told her about his

daughter in the first place. In fact, there was a lot she wished he had told her.

'You're not keen on horses, then?'

'On the contrary, I think they're magnificent animals. They don't seem so keen on me, though.'

She smiled and looked out of the window, as a sudden gust sent a flurry of leaves against the pane. 'That wind isn't showing any signs of dropping. I think I'd better get my washing in before it disappears over the hedge.'

'I'll do it.' He placed his mug on the table and stood up.

'There's no need.'

'There is. You're waiting for a phone call. Here, give me the basket.'

She watched him un-peg her sheets and folding them with difficulty in the blustery breeze. He seemed relaxed and unhurried, as if nothing was too much trouble; a far cry from the terse and short-tempered man who had stayed with them as a guest all those months ago. Maybe he was changing, she thought. She knew she was.

The trouble was, the more she saw of him, the more she liked him. She'd give anything to know where she stood with him. Nothing hurt more than unreciprocated love. Living with Vanessa all those years had taught her that much. Until her sister met Jed, there had been no shortage of crushes and disappointment. Vanessa used to fall for the most unreliable men and ended up being heartbroken when they dumped her.

She'd never had that experience. She had gone from an unhappy childhood to a miserable marriage and had little experience of the dating highs and lows that usually preceded such an arrangement. Marcus had been her one and only boyfriend. Her experience with men was negligible. No small wonder she couldn't read the signs.

She had the small and sneaking fear that Grant might not be attracted to her, and it could all be in her imagination. But then he would show her his tender, caring side, like now, and she didn't know what to think.

Her phone rang as she was about to fill the kettle for another cup of tea. It was Jed.

'How is she?' she said, her heart thumping.

'They're keeping her in,' he told her. 'For observation and rest. Her blood pressure is higher than they'd like it to be.'

'And the contractions?'

'False alarm. Something called Braxton-Hicks. It's like a practice run for the real thing. Quite common, apparently. Anyway, she's okay, but she needs to rest. I knew she was doing too much. She wants to know if you're fine with running the shop.'

'Of course, I am.' Caroline smiled over at Grant, who brought the washing in, left it in the basket by the door and retired to the settee. Monty was sitting on his lap. The dog looked extremely comfortable, sprawled across him, with his head hanging over his knees. 'False alarm,' she mouthed. He grinned.

'Can you let your mother know?'

'If I must,' she said. 'Thanks, Jed. Give her my love.'

'Panic over?' Grant said, pushing Monty to one side and getting to his feet. The spaniel gave him a mournful look.

'Yes, thank goodness, but they're keeping her in. Something to do with her blood pressure. She needs to rest, and she won't do that when she's at home.'

'Like most women I know.' He grinned.

Caroline wondered what that meant, and how many women he knew, but pushed the uncharitable and jealous thought to the back of her mind. 'Thanks for staying, Grant. I hope I haven't kept you too long. Your daughter will be wondering where you've got to.'

'I doubt that.' He picked up his veterinary bag. 'She's gone shopping for cushions and curtains and stuff for her room, so I'm not expecting her back anytime soon. I told her to wait until the weather improved, but she can be pretty impetuous at times. It's her own fault if she can't get back because the road's blocked.'

'It should be cleared by now, surely.'

'You'd like to think so, but I guess these country roads

aren't a priority. She hasn't rung me, so I'm guessing she's fine. I'll start worrying after the shops close.' He paused by the door. 'Want to drop Monty off with me tomorrow?'

'Are you sure?'

'Yes, no problem.' He stooped to stroke the spaniel's silky head and then straightened up. 'Half nine?'

'Perfect. Thanks.' She watched him go striding away, up the long drive. Where did she stand? Was he being neighbourly, or did he enjoy being with her? She couldn't tell. 'Ring me if you change your mind,' she called.

He gave her a wave over one shoulder to show he had heard her, but he didn't turn round.

She looked down at Monty. 'Think you've made a friend there?' She ruffled his ears. 'It's obvious he likes you, but he is a vet. He's supposed to like animals. And,' she added, straightening up and gazing wistfully towards Grey Lodge. 'I really like him, but that's our little secret. Don't tell him I told you so.'

**

Grant stepped around the clutter of boxes and bags that Sabrina had left in the hall upon her arrival the previous afternoon. She had promised to move them upstairs before the workmen arrived on Monday. Since it was mid-afternoon, and she still wasn't back from her shopping expedition, he thought he might as well move them himself.

His daughter had opted for the attic rooms, as Grant suspected she might. It gave her a suite of rooms to herself, including her own bathroom. One of the smaller rooms, she planned to convert into an office, complete with kettle, mini fridge and microwave. (It would save her trailing downstairs to the second-floor kitchen, when she was doing admin work and wanted a hot drink or a snack). Plus, she would have the use of two further bedrooms and a sitting room, which would be useful if she had friends come to stay.

Grant wondered if he should include a male friend in

that scenario but decided it wasn't wise to speculate on his daughter's first day. He'd let her get settled in first, before he probed her with questions.

The narrow wooden staircase wasn't best suited for the carrying of heavy boxes. The treads were steep, and the steps felt slippery. Grant found himself sliding his back along the bannisters for support, the cardboard boxes clamped against his chest. No wonder Sabrina had left her stuff in the hall, he thought. She probably expected 'dear old Dad' to do it, old, being the operative word. Grant felt every one of his fifty-two years.

He wished Helen was here. She would have loved the excitement of moving in, and unpacking and deciding what went in each room. And she would have been first in the queue to buy cushions and soft furnishings, along with all the knick-knacks that made a place feel like home.

Sabrina was like her mum, in that respect. But unlike her mother, she seemed to thrive on what she called organised chaos.

'It'll get sorted, Dad. There's no rush. I'll unpack later, I promise.'

But Grant was a perfectionist. He hated the mess. He wanted things done, and he wanted them done now. Which was why he carted his daughter's stuff up two flights of stairs, in order to get it tidy and out of the way.

In hindsight, he should have waited. It had been a long day. He'd spent the morning putting the first coat of paint in the consulting rooms, which had been plastered earlier in the week. Then he'd had to rush down to Caroline's cottage, thinking her sister was about to give birth, and when that hadn't happened, had decided that moving ten million boxes up a narrow staircase was a wise idea, and in leather-soled shoes as well. Any practical person could have told him it was a recipe for disaster.

Still, the fall, when it came, was unexpected. So too, was the sensation of crashing backwards, unable to save himself.

As he lay, spreadeagled on the landing, a shattered carton of files and books upended on his chest, and a searing pain in his left wrist, he had the horrible feeling that he'd fractured something, and it wasn't just the cardboard box.

'For God's sake! He pushed the box away from him and tried to sit up, but the agony in his wrist was excruciating. He had to bite his lips to stop from crying out. Shuffling backwards, he leaned against the landing wall and fumbled in his pocket for his phone, hoping it had survived what had been a pretty heavy fall.

He sucked in a deep breath, gritted his teeth, and called his daughter.

'Hi Dad.'

'Hi.' He swallowed hard. 'Um, are you nearly home?' He could hear music in the background and voices, lots of chatter.

'What? Sorry, I can't... Hang on a minute.' After a brief pause, she came back to him. 'That's better. Sorry, what were you saying, Dad? I'm at the retail park. I never thought it would be this busy, but I've got loads of brilliant stuff for the house. I've bought this amazing lamp—'

'How long will you be?'

'What?'

Grant ground his teeth together. He really was in a lot of pain, and shouting to make his daughter hear him wasn't helping matters. 'I said, how long will you be?'

'I'm not sure. An hour, maybe. Are you all right, Dad? You sound a bit strained.'

'I'll live.'

'Okay, well, it's an awful line, and I didn't get that. Dad? Hello, Dad? Are you still there? I can't hear you.'

He ended the call. This was useless. He needed to get to the hospital because he was positive that his wrist was broken. Besides that, he had to have some strong painkillers. He was in agony. He managed to stand up and tuck his injured hand into the front of his shirt for support. Then he lowered himself, step by step, to the ground floor of the house, where he opened the front door. It was all he could manage before he had to stop and rest. Red hot rods of pain were shooting up his arm. If he could get to the cottage, he was sure Caroline could give him a lift to A and E. After all, he'd do the same for her.

By the time he had battled the buffeting wind and dragged himself down the drive to the gatehouse at the end, he was sweating profusely. But he made it. He rapped sharply on the door. Monty launched himself at it with a volley of barks. He hoped he didn't launch himself at him in the same way. He didn't fancy toppling over a second time and breaking the other wrist.

Caroline opened the door, one hand anchoring the dog to her side. Her face visibly drained of colour. 'Grant? What's happened? Oh my God, what have you done?'

'Had a fall,' he said. 'Think I've broken my wrist.' He coughed and cleared his throat. 'I don't suppose you could take me to the nearest A and E?'

'Yes, of course. Oh, you poor man. Monty, get down. Come in, come in.' She was hustling him into the lounge as she spoke. 'I'll just find my keys. Monty, No!'

Grant gave a groan as the dog jumped up, his paws landing on the hand that was tucked into the front of his shirt. He could feel his eyes watering from the pain.

Caroline chucked a handful of biscuits in the dog's bowl, by way of distraction. (She'd think about his expanding waistline another day) and grabbed her car keys. 'Right. I'm ready. Let's hope they've cleared the road by now.'

Fortunately, one of the local farmers had been round with a chain saw, and all that remained of the fallen tree was a scattering of leaves and branches and a pile of sawn up logs by the side of the road.

It was a twenty-minute drive to the hospital. The suspension in Caroline's small car was not a match for the smooth luxury of his BMW. He felt more than battered and bruised, by the time she drew into the hospital carpark, managing to find a space the moment a car vacated it, and ignoring the angry look from another motorist who had hoped to do the same.

'That was lucky,' she said.

Grant wasn't sure the other driver thought so, judging by the unwelcome hand gesture he gave them.

Caroline, if she noticed, ignored him. 'Come on. Let's get you in there.'

The estimated waiting time was four hours but he was fortunate enough to be seen within two. After a brief (and painful) examination, he was helped into a wheelchair, despite insisting he was perfectly capable of walking, and wheeled down to the X-ray department for another wait.

Caroline took the opportunity to nip over to the maternity ward, to visit her sister. 'I won't be long,' she told him. 'But it makes sense to see her while I'm here.'

Grant could not agree more. The way things were going, it looked as if he would be there half the night. He used her absence to ring Sabrina again. Fortunately, she had completed her shopping trip and had finally arrived home.

'Where are you?' she said. She sounded puzzled. 'There's boxes and things halfway down the stairs. Are you okay?'

'I took a bit of a tumble,' he said.

'Dad!'

'I know. But I'm all right. I'm waiting for an X-ray. They think I've broken my wrist.' He gave a dry laugh. 'I could have told them that.'

'Oh, Dad! Do you want me to come and wait with you?'

'No, it's fine. Caroline gave me a lift.'

'Caroline?'

Of course. Sabrina didn't know who she was. Well, how could she? They hadn't been introduced yet. 'She's the woman who lives in the gatehouse cottage,' he said. 'Ella Trevelyan's stepsister.'

'And she's happy to wait and give you a lift home?'

Grant hesitated. He presumed she was. Then again, was he presuming too much? No, it would be fine. They were good at doing each other favours. Caroline wouldn't mind, he was certain. 'Yes,' he said. 'She'll bring me home.'

By the time he had been X-rayed and the break confirmed,

then wheeled back to the nurses' station to wait again to be strapped up and plastered, his patience was wearing thin. They had given him painkillers, which he suspected had worn off.

Caroline bought him a cheese and ham sandwich, and a watery cup of coffee to sustain him. She opted for a packet of crisps and a bottle of water.

'Talk about fine dining,' he muttered. 'One of these days I'll take you out for a proper dinner, to say thank you.'

'I could say the same thing,' she said. 'And, for the record, I'm sure you would have made a brilliant midwife. Vanessa says they'll likely send her home tomorrow, but only if she promises to stay in bed and rest.'

'And will she?'

'I'll send mother round.' She tilted her head back and tipped the last few crisps into her mouth. 'She'll make sure of it.'

Grant smiled despite his discomfort. The more he got to know Caroline, the more he warmed to her. She was funny in a self-deprecatory kind of way, and he found that endearing. And yes, he would take her out for dinner… soon. In spite of his previous misgivings, he was growing fond of her.

One thing was certain, she was proving to be a valued neighbour and a delightful friend.

Chapter Twenty-Five

Ursula discovered that retirement living was not as amazing as it had been made out to be. The sales pitch of a spotless apartment with stunning views over the river, which had convinced her to opt for one of the last remaining flats, had done its job. She was here, and the view was pleasant, but she had no intention of siting on her balcony, gazing out at the river day after day.

She flicked a feather duster over her dust-free furniture. Everything in her apartment was new, clean, shiny or low maintenance. It was a little after nine o'clock in the morning, and she had nothing to do, and nothing planned.

She switched on the coffee machine, and while she waited, flicked through the local paper that had just been delivered. There wasn't much in it. Everything was old news, since most stuff had been reported online the day before. But she enjoyed checking through the classified ads, and the notices of deaths, births and marriages.

She stirred a spoonful of sugar into her coffee, and sat down to drink it, the paper spread out on the table in front of her. An article about the strong winds and local damage ran to a couple of paragraphs. There was a photograph of a car with a branch on its roof and a fence on its side in someone's back garden. Nothing too dramatic. She wondered if Ella had suffered any damage at Hollyfields. She would ring her later to find out.

Turning the page, she came to the Situations Vacant section, and was surprised to see a picture of her old house, under the headline, 'Dalton Veterinary Practice. Opening soon. Applications welcome for the following positions…' She scanned the rest of the advert, her thoughts working overtime. Now there was an idea.

***

'What do you mean, you're bored?' Caroline said. 'You're supposed to be retired and taking things easy.'

'I know, darling, but you know how I like to keep busy.'

Caroline watched dubiously, as her mother began re-arranging the counter display of horse and dog treats, and assorted pencils, rubbers and notebooks in the tack shop.

'This would be the perfect little job for me.'

Caroline gaped at her, mortified. She didn't think Vanessa would see it that way. And besides, what was she supposed to do if her mother swanned in and took over, as she was patently angling to do?

'It's quite physical, you know. Lots of moving heavy bags of feed around, and some of those saddles weigh a ton.'

Her mother picked up a tray of assorted riding gloves and positioned them at the far end of the counter. 'There,' she said, standing back to admire her work. 'That looks better.'

'Mother, I said it's…'

'Yes, I know. I heard you the first time. Well, Adam helps out, doesn't he? He can do the heavy lifting.'

'Yes, but…'

'And anyway, I'm sixty-seven, not eighty-seven. I think you underestimate my capabilities.' Her mother gave her a scathing look, which had Caroline wondering if she was really having this conversation, or whether it was a dream and she hadn't woken up.

'Mother,' she said. 'This is my job.'

Ursula plonked herself down on a stool and slapped the newspaper she had brought with her onto the counter. 'It is for now,' she said, 'but I happen to think this…' She jabbed her finger at the open page. '…will suit you much better.'

With a resigned sigh, Caroline picked up the newspaper. 'Dalton Veterinary Practice', she read. 'Receptionist required.' She glanced across at her mother, who sat, arms folded across her ample chest, and nodding eagerly.

'Yes. Yes, that's the one. Don't you see? That would be perfect for you. And there'd be no travelling. You're literally on the premises.'

'Mother, I am not a receptionist.' She slapped the paper on the counter.

'Oh, rubbish. You were doing reception duties at that office job you had.'

'Not really.' She glanced back at the advert. 'Anyway, they want someone with experience of working with animals.'

'Exactly.' Her mother looked fit to burst. 'Think of all those years where you worked at the riding school. You've got oodles of experience. I think you should apply for it.'

Caroline stared across at her. 'But I like working here.'

Her mother had apparently thought of that. 'Yes, of course you do, darling. But at the end of the day, this is only a temporary job. I'm quite sure once Vanessa is back on her feet, she'll want to come back, and then what will you do? I mean, I'm perfectly willing to help out now, and once the baby is old enough, I can do a spot of baby-sitting to help her. I have my pension to fall back on.' She paused to catch her breath. 'But you don't have a career plan, do you darling, and this…' She jabbed a manicured nail at the advert, '…might be just the job you're looking for.'

It was too much to take in at this time of day. She'd barely had a chance to open up the shop before her mother had swept through the door, announcing that she was fed up of sitting in her apartment all day long, and wanted something to do. She never, for one moment, expected her to want a job, and her job, at that.

'Well? What do you think?'

Caroline drew in a deep breath. Her mother's eager expression showed that she had already decided. This was what she wanted, so this was what she would do. Well, Caroline had had quite enough of being walked over by her mother, Marcus, and anyone else who thought she was a doormat.

'I think,' she said, reaching under the counter for her

handbag, 'I'm going to have a word with Vanessa. She should be home by now. And, since you think it's so easy, you can look after the shop.' She snatched up the paper as she spoke. 'Is that all right with you?'

'Of course, it is, dear.'

'Good.'

The small satisfaction she received at slamming the door behind her, causing the bell above it to jangle noisily, was only a temporary thing. She was fuming. How dare her mother march in and treat her like she was an adolescent who didn't know her own mind? Well, she'd soon wipe the smug smile off her face. Just wait till her sister heard what their mother planned to do.

***

Vanessa had been discharged from the hospital first thing and was spending a lazy morning on the sofa, flicking through the pages of a parent and baby magazine, under strict instructions from Jed, that she wasn't to do a thing.

The twinges and niggles of pain that had resulted in their dash to the maternity unit the previous day had subsided. As long as she rested, and didn't exert herself, all would be well. The midwife had been reassuring on that front, at least.

'It's just your body having a little practice,' she said. 'And you know what they say; practice makes perfect.' Her warm Scottish lilt was soothing. 'You'll be fine, my dear. Baby will come when it's ready. I'm not worried, so you mustn't worry, either.'

Ella had popped in to see her and brought a bunch of flowers Rosie had picked from the wildflower meadow, and a home-made lasagne.

She could get used to this, she thought. She picked up the remote control and flicked on the television. Maybe she could find a nice film to watch.

Or maybe not. The insistent knocking on the front door suggested that whoever was outside would not go away.

Vanessa heaved herself off the settee and padded through to the hallway in her fluffy slippers. 'Who is it?'

'Me!'

'Caroline?' She unlocked the door. 'What are you doing here?'

Her sister marched past her and tossed the newspaper she held onto the table. 'It's mother.'

'Is she all right?'

'That depends what you mean by all right,' she snapped. 'Oh, how are you, by the way?'

'Fine. Thanks for asking.' Vanessa followed her sister into the lounge. Caroline had perched herself on the edge of a chair. She looked as if she was about to burst into tears.

'She's at the shop.'

'Who is? Oh, you mean, mother is?'

'Yes.'

'She wants to work there. She wants my job.'

Vanessa lowered herself onto the settee again, her thoughts whirling. She wasn't sure if she had heard her correctly. 'She wants your job?'

'Yes. Yes, that's what she said. She wants to run the tack shop until you come back to work, and then she'll do some baby-sitting to help out, and me...' Her voice had risen an octave. 'Well, I'm supposed to apply for this job at the vets, because, apparently, that's the perfect job for me. Not that I get a say in the matter.'

'She wants your job?' Vanessa found herself repeating. Her sister's cheeks had gone quite pink. 'And you've got to work at the vets. What vets?'

'The new practice at Grey Lodge. The one Grant and his daughter are setting up.'

Caroline tossed her the newspaper. 'It's in there. The Dalton veterinary practice.'

It took Vanessa a moment to find the advert. 'Veterinary receptionist,' she said. 'Hmm, that's a generous rate of pay. And flexible hours. That's handy.'

'Are you listening to me? Mother wants to run the tack shop.'

'Hmm. You said.' She finished reading and folded up the

newspaper. 'Actually, that's not a bad idea. I think you should go for it.'

'What!' Caroline looked incensed.

'The job at the vets.' She put her feet up on the settee and rested her hands on her stomach. 'It would be more convenient for you than traipsing over to the shop every day, and if mother is happy to cover for me, I don't see the problem.'

'You don't?'

'No. Anyway, you might not get it. There's bound to be loads of applicants.'

Caroline pulled a face. 'Thanks for the vote of confidence.'

'You're welcome.' She patted her stomach. 'Rest your hands here a minute. Baby is moving.'

Caroline did as she was instructed, her eyes widening. 'That's so weird. What does it feel like?'

'Weird.' Vanessa smiled. 'You'd be good at the vets. Just think, you'd get to work with the dishy Grant every day. You can't say you don't fancy him. I've seen how you look at him.'

'Oh, alright, so what if I do?' Caroline said, twiddling with one of the buttons on her jacket. 'But it doesn't mean he fancies me.'

'He might, if he has to work with you every day.'

Her sister gave her a sudden, thoughtful look. 'Do you really think I should apply for the job?'

'I do.'

'And you don't mind that mother will be in charge of the tack shop?'

'She won't be in charge. She'll just be running it for me and, in fairness to her, she did buy it. I can hardly object if she wants to help. No, I think you should go for it and see what happens. What do you need to do?'

Caroline studied the newspaper again. 'There's an online form to complete.'

'So, what are you waiting for? Just do it. You've got nothing to lose. And possibly,' Vanessa smiled at her. 'Everything to gain.'

Chapter Twenty-Six

Breaking his wrist could not have come at a worse time for Grant. Fortunately, it was his left wrist, and he was right-handed, but it meant he couldn't drive anywhere, nor do all the moving of equipment and clearing up he had planned.

Sabrina took over with enthusiasm, probably because she felt guilty, he thought. If she'd moved her stuff in the first place, his accident might not have happened.

'You can still do the painting,' she told him. 'You only need one hand to hold a brush.'

He admired her logic. The reality wasn't so cut and dried. Especially if he was required to climb a stepladder, but he did what he could manage. The builders assured him they could find someone else to do the rest.

The plans were coming together. By the end of the following week, he had two operating theatres, three consulting rooms, and a reception and waiting area. All that was needed was the equipment he'd ordered and the furnishings to go with it.

Sabrina had been in contact with the laboratory and arranged a rota for collecting and processing the various tests, blood samples and swabs they expected and had set up an arrangement with a drugs company for medications to be delivered daily.

Things were progressing as well as expected, but there was still much to do. Everything from stationary, scrubs, and supplies needed to be sourced and ordered, as well as recruiting new staff.

His daily walk with Monty through the woods and fields

was a welcome interlude from all the planning and organising. Thankfully, he could still manage that one-handed. Monty's training was going well. He liked to think that his recall was better than it had been. It certainly couldn't be any worse. But once the spaniel found the scent of something interesting, he easily got distracted, and there was always something for him to find in the woods. Today's treasured retrieve was a navy jumper, which he dragged out from under a thicket of ferns, and came trotting towards him, with said item hanging from his mouth.

Grant took it from him, in exchange for a handful of dog biscuits, and examined it carefully. It was a school jumper. The badge had the emblem of the local secondary school on the front. The name tag inside was for an A. Trevelyan.

'That must be Ella's son,' Sabrina said when he showed it to her. 'He's called Adam.'

'Really? Oh, well, in that case I'll give it to Caroline, when she collects Monty. She's his aunt,' he added, in response to her quizzical look. 'He helps her in the tack shop.'

'There's no need. I'm seeing Ella later. I did tell you.' She folded up the jumper as she spoke. 'We're going out for dinner. Her husband is still in Edinburgh and Rosie; that's her youngest, is at a sleepover with one of her friends.'

'Guess it's beans on toast for me, then.'

Sabrina laughed. 'Dad, don't make out you're useless just because your wrist is in plaster. You could always ask Caroline for help.'

'I'm sure she's got other things to do.'

'Yes, and you've been looking after her dog all day. She should treat you to dinner. I know I would, if I was her.'

'She's done enough for me already.' He would not elaborate further, though he could see by the enquiring look on his daughter's face that she was curious.

'You like her, don't you?'

'As a friend, yes.'

Sabrina tilted her head to one side.

He'd seen that look before. The kind of look that said she

didn't quite believe him, but she wasn't going to argue.

'I'm old enough to be her father,' he said.

'I don't think you are.'

'You know what I mean. I must be a good twelve or thirteen years older than her.'

'So? Some women like older men.'

'Yes, and some men like to be on their own. Your mother was quite enough for me. Now go and get ready for your night out; and stop badgering me.' He gave her a gentle shove. 'Go on. Haven't you got to wash your hair or put your face on?'

'Mum wouldn't want you to be lonely, you know.' Sabrina scuttled out of his reach before he could give her another push. 'She'd want you to be happy.'

'Go!' he said. But he was smiling, just the same.

***

'Dinner?' Caroline said, surprised. She had called round to collect Monty on her way home from work, and now Grant was suggesting she join him for dinner.

'I was thinking of ordering a takeaway,' he said, 'but it seems extravagant for one person, and I wondered if you'd like to join me.'

She hesitated on the doorstep, with Monty jumping up at her.

'Sabrina's out,' he added. 'She's gone to see Ella, and I didn't fancy cooking.'

'All right,' she said. 'That would be lovely. Thank you.'

She followed him into the house. It felt strange being back there and seeing all the changes he'd made in such a short space of time. The hallway now had rooms on either side of the staircase, with a long glass fronted counter in front of it.

A private doorway and corridor led to the foot of the stairs, ensuring residents didn't have to walk the length of the waiting room to gain access to the upper floors. The smell of paint and varnish hit her the moment she stepped inside.

'Careful, you don't brush against that wall,' he said as he

ushered her through. 'I think it's still damp.'

'I'm surprised Monty isn't covered in it.'

He smiled. 'He's slept in the lounge most of the time. Although we had a couple of long walks through the woods. Didn't we, boy?'

Monty wagged his tail in agreement.

'And he brought me a present.'

Caroline screwed up her face. 'Not a rabbit carcass?'

'Better than that.' He paused at the top of the stairs and held the landing door open for her. 'A navy jumper. A school jumper, actually. I think it belonged to your nephew. Sabrina's taken it over to Ella now. He dragged it out from under a clump of ferns,'

'In the woods?'

'That's right.'

'He must have left it one time he was over there. I mean, before you moved in,' she added.

'I expect so, though it didn't look as if it had been lying around for months.'

Caroline swallowed and glanced out of the window. Surely Adam hadn't been sneaking into the woods with his mates again? Not after she'd had words with him. She'd have to talk to him about it when he next showed up at the shop.

'What do you fancy?'

He brandished some takeaway menus at her. 'Pizza, Chinese, Indian—there's quite a selection, surprisingly, and they all deliver.'

'I don't mind.'

'Pizza, then? There's salad in the fridge, and I can open a bottle of wine.'

'Sounds lovely.'

They ate in the new kitchen diner on the second floor. What had once been a bedroom was now a fitted and functional modern kitchen, with a glass-topped dining table and chairs at one end, and units and appliances at the other. It was spotlessly clean. Dimmed spotlights over the table gave it a cosy, relaxed feel.

While waiting for the pizzas to arrive, Grant gave her a tour of the rest of the house, including Sabrina's attic suite of rooms.

'When mother first moved in here, this attic space was empty and Vanessa used to think it was haunted.' She smiled, remembering. 'After Michael died, she had it converted into extra bedrooms for the bed-and-breakfast business. But what you've done here is nothing short of amazing. It's beautiful.'

'Thank you.'

She followed him down the stairs.

'Does it feel strange, being back in your old home like this?' He uncorked the bottle of red wine and poured her a glass.

'Yes, and no. It's better to be a guest than a chambermaid. I think I've scrubbed every corner of these rooms.'

'And a grand job you made of it, too.' He raised his glass in a toast. 'Otherwise, I wouldn't have wanted to buy the place.'

The ringing of the doorbell heralded the arrival of their pizzas. She took the salad from the fridge, and found some cutlery in the drawer, while Grant went downstairs to collect it.

While she waited for him to come back, she wandered into the lounge, which had been the front guest bedroom. He had hung up pictures on the walls. A framed photograph of himself, his wife, and two teenage children took pride of place on the sideboard. She peered closer. His daughter and wife looked similar, both with dark hair and eyes. The boy had lighter hair and looked more like his father. It was a beautiful picture.

She wondered what had happened to his wife but knew she would never ask. Some things were best left unsaid.

'I got garlic bread, too. Hope that's okay.'

'Perfect.' She smiled and followed him into the kitchen. 'It'll keep the vampires away.'

They ate their meal in companionable silence. He seemed as comfortable with her presence as she was with his.

Caroline was surprised at how hungry she was. The pizza,

with extra toppings of mushroom and ham, was delicious. She helped herself to a piece of garlic bread, while he topped up their wine glasses with a rich-bodied but smooth Merlot.

'Not too much for me,' she said. 'I've got work tomorrow, unless Mother decides to take over again.' If her voice sounded sarcastic, she couldn't help it.

He raised a quizzical eyebrow at her.

'She's not ready for retirement yet. Apparently, she thinks running the tack shop will suit her down to the ground.'

'I see.' He nodded, looking serious. 'And what do you think?'

'It doesn't matter what I think. If she's made up her mind to do something, she invariably does it.'

He smiled. 'I gathered that. Well, if you're at a loose end, you can always help me with the decorating. You made a pretty good job of the cottage.'

'Thanks.' She chewed on a piece of garlic bread. She wondered if she should tell him she had applied for the receptionist's job. Vanessa had helped her to fill out the online application form and had pressed send before she could change her mind. She presumed he must have seen it. Then again, maybe he wasn't mentioning it because he didn't think she was suitable. Like Vanessa said, they were bound to get loads of applicants. She wouldn't spoil things by bringing it up.

'Have you had any more problems with people in the woods?' she asked.

'I've seen no one, but I'm still finding rubbish strewn about. I think it's a hotspot for the local youth.'

'It always was.' She helped herself to more salad. He had dressed it with a particularly tasty chilli oil. She would ask him for the recipe later.

'I'm thinking of hiring someone to keep an eye on the grounds.'

'What—like a security firm or something?'

He nodded. 'Just so they get the message, it's a no-go area. Once the practice is up and running, I can't have strangers wandering about the grounds.'

'No,' she said, inwardly resolving to have that chat with Adam sooner rather than later. 'That was delicious.' She wiped her lips with a paper napkin. 'But I really should get going.' She rose from her seat.

'You're welcome to stay.'

She hesitated.

'At least until Sabrina gets home,' he added. 'You haven't met her yet, and I'm sure she'd like to be introduced to you. Seeing as how you were the one who came to my rescue.'

'Hardly.' She lowered herself back into her chair.

It was, she reflected later, a perfect evening.

They chatted easily, drank more wine and took Monty for a walk over the fields, with Grant showing her the progress he was making with his recall. 'He's not perfect, but he's getting there,' he said.

When he realised that his daughter planned on staying out much later than he expected, he walked them both back to her cottage and saw them safely inside.

She closed the door and locked it, her heart thumping. It had been like a date. They'd spent a whole evening together. Good food, wine and company. When he'd waited in the front garden for her to go inside, she'd thought he might kiss her. Had hoped he was going to kiss her. But he'd bent to stroke Monty instead, before turning to walk away.

Was he too shy? Was it too soon? She had absolutely no idea. But the longing she felt was real enough. He was gorgeous, and she fancied him like mad. If only she could get him to feel the same way.

Chapter Twenty-Seven

Adam had got himself a girlfriend. It was all he could talk about, and Caroline didn't know whether she felt pleased, or downright miffed. Why was it so easy for youngsters, and not for her? He'd been seeing Jessica Marchant for a few weeks on a purely friendly basis, but now they were officially dating. He was her boyfriend.

The fact that Max Bradshaw also had designs on the same girl was neither here nor there, as far as Adam was concerned, but Caroline wasn't so sure. She felt certain the youth in question would not handle rejection well. Max Bradshaw didn't seem the type.

Still, it wasn't her problem. She had more pressing things on her mind. The lack of communication from Grant Dalton, being the main one. Since their lovely evening together, she had barely seen him.

Now that her mother was practically forcing her out of the shop, she didn't need to rely on him for doggy day-care. She could spend a leisurely morning walking Monty, before going to the shop for a couple of hours so her mother could have a lunch break, and then it was more of the same in the afternoon, unless her mother had an appointment, or other plans. Like today, when she had swanned off to the hairdressers for a couple of hours and left her and Adam to sort out the feed delivery.

Caroline ticked off the items on the invoice while Adam stacked the heavy bags in the storeroom, putting aside the ones customers had ordered in, to be collected later.

It had been a hectic morning. Saturdays were always busy,

and she was glad of the extra help. The equestrian show season was in full swing, and Vanessa had ensured they had enough clothing and tack items to suit every pocket. Gloves, hats, and show jackets were in high demand.

'Where do you want me to put this box of rosettes?' Adam asked. 'Shall I leave them on the counter, where people can see them?'

'Please.' She ducked back into the storeroom to see if she could locate a child's riding hat that a customer had rung in about earlier.

The shop door banged open; causing the bell above it to jangle noisily, just as she was kneeling over a large cardboard box marked "hats" at the back of the room.

'Won't be a minute,' she called, delving in to the bottom of the box. Why were the things she wanted always the last things she could find? The smaller, toddler sized riding hats were underneath everything else. She lifted some of the larger sizes out and balanced them precariously in a tower until she reached the one she wanted.

The crashing of a display stand was the next thing she heard. 'For goodness' sake,' she muttered, straightening up. What had happened now?

She heard a shout, and the unmistakable sound of breaking glass.

'Adam?' She jumped to her feet. Somebody was swearing, and it didn't sound like her nephew. The heavy thump, and the sound of a hissed intake of breath, caused her to reach for a riding crop, as she dashed to the door of the storeroom. 'What on earth...'

Her words tailed away as she saw her nephew sprawled on his back on the floor, blood trickling from his nose, and the hooded bulk of Max Bradshaw towering over him, fists raised. The front door had a smashed pane of glass, leaving shards of jagged edges sticking out at all angles. Glittering pieces of it covered the floor.

'What the hell do you think you're doing?' she shrieked,

whacking the riding crop down hard across Max's clenched fists.

The youth swore, and spun round, eyes glaring like a madman.

Caroline brandished the whip at him, striking him on his arm, and again on his leg. She'd never felt so frightened in her entire life, but she refused to stand back and watch this young lout batter her nephew.

It gave Adam time to scramble to his feet. Blood dripped from his nose, and he smeared it away with the back of his hand. She suspected it might be broken.

As he did so, he stared with outraged fury at his attacker.

To Caroline's horror, she watched him raise both his fists in some kind of choreographed battle pose, and start dancing from side to side, like a cage fighter, his feet scrunching over the shattered glass.

'No! Whatever this is about, just stop it.' Caroline hoped the sound of her most authoritarian voice would restore some kind of order. It didn't.

Both boys were facing each other in a sort of stand-off. She saw pure rage blazing from Max's eyes. A stark red mark was forming on the back of his hand, and she felt a twinge of guilt. Maybe she shouldn't have hit him so hard. Then again, what was she supposed to do? The boy was out of control. They both were.

Adam wiped a sleeve over his bloodied nose, his eyes not shifting from Max's murderous glare. Crimson stains covered his shirt.

'Stop it! Stop this right now!'

Her words fell on deaf ears. The boys were weaving from side to side, fronting up to each other. Both looked ready and able to kill.

Caroline felt petrified. She didn't know what to do or how to stop them. 'Adam, calm down,' she said.

He beckoned Max towards him, goading him. 'Come on. Come on, just try it.'

Blood trickled from his nose, down his chin, and dripped onto the floor.

Max crouched like a cat, waiting to spring.

'This is ridiculous!' She planted her hands on Max's chest and tried to push him away, but he grabbed her wrist and spun her round, forcing her in front of him. His breath smelt of stale beer. One arm looped itself round her neck, yanking her backwards, and she screamed.

Adam launched himself at Max in a flurry of fists. It all happened so fast. One minute, she was between them, and the next thing, Max had hurled her away from him. She staggered sideways and fell against the door frame. In that same moment, she felt a punch in her side. (She really did think it was a punch) As she prepared to unleash a stream of obscenities at him, the air suddenly seemed to escape from her lungs. A startled glance downwards, and she could see a pool of red spreading across her cream blouse. Puzzled, she looked at Adam. The look of abject horror on his face told her all she needed to know. That, and the fact the room was swimming woozily around her.

'Shit.' Max froze, his face ashen. Without another word, he turned and bolted for the door.

She slumped against the wall, slithered down it, taking a rack of greetings cards and notelets with her, and collapsed onto the floor with a gasp. The room was becoming hazy.

Adam stared at her, his eyes wide with shock.

She was vaguely aware of him snatching down a padded blue numnah from one of the shelves and rushing to press it against her side. The small brass bell above the broken door jangled like crazy.

Her last conscious memory was of Adam, crouched beside her, sobbing, and saying she was going to be fine. It was all going to be fine.

Chapter Twenty-Eight

'This one sounds all right.' Sabrina handed him a sheet from the top of the pile and Grant scanned the page. He had left his daughter to sort through the applications, since she was better on the computer than him, and she had printed out a short list of candidates for the veterinary nurse and receptionist posts.

'Bit young,' he muttered. 'Not a lot of experience.'

'She's twenty-three and had five years at Prentice Hall vets.'

'So, why is she leaving?'

Sabrina stuffed a lock of dark hair behind one ear and re-examined the sheet of paper. 'Doesn't say.'

'And why does she want to come here?'

'Doesn't say.' She sighed. 'Dad, those are the sort of things you can ask at the interview stage.'

'If we ask her for an interview.'

'Well, we've got to ask some of them, otherwise it will be just you and me, and no one else.' She plucked another form from the pile and handed it to him. 'Here, try this one, and see what you think. I'm going to make us a coffee.'

He wasn't in the mood for this. A visit to the hospital that morning had confirmed that, although his wrist was healing well, the cast would need to stay on for at least another two weeks, just to be on the safe side. Two more weeks of not driving, and precious little to do apart from watch the workmen and his daughter do all the things he wanted to do himself. Swanning around with a paintbrush all day was wearing a bit thin.

He had hoped that Caroline would drop Monty off. He'd enjoyed their training sessions, and it helped to fill the time. But since Ursula had descended on the tack shop, there had been no need for him to look after the dog, more's the pity.

He glanced down at the application form. He was sure Lucy MacDonald did love all animals, but he didn't think that was a good enough reason for her to want to work at a vet practice. It wasn't all fluffy kittens and cute puppies. There was blood, gore, distress and heartache. And stress. No one ever mentioned the stress. Difficult customers, those who refused to pay, those who paid and then complained of the cost; it all added up.

There was no National Health Service for pets. Drugs and tests were expensive, which was where insurance companies came in. This idealised image people had of the veterinary service was usually because of soppy dramas and fly on the wall documentaries, all carefully sanitised for the viewing public. In his opinion, obviously. Others might disagree.

'Oh, my God! Dad!'

He jerked his head up as his daughter came rushing back into the office, her eyes widening as she stared at a message on her phone. 'Caroline's been hurt.'

'What?'

'This message. It's from Ella.'

'What!' He was on his feet in an instant. A cold, icy dread flooded through his veins. 'Is she okay?'

'Hang on, hang on.' She scrolled down the phone. 'It was in the tack shop. She fell onto broken glass, trying to break up a fight.' Sabrina raised her eyes to meet his. 'Adam was with her. They've gone to the hospital.'

'Is she badly hurt?' His heart was racing.

'I don't know.' Sabrina looked back at her phone. 'She doesn't say. Just that they're at the hospital now and she's been taken to theatre.'

'Oh God!' He slumped back in his chair. 'Oh God! No.' He couldn't believe what he was hearing. 'A fight? What was it, an attempted robbery?'

Sabrina shrugged. 'I don't know. Bloody hell.' She shook

her head in disbelief. 'Do you want to go there? I can give you a lift.'

'No, I can't. It'll just be family, if… if it's serious.' He could hardly bear to say it, let alone think it.

'Dad.' Her voice lowered. 'You should go.'

He sucked in a breath, his thoughts whirling. Of course, he wanted to see her. He couldn't stand the thought that something bad had happened to her, and he hadn't been there to help her, protect her.

'I know how much you think of her. I'm not stupid.'

He glanced sideways up at her. Did she know? Did she really? When he hardly knew himself what he thought, only that he didn't want to lose her. He couldn't bear to go through all that trauma again, and not like this, not when she didn't even know how he felt.

He scraped back his chair. 'Okay, but just to make sure she's all right.'

'Of course.' She snatched up her bag and keys. 'Come on.'

***

Ursula stared at her reflection in the mirror and came to the conclusion that ash blonde was definitely her colour, and the girl had done a professional job, which accounted for the eye-watering price. 'Very nice,' she said, turning her head one way, and then the other.

The stylist hovered behind her, holding a large circular mirror so she could see herself from all angles.

'I've kept the length a bit longer at the back, so see how you get on with it. We can always go shorter next time, if you prefer.'

She had opted for a layered bob-cut, more in keeping with her age, having grown tired of the bun she usually favoured, which was, she thought, rather ageing. She rather liked the shorter cropped look. It gave her a look of Prue Leith. Perhaps coloured glasses would be her next step. It was time she changed her image and her new job was the perfect opportunity for her to make that change.

The hairdressing salon was situated in a side street, a short walk away from the tack shop, but Ursula didn't see the point in hurrying back. She reasoned that Caroline could manage perfectly well with the delivery, since she had Adam to help her with the larger bags.

She took the opportunity to loiter in the dress shop, the newsagents, and then the bakers, where she purchased a box of iced eclairs to go with their afternoon cup of tea. It was a beautiful afternoon and she strolled back in her own time, enjoying the warmth of the summer sun and the gentle breeze.

The two police cars, and the strip of blue and white tape that cordoned off the area, should have alerted her to something amiss, but Ursula was in her own little world, and it didn't occur to her that something might have happened at the tack shop, until she reached the corner of the street and found her way blocked by a uniformed police officer.

'I'm sorry, Madame, but you can't go this way.'

'I think you'll find that I can,' she said. 'That's my shop over there, and I'm here to relieve my daughter, so she can go on her break.'

'And your name is?'

'Mrs Lloyd-Duncan,' she said.

The policeman planted his legs apart and held one hand up as he reached for his radio. 'One moment, please.'

Ursula glanced at her watch and gave him an irritated look as he spoke into his radio in muffled tones. She tried to peer beyond his shoulder, but the police car blocked her view. 'What's going on?' she said. 'Has something happened?'

'There's been an incident, yes.' He beckoned to his colleague, and a young policewoman, looking no older than about fifteen, in Ursula's opinion, came walking briskly towards them.

'Mrs Lloyd-Duncan? If you'd like to come with me.'

'Why? What's happened?' she said.

'I'm afraid I've got some bad news. If you'd like to step this way.'

***

Grant decided it was a good job he wasn't fit to drive. He didn't think he could have kept to the speed limit on the country lanes, like his daughter was doing. He drummed his fingers on his knee, willing her to hurry up. He was desperate to get to the hospital to find out what had happened to Caroline. It was ridiculous, beyond belief. How could she have been injured breaking up a fight? A shop assistant in a country saddlery? In this sleepy part of Suffolk?

'Can't you go any faster?' he muttered.

'Not safely.' Sabrina shot him a look. 'You want to get there in one piece, don't you?'

He grunted.

It seemed an age before she pulled into the hospital car park and found a space some distance from the main entrance.

Grant didn't wait for her to follow, but ran to the main building and burst through the doors. Sabrina caught up with him as he was blurting out the details to a startled looking receptionist.

'Are you family?'

'No, but…'

'Yes,' Sabrina lied, resting one hand on his arm and squeezing it. 'We're part of her extended family. I believe her stepsister is already here.'

The woman stared at her computer screen. 'Ah, yes.' She pointed along the corridor. 'You need to go through those double doors, turn right, follow to the end, then left. There's a waiting room…'

Grant set off before she could finish, barging his way through the double doors. He hated hospitals; the smell of them, the pale, insipid walls and rubber floors, the abstract art put up to make the place look more homely, the trolleys, the smell of overcooked food and disinfectant. It brought everything back to him. The endless hours of waiting, feeling helpless, and knowing the inevitable outcome. But not this time, please, not this time.

'Dad, wait.'

He quickened his stride, his heart hammering like a sledgehammer inside his chest.

Sabrina came jogging up to him, her cheeks pink. 'There's Ella. Look.' She pointed.

Caroline's stepsister was standing in the corridor, phone clamped to her ear, nodding her head, but she glanced up and gave them a hurried wave, before finishing her call, and coming towards them.

'She's okay,' were the first words she said, and Grant could have hugged her. Could have swept her off her feet, swung her round, and hugged her.

'What happened?' His gaze went beyond Ella to where a young man stood, leaning back against the wall. His shirt was stained with blood, and he had bloodstains on his hands and arms. A policeman was standing talking to him, notebook in hand. 'Is that...'

'That's Adam. My son,' Ella explained. 'He was with his aunt when she got hurt. But she's going to be okay, thank God. She tried to break up a fight between him and another lad.'

'She did what?' Grant sucked in a breath.

'I know. Mad or what? She got between Adam and the other bloke. Some fight over a girl, I believe.' She glanced back at her son. 'He's got some explaining to do.'

'So, how is she?'

'Well, she's lost a lot of blood, but the doctor seems to think she'll be fine.' Ella gave him a half-hearted smile. 'She was lucky. There was no harm done to any major organs. They stitched her up, and that's about all I can tell you, really.'

He exhaled with a sigh, realising that he'd been holding his breath the whole time she was speaking to them. 'Can we see her?'

'I don't think they're letting anyone in just yet.'

He gazed around. 'There must be someone I can ask?'

'They're pretty short-staffed. Anyway, I need to stay with

Adam, but I thought I'd let you know.'

'Thanks,' Sabrina said. She caught hold of his arm. 'Dad, don't harass the nurses.'

'I'm not,' he said.

He didn't need to. Ursula was doing enough of that for all of them.

'What do you mean, I can't see her? She's my daughter, and I demand to see her right now?' came the highly aggrieved voice from somewhere down the corridor.

He turned in time to see Ursula Lloyd Duncan marching towards them, with a young girl in pale blue scrubs following in her wake.

'She hasn't come round from the anaesthetic yet,' the girl was saying. 'I really don't think...'

'Let me be the judge of that. Oh!' She pulled herself up short and stared at him. 'Mr Dalton. What are you doing here?'

'The same as you,' he said.

'You've come to see Caroline?' Ursula's eyes narrowed. 'Why would you do that?'

'I would have thought that was obvious,' he muttered. He glanced at the young nurse and gave her a sympathetic smile. 'Could you let her know that Grant Dalton is here?' he said. 'I'd really like to see her, if she's well enough to have a visitor.'

'Yes, well, I intend to see her first,' Ursula said, somewhat haughtily.

The nurse hesitated, looking from one to the other. 'Give me a moment,' she said.

As they waited in the corridor, Ursula's beady gaze rested on her grandson, her eyes widening in horror. 'Adam! Oh, my dear boy.' She hurried over, ignoring the look she got from the policeman and Ella. 'What on earth has happened to you? Will someone please tell me what is going on?'

The nurse tapped Grant lightly on the arm and tilted her head at the door behind her. 'You can go in now,' she said. 'But make it quick. She's very sleepy.'

'Thanks.'

Grant dodged behind her and through the door to the room on the right, where he could see Caroline lying on the bed, a thin blanket pulled over her, a monitor bleeping at her side.

'Now then, crazy lady,' he murmured, sitting beside her and reaching out to take hold of her hand. 'What have you been doing this time?'

She blinked sleepily up at him.

'It's okay. You don't have to talk.' He stroked her fingers, reassured by the gentle squeeze she gave him. 'I don't like talkative women.'

A flicker of a smile tugged at the corners of her lips.

'The things some people do to get attention, hmm,' he murmured. 'It was bad enough me breaking my wrist, but you had to go one better.'

Her eyelids fluttered open. 'Grant,' she sighed. She breathed out slowly. 'You're here.' Her voice sounded weak and shaky.

'Yep, I'm here.' He leaned forwards to push a lock of hair away from her eyes. She looked peaceful and serene. Beautiful, in fact, and he found it hard to resist the urge to sweep her into his arms and never let her go. 'I'm going nowhere.'

'She's my daughter, and I have every right…' Ursula's enraged words came thundering along the corridor to greet them. 'In here?' The door banged open. 'Caroline! Oh, my darling, how are you?'

Grant stood up, to prevent the sudden onslaught of Ursula sweeping into the room and taking over, as she always did. 'She's fine, Mrs Lloyd-Duncan, but she needs to rest.'

'Well, yes, of course she does. But she'll want to see me. Caroline, dearest….'

Grant politely, but firmly, steered her back the way she had come. 'And she will see you, but not right now.'

'Excuse me?'

'I said, not right now.' He glanced back at Caroline, whose eyelids had fluttered shut again. Possibly deliberately, he thought.

'Well, really.' Ursula sounded flustered, but Grant gave her no room to manoeuvre.

'Why don't you go and get a nice cup of tea, hmm? And come back later.'

Ursula peered over his left shoulder. 'Well, she does look a bit tired.'

'That will be the anaesthetic,' he said. 'It'll take her a while to come round. I don't mind sitting with her while you talk to your grandson. I'm sure you're as keen as I am to find out what actually happened. She'll be more than happy to see you once she's fully awake.'

Ursula looked undecided, but Grant's concerned and understanding look seemed to do the trick.

'Later, darling,' she said. 'I'll just have a quick word with Adam. You rest up, now.'

Caroline lay silent and still. Her eyelids twitched but remained closed.

He sat back down and caught hold of her hand. It felt warm to the touch.

'Thank you,' she said, her voice barely a whisper.

'That's what friends are for.'

'Friends,' she repeated sleepily.

'More than that, hopefully.'

He didn't know if she heard him or whether she had drifted off again. Her eyes stayed closed and her breathing was slow and regular.

But, to his amazement, considering everything she had been through and all that had happened to her, he could swear she was smiling.

Chapter Twenty-Nine

'I'm beginning to think we should turn this place into a convalescent home, rather than a veterinary practice,' Sabrina said.

Grant poured a dash of milk into his coffee and carried it over to the table, where his daughter was ploughing through the application forms. 'You don't mind her staying here, do you?'

'Not at all,' she said. 'You can keep an eye on each other while I sort this lot out.'

He had decided that Caroline should move into Grey Lodge while she recovered from the injury that had temporarily put her out of action. With her sister due to give birth any day now, and her mother living in a one-bedroom retirement apartment, it had seemed the obvious solution.

'We've got plenty of spare rooms, and Monty can come with you. It's not a problem,' he assured her.

She had been reluctant at first. He understood that. She valued her independence, and he admired her for that. But he also knew it would take her a while before she got her strength back and he wanted to be there for her. No more pretending. He cared about her, more than she knew, and he intended to put that straight, sooner, rather than later. In the meantime, he was letting her rest as much as she liked.

His gaze went to the window. Caroline lay on one of the sun loungers in the garden, a large straw hat shading her eyes from the sun. She was reading a book. Monty dozed in a shady spot on the patio beside her, his head resting on his paws. Every so often, his ears and nose twitched.

'There's a candidate here, I think you'll be interested in,'

Sabrina said, sliding a form across the table to him. A wicked glint twinkled in her eyes.

'Mature, honest, excellent references.' Grant raised his eyebrows. 'Well, I'll be.' He smiled as he read on. Caroline had applied for the post of veterinary receptionist, and she'd never said a word to him. Not even a hint that she was interested.

'I take it she'll be going on the short list,' Sabrina said.

'What short list?' Grant grinned and stood up.

Sabrina shook a warning finger at him. 'You said you wouldn't mix business and pleasure.'

'I said a lot of things. Some, I wish I hadn't. Some I wish I had.' He folded the paper in half. 'Are we agreed?'

'I'm happy, if you are.'

'Good.' He drained the last of his coffee. 'Now all we need to do is find a couple of qualified vet nurses, and we'll be sorted. Think you can manage that for me?'

'Dad…'

He glanced back at her.

'It's good to have you back.'

He knew exactly what she meant. He'd been wallowing in self-pity for far too long. But having someone else to worry about instead of himself made him realise that life really was too short; that things could change in an instant, and fate could turn plans upside down in a flash. It was time to live in the moment and enjoy every second.

With that thought in mind, he strode across the room, pushed open the double doors, and stepped out onto the stone patio.

Caroline raised her head, tilted her sun hat back, and smiled at him. It was the most beautiful smile he had seen in a long time.

'Mind if I join you?' he said, pulling up a chair.

'There are things we need to discuss.'

***

Caroline was in love. Hopelessly, helplessly in love. It

had taken her a while to realise that. Her initial dislike of the brusque Yorkshireman who had stayed with them at Grey Lodge had turned into a creeping admiration for him, and then into a longing that she'd never felt before. She loved Grant Dalton, and she could hardly believe it when she realised he had the same feelings for her.

He had told her so when he offered her the receptionist's job. He loved her and he didn't want to lose her, so could she please come and work for him, and they'd take it from there?

'It's so romantic,' Vanessa said. 'Two lost and lonely people, forced together through life and death circumstances, finally finding love.'

'It wasn't quite like that,' Caroline said, leaning over the crib to coo at her sister's baby. Vanessa had given birth in the days following her operation, and she felt as if she had missed out on the most exciting time in her sister's life. Baby Emily was three weeks old, and mother and child were doing well. Very well, in fact. Caroline couldn't remember when she had seen Vanessa look so happy; tired, obviously, but contented beyond measure.

'Motherhood suits you,' she said, marvelling at the baby's tiny fingers, which were wrapped round one of hers.

'Being in love suits you.' Vanessa said.

Caroline straightened up and smiled. 'We're taking things slowly.'

It was her choice, not because she wasn't sure of her feelings for Grant, but because she was frightened it was all happening too fast, and she didn't want him to have any regrets.

Would he have revealed how he felt about her if she hadn't been injured? The shock of her accident and seeing her so helpless in a hospital bed must have stirred up memories of his wife, and she couldn't blame him for that.

It was the reason why she'd moved back into her cottage as soon as she felt strong enough, despite him asking her to stay with him at Grey Lodge.

'I can't just move in with you,' she said. 'We haven't even

been on a date yet, and you hardly know me.'

'I know enough.'

'Please, Grant. Let's not rush things.'

'Okay. Have it your way,' he said. 'But I warn you, I'm not very good at this dating lark.'

'Me neither,' she said and laughed. 'But it'll be fun trying.'

So that's what they were doing, going on dates together. A trip to the theatre to see a play she loved (and he hated), a candle-lit dinner in a riverside pub, an early evening stroll along the beach eating fish and chips whilst trying to ward off hungry seagulls, and several long dog walks with Monty scampering and sniffing alongside them. They were like two best friends going on trips together, and yes, it was fun, she conceded. It was also very frustrating.

'Well, I think you're being sensible,' Vanessa said, tucking the white knitted blanket around baby Emily's waving legs. 'There's nothing wrong with that. Whirlwind romances aren't everything they're cracked up to be. A solid friendship is the foundation for a happy marriage.'

'Like you and Jed?' she teased, remembering how her sister had fallen in love with Jed from the moment she set eyes on him.

'We were friends before we became lovers, I'll have you know.'

'And now you're parents.'

'I know.' Vanessa straightened up and smiled. 'How times change. When do you start your new job?'

'Next week. Grant wants me to be up to speed with the computers before the practice has its official opening at the end of the month.'

'Yes, I saw that in the local paper. It looks like he's organising quite a do. A guided tour of the facilities, barbecue, live music, and complementary drinks. I'm sure it said free fizz. You'll have to rehearse your telephone voice. "Dalton Veterinary Surgery. How can I help you?" Vanessa spoke with a prim and proper cut-glass accent.

'Don't mock.' Caroline said, bending over the crib again, entranced by her tiny niece. Emily's thick, dark lashes were fluttering as her eyes closed. 'I'm really nervous about it.'

'Oh rubbish. You'll be fine. Anyway, I'm sure Grant and Sabrina are going to be more stressed than you.'

'I don't think so. Grant seems to be positively thriving on it.'

Vanessa placed a finger to her lips, and gently pushed her towards the kitchen, indicating they should leave the baby to sleep undisturbed.

'Does he know it's on the same date as your birthday?'

Caroline shook her head. 'I haven't told him.'

'But it's your fortieth.'

'Don't remind me. Here, you sit down. You're supposed to rest when the baby sleeps. I'll make us both a cup of tea.'

Vanessa sighed and sank onto one of the padded kitchen chairs. 'Thanks. Although I really should put some washing on.'

'I can do that. You need to relax.'

'So do you. It's not that long since you had life-saving surgery.'

'Hardly.' Her hand went automatically to her side. A slight tenderness remained, but the wound had healed perfectly, leaving only the faintest of scars. It was the tiredness that affected her the most; the feeling of utter exhaustion that had taken a long time to shift.

Staying at Grey Lodge for those first few weeks had helped her recover quicker than she could have hoped for. Grant had been the perfect host, nurse, and companion, but she meant it when she said she wanted to take things slowly. He needed time to get his business off the ground, and she didn't want to distract him from that.

Working together would help her understand the sort of man he was, though she felt she knew that already. He was kind, patient, and a devoted family man. She could see that by the way he fussed around Sabrina, and worried over his son, Greg, who was touring with his band in the States.

'He's actually quite good, but don't tell him I told you so,' he said. 'I was gutted when he packed in his course at Uni to form a rock and roll band. It was Helen who encouraged him to follow his passion for music. I wasn't exactly supportive,' he added, with a rueful smile. 'But he's doing okay. They're a big hit in Japan, apparently. I guess I'm honoured he's found a break in his busy schedule to come to our opening ceremony.'

She could tell he was pleased. He talked of little else, and it was lovely to see his enthusiasm in planning the event. Sabrina had sent out flyers advertising the date and had arranged for a marquee to be erected on the front lawn in case of wet weather. Ella had been roped in to cut the ribbon and give a speech. Since she was a well-known person in equestrian circles, both here and nationwide, she was bound to attract interested spectators and well-wishers, to say nothing of the local press.

She could hardly tell him her fortieth birthday fell on the same day and steal his thunder. Perhaps she would celebrate it the week after.

'You'll do no such thing,' Vanessa retorted, when she ran the idea by her. 'This is a milestone birthday. Mother's not likely to forget it, and neither will I.'

'I'm not bothered, really. It's just another day.'

'It's not just another day. It's one that deserves to be celebrated. Leave it with me,' her sister added, tapping the side of her nose.

'Vanessa, you won't say anything, will you? Please don't tell Grant. This day is so important to him.'

'I won't,' she said.

But by the thoughtful look on her sister's face, Caroline wasn't convinced.

***

Two weeks later, and the builders had finished the alterations, and it was just a case of fitting in the various equipment and veterinary supplies before the practice was fully operational.

Sabrina had organised a training session for Caroline, and

the two veterinary nurses they had taken on, so she could run through the computer software and booking system for the practice with them.

'It's fairly straightforward,' she explained. 'Each vet and nurse has their own lists, and it's just a case of booking appointments in the relevant spots, and if they're transferring from another practice, making sure you get them to request the clinical history of each animal. Details of medication, treatment and that sort of thing.'

Caroline thought it was anything but straightforward. She sat at the reception desk, staring at the screen, and trying to take notes. Of the two nurses, Josie, the older one, with a pronounced Suffolk accent, had experience of the same programme and knew what she was doing. Lauren, the younger girl, fresh out of training, didn't, but had the knack of picking things up easily.

'What does this do?' Caroline asked, for the umpteenth time. She was sure Sabrina must be regretting her father's decision to employ her.

'That's if you want to add another animal to the client's account. Don't worry. You'll soon get the hang of it.'

Caroline wasn't so sure. She was used to computers, but this was unlike anything she had worked with before.

'I don't think I'm going to be any good at this job,' she told Grant later, as they took Monty for a walk through the woods together. 'The girls make it look so easy, but I feel useless. I'm forever asking Sabrina what to do.'

'Which is a whole lot better than not asking,' he said, grinning. 'No one expects you to know what to do straight away.' He stooped to pick up the ball Monty had retrieved from the undergrowth and threw it hard; the spaniel bounded after it with an excited volley of barks. 'I have every confidence in you.'

'You must be the only one who has.'

He slipped an arm around her waist. 'You worry too much. There's still a week to go before the opening.'

'I know, but I don't want to let you down. This is important to you.'

'And so are you.' He turned her to face him and looked at her, his eyes crinkling with amusement. 'So,' he repeated slowly, 'are you.' He gave her a brief peck on the cheek. 'Come on. Let's get back and I'll run through it with you. I don't charge for private tuition,' he added. 'But don't tell the others, in case they get jealous.'

Caroline felt a surge of emotion as he caught hold of her hand. Gratitude and longing and a sudden rush of desire. She could feel the colour flooding to her cheeks. Oh, how she wanted to get closer to this man, but she had to hold back. She had to. For his sake, and for hers. He'd know when the time was right to take their relationship further, and she wasn't going to pre-empt that. It was enough to know that he wanted to be with her, and he cared.

'Where is that daft dog?' he said, seemingly oblivious to her concerns. 'Monty? Come on, boy. Home.'

The spaniel came bounding up to him, pink tongue lolling from one side of his mouth. The ball was missing.

'Where is it?' he said, stooping to stroke the excited dog. 'Go on, find it.' He pointed into the trees.

'I'm impressed,' she said, as Monty reappeared a moment later, with the ball in his mouth. 'I think he understands you.

Grant gave her a wry smile. 'At least someone does. Come on. Let's go.'

Chapter Thirty

How could she possibly be forty? That was four decades old, and so much had happened to her over the years, so why was she feeling like a gawky teenager starting her first job?

Caroline stared at her reflection in the full-length mirror which hung from the wall in her tiny bedroom. The practice uniform of a navy polo shirt, with the logo "Dalton Veterinary practice" embroidered on the front, fitted her perfectly. She turned sideways, checking her black trousers for dog hairs, though she didn't suppose it mattered, considering the nature of the business.

Scraping back her hair, she secured it with a band at the nape of her neck.

She could hear the scrunching of tyres on the gravel drive and crossed to the window in time to see her sister clambering out of her car. She was struggling to remove a large box from the boot.

Caroline opened the front door, one hand on Monty's collar.

'Happy birthday,' Vanessa said, balancing the box on her hip. 'There are some flowers from mother on the back seat. My, you look smart.'

'Thanks,' she said, hurrying to help her. 'Where's Emily?'

'Oh, she's fast asleep. I've left her with Jed, so I can't stay long.'

Caroline took the box from her. 'What's in it?'

'You'll have to open it and see.' Her sister scooped the bouquet and a bottle of champagne from the back of the car and followed her up the path to the cottage. 'Mother says she'll see you later at the opening ceremony, but she wanted you to have these.'

'Is she going to the tack shop?"

'Of course, but only in the morning. She's closing early so she can be at Grey Lodge. You know she wouldn't miss that for the world.'

'That's what I was afraid of,' Caroline sighed. 'Oh dear. I'm so nervous.'

'Why?' Vanessa laid the flowers on the kitchen worktop. 'You look great. Oh, and there's a card from Ella and Lewis, and there's one here from Adam and Jess.' She raised an eyebrow at her. 'Young love. Don't ask. And Rosie's made you one with a picture of Merlin on it. Or at least, I think it's Merlin.' Her sister peered closer at the hand-drawn card with the grey horse grazing in a green field on it. 'It's not a bad likeness.'

'Adam said Rosie was good at art,' she said. 'It's lovely.'

'Go on, open the box.'

Caroline pulled at the wrapping paper. The parcel was heavy, and when she lifted the lid, she could see a jumble of polystyrene padding surrounding the object inside. 'What on earth is this?' She delved deeper and felt something hard and smooth and shiny. 'Oh, my goodness, this is gorgeous!'

The brass statue of a Springer spaniel mounted on a polished wooden base was the image of Monty.

Vanessa's face beamed, as she watched her lift it from the box. 'Thought you'd like it.'

'It's beautiful. Thank you so much. I absolutely love it. What do you think, Monty?'

The spaniel was more interested in sniffing the cardboard box, than what it had contained.

Caroline ruffled his ears.

'I've put the champagne in your fridge,' Vanessa said. 'And I can come round later tonight and help you have a little celebration, if you like? That's if you're not too exhausted after the events of the day. I mean, you are forty now.'

'Hey, less of that.' She laughed. 'I can hardly believe it,

myself. Where did all those years go?'

'Getting us to here, that's where.' Vanessa glanced at her watch. 'I've got to go, but good luck, and I'll see you later. You'll be amazing. Break a leg, and all that.'

Caroline stood at the door, waving her off. Her sister's visit had been an unexpected surprise and had lifted her mood no end.

'Right, Monty,' she said, reaching for his lead. 'It's time we were making a move. Some of us have work to go to.'

***

Grant had scheduled the official opening of the Dalton Veterinary Practice to take place at two o'clock. This would give them plenty of time to make sure the catering arrangements were all in hand, and that the balloons and bunting Sabrina had insisted upon were in place. It would also ensure that his son, Greg, who flew in the previous night from the States, and who Caroline had yet to meet, could recover from his flight.

By mid-day, everything was ready, and Grant had gathered them in the waiting room to give them a last run through of the schedule, before they took a welcome break for lunch.

'I'd like you, Lauren and Josie, to give conducted tours of the consulting rooms and operating theatres to potential clients. Sabrina and I will be on hand to answer questions, and Caroline, you'll be in charge of the reception desk. I'm not expecting any phone calls today, but you never know. Does that sound okay to everyone?'

They all nodded, though Caroline couldn't help feeling apprehensive. Although she had got to grips with the computer, thanks to Grant's patient tutoring, she was worried someone might ask her something she didn't know.

'If that happens, you just send them to me,' he said.

'Or me.' Sabrina poked her head around the first consulting room door. 'It's all set up, Dad.'

'Excellent. Right, well, if you'd all like to come this way, there's something I want to show you.'

Caroline trooped after the two younger nurses, expecting to be shown some new equipment that she needed to know about.

What she didn't expect to find was the room decked out with 40th birthday banners and balloons, and a large cake box in the middle of the consulting room table.

'Surprise!' Josie said, pushing her through the door, as Lauren set off a party popper, making her jump. Shreds of coloured paper floated down around her head.

'Happy birthday,' Sabrina said, presenting her with a beautifully wrapped rectangular parcel with a blue silk ribbon around it. 'This is from all of us.'

Caroline was stunned. 'Thank you,' she said, her voice quivering. 'But… but how did you know?' She glanced at Grant. 'Did Vanessa tell you?'

He shook his head, smiling, and winked at his daughter. 'No, but I'm surprised you wanted to keep it a secret. It was Ella who mentioned it.'

'She told me when we were talking about the opening ceremony,' Sabrina said. 'She was surprised Dad didn't know.'

Caroline blushed. 'I didn't want to say anything. You were so busy planning this event. I thought I'd celebrate it later.'

'Well, the secret's out now,' Grant said. 'Happy birthday, old woman.'

She pulled a face at him as she ripped open the slim parcel and found an envelope containing a voucher for a spa day for two. She would need to relax in a spa after the excitement of today, she thought. 'Thank you,' she said. 'This is perfect.'

'And there's more,' Grant said. 'I've got a little present for you, but first, you need to cut the cake. We're all starving here.'

The caterers had supplied the cake, complete with a 40th birthday candle, and delivered it when they were setting up the buffet and barbecue. Sabrina had sneaked it into her consulting room and hidden it under a pile of scrubs.

It was, Caroline told them, the nicest birthday cake she had ever had in all her forty years.

'I'll put the kettle on,' Sabrina said. 'I think we could all do with a hot drink before everyone arrives. The champagne will have to come later. Lauren, can you give me a hand? Oh, and Josie, can you bring those plates to the kitchen with you?'

'Goodness, yes, we'd better tidy up this room,' Caroline said.

Grant grinned at her as she patted her lips with a paper towel.

'What? Have I got icing on my nose, or something? Why are you looking at me like that?'

'Because I'm trying hard to be professional and finding it very difficult.'

'Grant,' she sighed, as he stepped forward and drew her close. 'We're at work.'

Her protests were half-hearted because she wanted nothing more than to be swept up in his arms. She raised her hands and rested them round the back of his neck. 'Thank you,' she said.

He planted a kiss on the tip of her nose. 'I've got something else for you. I didn't want to give it to you in front of the others, just in case you didn't like it.' Drawing back a step, he reached into his pocket and produced a small, velvet-covered box. 'I'll understand if you say no…'

Caroline sucked in a breath. He wasn't going to propose, was he? Oh, my goodness. He was. He really was! She stared in disbelief at the exquisite diamond solitaire ring nestling on a blue velvet cushion.

'I was… er… wondering if you would marry me?'

With a squeal, she flung herself at him, wrapping her arms round him and hugging him almost as tightly as he hugged her. 'Of course I will,' she said. 'Grant, I love you so, so much.'

'Well, that's a relief.' He seemed to exhale, visibly.

In case he had any doubts, she cemented them with a long and lingering kiss. 'And now we've got that settled,' she said, drawing apart and gazing up at him, 'let's get back to business. You've got an important event scheduled for today.'

'Indeed, I have,' he said, pulling her close. 'But nothing, is more important than this.'

***

Caroline wasn't sure how she got through the next few hours, trying to maintain an air of professional calm and efficiency, when her thoughts were whirling all over the place.

The permanent grin that seemed to be cemented on her face wasn't a false one. She was happier than she'd ever been in her entire life. Grant Dalton had asked her to marry him. It was more than she could have dreamed of, but she had the ring to prove it.

She watched in a daze as Ella made her speech and cut the ribbon on the door to the practice. She smiled and nodded, and directed people to the toilets, or the marquee, or pointed them toward the conducted tour. And every so often, she caught Grant watching her with a knowing look on his face, and she would smile back at him, wondering how it was she had managed to win the heart of this man.

'How's the birthday girl doing?' Vanessa said, wandering into reception, pushing baby Emily in her pram.

'You're not going to believe this.' Caroline rushed out from behind the desk and clutched at her sister's arm. 'He's only gone and asked me to marry him.'

'Who has?'

'What do you mean, "who has?"'

'Only kidding,' she said, and laughed. 'Sorry, couldn't resist. That's amazing.'

'And he's bought me this.' She showed her the ring. 'Honestly, I can hardly believe it.'

'Looks like he's serious, then. About blinking time. You've been tip-toeing round each other for ages.' Vanessa examined the ring and nodded. 'Well, congratulations, Sis. I'm really happy for you.'

'Thanks. I'm glad. I suspect mother isn't going to be too impressed.' She could see Ursula making her way across the crowded entrance hall, a glass of something in her hand, and an elaborate pink fascinator on her head. 'She never did see eye to eye with Grant.'

'She'll get over it,' Vanessa assured her. 'After all, he's the one with money and influence. That's always a plus point in mother's book.'

Which, indeed, it was.

'Well, it's your choice, darling,' Ursula said. 'As you know, I'm never one to interfere? Besides, I've always liked a society wedding. I'm sure Petunia Fitzgerald will be delighted when I tell her that the owner of the new veterinary practice is going to be my son-in-law.'

***

She smiled, remembering. Her mother would never change, and it would seem strange if she did. She wondered if she'd been so keen to tell Mrs Fitzgerald about her grandson's involvement in the fight that had hit the front page of the local newspaper, with names omitted because of their age.

Max Bradshaw faced charges of assault and was lying low until his case reached the magistrate's court. His reputation as the school bully would not go in his favour. This wasn't the first time he had used fists instead of words.

Caroline wasn't sure if she wanted to press charges over an argument between two teenagers. Her injuries had been an unfortunate side effect. But Grant believed that giving the lad a stark warning might steer him away from the path he was headed. At least he wasn't bothering Adam now. Her nephew seemed to have settled down to his studies, helped, no doubt, by the influence of his girlfriend, Jessica; her of the micro-mini denim shorts, who was actually a studious and remarkably pleasant young girl.

'Penny for them,' Grant said, coming to stand behind her as she stood by the reception desk, staring absent-mindedly at the computer screen in front of her.

The last tour had finished for the day, and most of the visitors were mingling on the lawn, taking advantage of the free drinks and entertainment.

She glanced back at him and smiled. He looked dashing and professional in his green scrubs, a stethoscope draped loosely round his neck.

'I was just thinking about something Mother said. It wasn't anything important.'

'No surprises, there.' His arms encircled her waist, pulling her back against his chest.

'Grant.' She leaned her head on his shoulder. 'I don't want a big wedding.'

'Me neither.' He kissed her ear. 'I want something memorable, just for us.'

'Sounds perfect.'

'But, in the meantime…' He leaned over and shut down her computer. 'I think you've done enough for one day. Come on, let's go outside and celebrate your birthday.'

'And our engagement.'

He grinned. 'Especially our engagement.'

***

The secret was out. Ursula, not known for her discretion, was happily telling anyone within earshot that she was soon to be the new vet's mother-in-law.

Grant pulled Caroline to one side. 'Promise me you won't bring her back here once we're married,' he said.

'I promise.' She laughed. 'I've spent half my life trying to get away from that woman. She's my mother, and I love her, but I don't always like her.'

'That's all I need to know. Now, where's that champagne?'

They made their way to the front of the marquee, where Sabrina was handing out glasses of bubbly and offering trays of nibbles. The aroma of meaty sausages and burgers from the barbecue made Caroline feel hungry. Apart from her slice of birthday cake, she hadn't eaten all day. She picked up a couple of canapes from the tray as she waited for Grant to join her with the drinks.

'I hear congratulations are in order,' Ella said, coming to join her. 'Sabrina has been telling me the news, and I'm so pleased for you. For both of you, actually,' she added, smiling as Grant strolled over, carrying two glasses of chilled champagne. I hope you have a long and happy life together. I can't wait for the wedding.'

'I'll second that,' Vanessa said. 'Oh, for goodness' sake, Monty.' She ruffled the spaniel's silky ears. 'I'm trying to take a photo here.' The spaniel, who had been shut in the kitchen for most of the day, was jumping up at her, his tail wagging joyously. 'Can't you get this dog to sit still?'

Caroline smiled, as Grant clicked his fingers, and the dog went bounding over to him, and sat obediently at his feet.

'We're working on it,' she said. 'I can't say it's been easy.'

'Nothing worth doing ever is,' Grant said. 'Here's to us, you, me, and Monty.'

Ursula was beaming. Her pink feathered hat sat slightly askew on her head, as she quaffed the last of her champagne.

'I brought them together, you know,' she was saying, to anyone who would listen, and when she realised no one was, wandered off in search of a refill.

'Sorry,' Caroline said.

'Don't be.' Grant slipped his arm around her waist and squeezed it. 'She's right, for once, and I'm actually grateful to her, but don't tell her I said that. Come on, Mrs Dalton-to-be. I think it's time we had a dance. My son and his band are waiting.'

The End

Acknowledgements

Grateful thanks, as always, to my lovely writing group friends; Jane Bailey, Sophie Green, Liz Ferretti and Ruth Dugdall, for all their support over the years.

Thanks also, to my editor Gemma Skelton, from The Write Word, for pointing out any errors and keeping me motivated, and to my talented narrator, Gill Mills, from Canopy Audiobooks, who brought my books to life.

And, a final thanks to my family and friends, for putting up with me while I invented my imaginary characters and wove them into stories.

Other novels by the same author, available on Amazon.co.uk:

Green Wellies and Wax Jackets ISBN 9798867251147

Muddy Boots and Mishaps   ISBN9781986315241

The CoachTrip.   ISBN9781985097315

A Love Betrayed (Morag Lewis). Robert Hale Ltd. ISBN 0709038860